Series in Fairy-Tale Studies

General Editor
Donald Haase, Wayne State University

Advisory Editors
Cristina Bacchilega, University of Hawai'i, Mānoa
Stephen Benson, University of East Anglia
Nancy L. Canepa, Dartmouth College
Anne E. Duggan, Wayne State University
Pauline Greenhill, University of Winnipeg
Christine A. Jones, University of Utah
Janet Langlois, Wayne State University
Ulrich Marzolph, University of Göttingen
Carolina Fernández Rodríguez, University of Oviedo
Maria Tatar, Harvard University
Jack Zipes, University of Minnesota

A complete listing of the books in this series can be found online at wsupress.wayne.edu

Erotic Infidelities

Love and Enchantment
in Angela Carter's *The Bloody Chamber*

Kimberly J. Lau

Wayne State University Press
Detroit

© 2015 by Wayne State University Press, Detroit, Michigan 48201.
All rights reserved.
No part of this book may be reproduced without formal permission.
Manufactured in the United States of America.

19 18 17 16 15   5 4 3 2 1

Library of Congress Control Number: 2014936569

ISBN 978-0-8143-3933-6 (paperback)
ISBN 978-0-8143-3934-3 (e-book)

Designed and typeset by Bryce Schimanski
Composed in Chapparal Pro

For my mother
Eloise Lau
who has always come to my rescue,
even if she's never disposed of a man-eating tiger

Contents

Acknowledgments ix

1. Enduring Narratives 1
2. Labyrinthine Structures: "The Bloody Chamber" 17
3. Beastly Subjects: The Feline Stories 42
4. Dangerous Articulations: "The Erl-King" and "The Snow Child" 73
5. A Desire for Death: "The Lady of the House of Love" 100
6. Erotic Infidelities: The Wolf Trilogy 122

   Epilogue: Enchanting Possibilities 145

Notes 153
Bibliography 169
Index 177

Acknowledgments

A humble attempt at expressing my profound gratitude:

To Angela Carter, for the unique pleasures of *The Bloody Chamber*.

To Donald Haase, for inviting me into the good company of the Series in Fairy-Tale Studies.

To Cristina Bacchilega and an anonymous reviewer, for productive and provocative challenges.

To Annie Martin, for her graciousness and phenomenal skill in shepherding *Erotic Infidelities* from concept to completion, and to Kristin Harpster, Mimi Braverman, and Bryce Schimanski for expert care and attention along the way.

To Wayne State University Press, for permission to reproduce previously published material for chapters 5 and 6.

To Kathy Chetkovich, for enriching and refining my ideas with her sheer brilliance, careful reading, and contagious enthusiasm.

To Francesca Caparas, for exceptional research assistance and meticulous indexing.

To the Committee on Research at the University of California, Santa Cruz, for financial support.

To Cristina Bacchilega, JoAnn Conrad, Anne Duggan, Carla Freccero, Pauline Greenhill, Martine Hennard Dutheil de la Rochère, David Marriott, Helene Moglen, Micah Perks, Kathryn Stockton, and Kay Turner for their generosity in sharing, teaching, discussing, reading, and pushing.

To John, my tender wolf, for everything.

1

Enduring Narratives

Enduring narratives: narratives that endure; the act of enduring narratives.

The love story. The fairy tale.

To speak of love is tricky. It is to fall into cliché, to ventriloquize, to diminish one's individuality. The words with which we hope to convey our most profound feelings—our supposedly unique experiences—are largely empty, transformed by custom and collectivity into worn platitudes and rote sentiments. Love stories suffer the same fate. As Roland Barthes observed, "Every other night, on TV, someone says: *I love you*" (2001: 151). *I love you* is all too familiar: at once a commonly shared *feeling* and a commonly shared *narrative*. Love is trapped by convention as well as by the limits of discursivity.

If language confines love to repetitive expression, then the fairy tale may well epitomize its narrative incarnation. With its highly formulaic structure, its bare plotting, and its minimal character development, the fairy tale is all tradition and trope. And yet the predictability of the fairy tale, like the love story, might very well be part of its allure. The comfortable structures—from form and plot to image and phrase—that hinder the possibility of thinking love and desire anew also sustain the cultural ideologies at the heart of the love story and the fairy tale, enduring narratives par excellence.

Fantasies of Difference/Different Fantasies

Angela Carter was savvy to the gendered politics of enduring narratives, and *The Bloody Chamber* is devoted to unsettling both its meanings. First published in 1979, *The Bloody Chamber* remains one of the most enchanting—and one of the most bewildering and provocative—collections of retold fairy tales. With their fantastically strange couplings and wonderfully disorienting endings, Carter's fairy tales work to free love from its existence as cliché. Love's entrapment in trope is especially dangerous, because the formulaic nature of the love story, of the fairy tale, of the romance novel—like pornography—imbues it with a mythic quality that structures gendered fantasies of sex and desire and denies the possibility of subjectivity, as Carter suggests in her critical work *The Sadeian Woman*: "At the first touch or sigh he, she, is subsumed immediately into a universal. . . . The man and woman, in their particularity, their being, are absent from these representations of themselves as male and female. These tableaux of falsification remove our sexual life from the world, from the tactile experience itself" (2006: 8–9). Although both *The Bloody Chamber* and *The Sadeian Woman* critique love's reduction to universalizing myth and women's complicity in the oppressive power relations it veils, Carter refuses to give up on love. Instead, she seeks to conjure it in previously unrecognizable ways. For Carter only a radically reimagined love has the power to liberate us—and our subjectivities, our sex, our desire—from enduring narratives, and this effort to retrieve love from cliché and convention lies at the heart of *The Bloody Chamber*.

The possibility of recuperating love calls for a simultaneous interrogation and reworking of foundational cultural myths and theories. As such, Carter's creative practice is also her critical project. "For me," she writes in the preface to *Come Unto These Yellow Sands*, "a narrative is an argument stated in fictional terms" (1985: 7), and she famously referred to *The Bloody Chamber* as "a book of stories about fairy stories" (1998c: 38). Her metatales are much more pointed than that, however, and they might best be described as fairy stories about gender and sexuality, language and desire. These themes recur in Carter's fiction, and their staging in relation to feminism and psychoanalysis has been widely recognized by critics.[1] Christina Britzolakis, for instance, claims that Carter's texts "lend themselves in an exemplary manner to the ongoing dialogue between psychoanalysis and feminism" as they "self-consciously engage with a wide range of post-1968 theoretical debates, and with a distinctively semiological conception of culture" (1997: 44). More specifically, Scott Dimovitz contends that "Carter's speculative fiction of the 1970s uses psychoanalytic theory to show the forces that construct the contemporary form of Western patriarchy" (2010: 4).

The Bloody Chamber contests Freud's theories of psychosexual development and Lacan's related theories of gender, language, and desire, a set of enduring narratives tightly bound to Carter's primary intertexts—fairy tales, Romantic poetry, and Sadeian pornography—and critical to the patriarchal construction and maintenance of gender, sexuality, and power. In a nuanced analysis of Carter's 1970s short fiction, of which *The Bloody Chamber* is the most well-known, Dimovitz argues convincingly that Carter's "main target is not merely psychoanalytic theory, but the particular form of poststructuralist psychoanalysis offered by Jacques Lacan" (2010: 4). Within this context Carter's fairy tales repeatedly interrogate and critique specific tenets of psychoanalytic theory; they challenge the sexist underpinnings of Freud's conceptualization of the Oedipal complex and Lacan's related theory of the phallus as privileged signifier as well as their implications for ideologies of gender and sexuality in Western culture.

At the same time, however, Carter seems to find a certain promise in psychoanalysis. A brief line from one of her notebooks captures this sensibility: "looking at this world, seeing it as utterly strange—psychoanalysis" (emphasis in original).[2] Here, Carter's definition underscores the mutual influences of Lacan and the Surrealists, whose theories she deeply admired but for the glaring problem of their overwhelming misogyny (Carter, 1998a: 512); with her brief journal notation, Carter distills what she might have called the "latent content"[3] from the convoluted and justificatory sex-based distinctions that underlie Freudian and Lacanian psychoanalytic theory. It is precisely this sense of psychoanalysis—to make our world utterly strange—that inspires the *Bloody Chamber* stories and their commitment to refashioning some of Lacan's potentially productive insights for feminism, a project Patricia Waugh attributes to all of Carter's fiction, which she characterizes as "grounded . . . in a knowing play with the ideas of the Freudian revisionist Jacques Lacan, for whom self is always an endless pursuit of reflections in the eyes of others, love a desire for the desire of the other" (1995: 195). In *The Bloody Chamber* Carter works and reworks these ideas in order to critique *and* revise the sexist assumptions that underpin Freudian and Lacanian theory. In their place she fantasizes different premises and different outcomes, different possibilities for women, for desire, and for an alternate erotics—the mutual pleasures of an expanded sensorium, an affective and reciprocal recognition, an identificatory metamorphosis.

Intertextual Multiplicities

Just as narratives of love and sex—fairy tales, romance novels, pornography—are prone to formulaic predictability, so too are most efforts to theorize them in fiction. The *Bloody Chamber* stories avoid such heavy-handedness, however, because they move away from expected feminist critiques and their anticipated fairy-tale revisions. Instead, Carter's stories are rich with paradox and play; they delight with their clever interventions into patriarchal narrative legacies and theoretical inheritances even as they disturb with their attention to women's complicity in such oppressive structures. Much of Carter's brilliance in creating subtle and nuanced narrative arguments derives from her remarkable intertextual range: not simply fairy tales but also Romantic poetry, Gothic novels, Shakespeare's plays, biblical mythology, visual art, literary pornography, folklore, and, of course, psychoanalytic theory as well as *The Sadeian Woman*, her own critical work published in the same year as *The Bloody Chamber*. In addition, as Martine Hennard Dutheil de la Rochère (2013) so convincingly demonstrates, Carter's 1977 translation of Charles Perrault's *Histoires ou contes du temps passé*, along with her extensive research for it, provides another rich source for her intertextual play. Hennard Dutheil de la Rochère's reading of the overlapping tales—those that Carter first translated for *The Fairy tales of Charles Perrault* and then transformed, primarily in *The Bloody Chamber*—highlights the way they make sly use of the slippages implicit in Carter's own translations, thus opening up opportunities to draw out, reimagine, and complicate the adult themes lurking around the edges of Perrault's seemingly child-oriented tales. Such intertextualities—the conscious references and allusions to other texts in order to comment on them—reveal the historical sediments and multilayered nature of enduring narratives, the cultural trappings that render them trite while also conveying the weight of their gendered burden.

At the same time, the *Bloody Chamber* stories provide their own productive intertextualities: from story to story, among stories within thematic and formal groupings, and over the course of the collection as a whole. As several critics have noted, *The Bloody Chamber* must be read as an interdependent set of stories that continually approach the collection's central concerns from different vantage points.[4] This shifting and multiple style is characteristically Carter. Lorna Sage identifies it in the way Carter's radio plays "would, within the same story, give you different versions, turn it around or inside out, transform it" (1994: 36), and Lucie Armitt sees in *The Bloody Chamber* "a single narrative which uses the short story medium to work and rework compulsive repetitions" (1997: 96). Always resisting even her own narrative enclosures, Carter instead opens the *Bloody Chamber* stories to speculation and possibility.

The rich internal intertextuality of the *Bloody Chamber* stories also gives rise to several narrative-theoretical arcs that emerge across the collection and exacerbate the multiple meanings of individual tales. Carter's spatial and temporal movement from story to story seems to offer its own narrative argument for an alternate erotics that might exist beyond the phallogocentric Symbolic Order, for instance. *The Bloody Chamber* thus begins with the highly cultured and civilized world of the Marquis's castle and slowly makes its way through spaces that invoke its demise and degeneration. Mr. Lyon's Palladian house may be a bourgeois instantiation of the Marquis's aristocratic fortress, a simple step down in class, but the Beast's palazzo is in ruins and finally crumbles at the following story's end. The Erl-King's labyrinthine woods imprison the heroine much as the Marquis's castle does, and Carter implies that "the natural world" is no safer for women than "the civilized world," because both are determined by patriarchal power. Even in disarray and without his physical presence, Nosferatu's mansion overwhelms the vampire Countess with its ancestral hauntings, with Nosferatu's patriarchal legacy. It is only in the space of geographic and ontological liminality—the zombie-werewolf Duke's abandoned castle, another denlike home for the feral Wolf-Alice—that an alternate erotics might come into being. In terms of temporality and the collection's female protagonists, Carter's fairy tales track women's development in reverse, beginning with a recently married heroine and regressing back to the presymbolic Wolf-Alice, a regression that seeks to undo women's incorporation into the Law of the Father and its enduring patriarchal narratives of love, marriage, and women's propriety.

Critical Enchantments

Given Carter's theoretical and critical preoccupations, it should come as no surprise that *The Bloody Chamber* has inspired an impressive body of criticism in the thirty-five years since its publication. Situated at the intersection of feminist, psychoanalytic, literary, and fairy tale studies, the critical engagement with Carter's tales follows their lead and delves into the same enduring questions of gender, sexuality, and desire. By privileging Carter's intertextual play and her particular, peculiar modes of adaptation, critical readings of the tales articulate the many ways they trouble—complicate, confound, deconstruct—the cultural narratives and discourses at their heart. At the same time, critical debates about the sexual representation of women in Carter's fairy tales make clear that they also trouble some of the more polemical feminist theories and approaches to women's sexuality and representation. The rich complexity of Carter's vast intertextual range, her investment in demythologizing, her preoccupation with the workings of desire, and her insistence on women's participation in their own sexual subjugation and oppression are all well established in the criticism, as is Carter's fascination with fairy tales.

Carter's lifelong attraction to the fairy tale coupled with her translation of Perrault's tales and her self-proclaimed identification with folklore confirms her centrality to contemporary fairy-tale studies. Not only have her tales shaped the evolution of feminist and postmodern adaptations of the genre, but they have also encouraged us to reconsider, rethink, and reframe—to revisit with a new and different consciousness—many of her source tales. Indeed, Carter's canonization in fairy-tale studies is so well established that Sonya Andermahr and Lawrence Phillips, editors of the

2012 volume *Angela Carter: New Critical Readings*, claim that Carter has been "overly categorized as a postmodern folklorist"; as a result, they call for her work to be "located historically" and "in a broader genre context" that will help establish her "not simply as a major female fabulist, but as a major late twentieth-century writer *tout court*" (1–2).

Implicit in such a call and in Andermahr and Phillips's subsequent contention that *New Critical Readings* "avoids the tendency to restrict discussion of Carter's narrative techniques to the demythologization of fairy tale discourse" (2012: 2) is the assumption that Carter's fairy tales do not lend themselves to historical and material analysis. Yet the dominant themes and concerns of *New Critical Readings*—Carter's investment in the social production and effects of gender identity and performance, her interrogation of psychoanalysis and philosophy, the affective work her stories accomplish—pertain in her fairy tales as well. To understand Carter as a "postmodern folklorist" is not to diminish her status as a public intellectual and "writer *tout court*"; rather, it is to understand how deeply her fairy tales are informed by, and how thoroughly they evoke, her materialist commitment to social critique and politics.

Although the *Bloody Chamber* stories continue to generate new analyses and interpretations with a regularity that attests to their theoretical and creative depth, most of the criticism dates from the late 1980s and 1990s and represents its historical moment: feminist critiques and reformulations of Freudian and Lacanian psychoanalytic theory, the sex wars, the disavowal of patriarchal literary canons, an interest in postmodern aesthetics. Although such theoretical questions and concerns may seem outmoded or irrelevant to contemporary cultural theory and Carter criticism, I return to many of them here because they frequently gesture toward, but stop short of articulating, the transformative political potential of Carter's fairy tales. By synthesizing and further extending this well-known critical literature, I seek to recontextualize it, drawing out its relation to the affective dimensions of Carter's fairy tales.

The fairy tale is a notoriously affecting genre. Many who are drawn to fairy tales and to fairy tale studies are enchanted by the tales themselves; fairy tales have a wondrous effect on us—an enticing sway over us—despite our critical recognition of their deeply patriarchal and heteronormative underpinnings. It is a challenge to reconcile what the tale *does* to us with what it *means* to us. Recent work in fairy-tale studies that privileges queer theory and queer approaches to the fairy tale, such as Kay Turner and Pauline Greenhill's edited volume *Transgressive Tales: Queering the Grimms* (2012), helps resolve this disjuncture between our critical and affective responses. Such interpretations allow us to recuperate traditional tales through slant readings that recover the queer desires and relationships just below the hegemonic surface, a progressive intellectual move that affirms our emotional relationship to the tales. Despite the true originality and political importance of reading traditional tales through queer theory, however, these approaches bypass the lasting problem of heterosexual love and desire at the ideological heart of the tales, a problem of hegemonic cultural mythologizing that continues to chafe at critics for whom the traditional tales also prove pleasurable.

In my reading of *The Bloody Chamber* as a *collection* and not just a set of individual stories, I attend to the ways that Carter takes up this problem, which has been overlooked in the criticism to date. By prioritizing the demythologizing of hegemonic cultural narratives in *The Bloody Chamber*, Carter's critics have not addressed the ways in which her fairy tales grapple with, and seek to overcome, the near impossibility of heterosexual love and desire under patriarchy. Given the cultural, political, and ideological dominance of heterosexuality, it may seem absurd to claim its impossibility or, at least, its extreme difficulty. Yet at least one queer theorist makes a similar claim. Kathryn Bond Stockton argues that the discursive construction of "same" sex love and desire as *unnatural* exposes the ideological work necessary to naturalize heterosexuality, in which the attraction of "opposites"—difficult to unite, according to virtually all other discourses—is made to seem *natural* and easy. Isn't an attraction to one who is similar to oneself, culturally as well as physically, at least as "logical" (if not more so), Stockton asks, even as she contests the idea of "same" sex anything and the figuration of men and women as opposites.[5]

Although Carter contends that heterosexual love and desire are nearly impossible for different reasons, Stockton's revelation of the naturalization of heterosexuality dovetails with Carter's problematic precisely because the ideological work necessary to maintain that naturalization also constrains the expression of heterosexual love and desire. Carter's devotion to the possibility of heterosexual love and desire outside of dominant cultural scripts—her commitment to exploring how we might recuperate love and erotic desire for heterosexuality—was, in many ways, a lifelong obsession. Her novels all take on heterosexual relationships of love and desire—from the oppressive, manipulative, and deadly to the sex-shifting and fantastic—and Sarah Gamble suggests that the arc of romantic possibility in the novels is imbricated with Carter's own romantic life (2006: 170–71).

Similarly, the recurrent trope of living dolls and female puppets in Carter's fiction might also be understood in this context. Although most commonly read as Carter's critique of femininity's construction and limitations within a patriarchal culture, her living dolls and female puppets also underscore the highly constricted possibilities for sex and love, and in Carter's fiction male doll makers and puppet masters are just as beholden to the limited scripts they force on their female dolls and marionettes as the dolls themselves. Carter once described her "passion for automata," like these living dolls and puppets, as being motivated by her own personal ontological questions: "I'm very interested in the idea of simulacra, of invented people, of imitation human beings, because, you know, the big question that we have to ask ourselves is how do we know that we're not imitation human beings?" (quoted in Crofts, 2003: 144). To be more than an imitation human being is, of course, to experience a genuine agency, to escape, even for a fleeting moment, the social, cultural, linguistic prison into which we are born.

How do we love, how do we desire, how do we have sex, even, without becoming "imitation human beings"? Such questions recur not only in Carter's fiction but also throughout the personal experiences she recorded in her journals over the course of her adult life. Carter's personal exploration of the possibility of another love, of another desire, of two people, two *subjects*, coming together in mutual recognition or mutual pleasure, perhaps even both, surfaces as a central, and lifelong, preoccupation. Contemplating the end of one romantic relationship, for instance, Carter casts it in terms of the patriarchal objectification of women she so frequently complicates in her fiction: "He does not see me as a subject but as an object on which he projects fantasies of lust & domination & aggression

& despair."[6] Later in the same journal, however, Carter recognizes her own complicity in serving as the object of men's desires, a complicity that winds—uncomfortably, for many feminist readers—through the *Bloody Chamber* stories: "The extent to which I function as a mirror astonishes me—all things to all men, indeed! A screen for the projection of fantasies & hence an icon; an object, a completely passive object—& is that why I fear to be alone, though the fear's growing less; passivity & narcissism." In another resonance with her fiction, Carter demythologizes love in an early entry: "All love is, at bottom, self-deceit; or, at least, what we call love is self-deceit. There can be no ultimate connexion [sic]."[7] But at the same time she also holds out hope for love's existence beyond trope and convention: "Love is the impossible but always magnificent and well-worth-attempting endeavor to peirce [sic] the veil of appearances."[8] I offer these examples not to suggest that Carter simply wrote her life into her stories and novels or that we should turn to her life as a guide to interpreting her work;[9] rather, I draw from Carter's journals to highlight her deep, lifelong investment in retrieving love, desire, and sex from their cultural constraints, their deceits and veiled appearances.

The difficulty of escaping the seemingly individual but ultimately universal language of love, of escaping the seemingly individual but ultimately universal performance of sex, of the erotic, is precisely what makes love and desire nearly impossible to think and to create and to perform, especially in their dominant mode of heterosexuality. This recognition of how love and sex are entrapped in language and culture perhaps accounts for Carter's attraction to, and critique of, Lacan's psychoanalytic theories, which posit both that "there is no sexual relation" because subjects can only ever approach each other in language and that feminine *jouissance* implies a possible break with(in) the phallogocentric Symbolic Order. In this book I set out to revisit the workings of language and desire in *The Bloody Chamber* within this context in order to foreground the political and ethical significance of Carter's ongoing investment in imagining unforeseen possibilities for heterosexual love and desire, for an alternate erotics.

Even as Carter insists on the separation of love and desire in *The Bloody Chamber*—indeed, their separation is foundational to her demythologization of the enduring cultural narratives that fix women's sexual desire within the frame of romantic love—she encourages their shared capacity to induce unexpected enchantments, the "affective force" and "sense of wonder" that Jane Bennett (2001) ascribes to the term. Here, I argue that it is in the very strangeness of Carter's fairy-tale enchantments—the moments when love or erotic desire exceed or escape the deeply familiar, habitual structures and ideologies that contain them—that we see momentary, fleeting possibilities for heterosexual love and desire. For Carter these enchantments are animated by what I call her erotic infidelities, by which I mean both an infidelity to her source tales and other intertexts through an erotic energy and an infidelity to a hegemonic and singular erotic (whether defined by patriarchal society or, in an alternate vein, by feminists). Infidelities always imply a certain intimate betrayal of what precedes them. As such, Carter's erotic infidelities work against our culturally determined expectations and longings, against what we think we know and what we think we want, and, in so doing, they usher us into fresh and welcome enchantments.

Erotic Infidelities

In the following chapters I privilege Carter's multiplicity and intertextuality—internally between and across the stories as well as externally with her theoretical and literary engagements—to explore the contours and possibilities of her alternate erotics. In place of the familiar tropes of both patriarchal *and* traditionally feminist notions of desire, Carter offers marvelous sexual couplings and imaginative hybridities: between tiger and girl-becoming-tiger; between girl and werewolf-made-wolf; between feral wolf-girl and zombie-werewolf. In reading *The Bloody Chamber* as a series of individual stories or groups of stories *and* as a complete collection, I trace Carter's narrative indictment of the oppressive constraints on thinking and writing (not to mention having) sex and desire even as she recuperates the possibility of both, at times alongside love and companionship.

In Chapter 2, "Labyrinthine Structures," I attend to the ways that Carter addresses gender and language as labyrinthine structures—complex cultural edifices constructed and augmented over time in ways that obscure their very constructedness—in the collection's titular story, "The

Bloody Chamber," which is a retelling of "Bluebeard." Carter's fairy tale is richly saturated with cultural allusions that bespeak the Marquis's highly "civilized" world, an intensely gendered world necessarily imagined and articulated through language. Through the story's intertextual accretion of the literary, musical, and visual arts, together with the heroine's tendency to read herself into these aesthetic representations, Carter establishes this world—instantiated by the Marquis's chateau—as a symbol of the highly structured and, for women, highly constraining nature of both aesthetic representation and phallogocentric language. Imprisoned within the chateau along with the Marquis's tortured and murdered ex-wives and haunted by the legacy of Bluebeard's grisly predilection, the heroine attests to women's entrapment in the dizzying mazes created by such literary and theoretical traditions.

Against these labyrinthine structures, Carter intervenes in the heroine's imprisonment (in the chateau, in literature, in language) by endowing her mother—clearly a phallic mother—with a telepathic knowing that allows her to rescue her daughter. This "maternal telepathy" is as much a commentary on gender as a critique of psychoanalytic theories about women's relationships to language and the Symbolic Order. As the first story of the collection, "The Bloody Chamber" also props up the structures of "civilization"—language, aesthetic representations, literary traditions—against which Carter writes with increasing force throughout the subsequent stories.

In the next chapter, "Beastly Subjects," I consider Carter's "feline stories"—"The Courtship of Mr. Lyon," "The Tiger's Bride," and "Puss-in-Boots"—as an initial move away from the labyrinthine structures discussed in Chapter 2 and toward an alternate erotics. Although Carter's feline stories do not function as a trilogy in the way that her later wolf stories do, their attention to feline-human relationships and their consideration of feline liminality (from the human perspective) warrant a joint reading, particularly because the intertextuality of the three tales sets off a slow crumbling of the supposed pillars of civilization—wealth, luxurious furnishings and objets d'art, decadent fashion and jewelry—that ultimately imprison women by defining and confining them as patriarchal property and objects of exchange.

As transformations of "Beauty and the Beast," both "The Courtship of Mr. Lyon" and "The Tiger's Bride" encourage a consideration of the animal desires lying just below the surface of the literary tale as well as how those desires are veiled and confounded by myths of civilization. As mirrored tales, "The Courtship of Mr. Lyon" and "The Tiger's Bride" are inversions of each other; the first is fairly traditional and historically grounded, whereas the second stages a fantastic reversal that exposes the trappings of the first story to be nothing more than façade, masquerade, and sleight of hand. Through this inverted and doubled retelling, Carter critiques the circulation of women within male systems of power and privilege and enables moments of an alternate erotics outside of hegemonic representations and phallogocentric language.

Carter's alternate erotics reimagines the sexual dynamics of looking and of singularity, two hallmarks of a phallogocentric culture and language. Instead, the hero of the second inverted "Beauty and the Beast" tale—the Tiger beneath the mask and masquerade of humanity, of masculinity, of propriety, power, and status—inspires another way of communicating, and his licking the heroine into her animal being is later picked up by "Puss-in-Boots," in which human and feline desires are conflated, echoed, and ultimately articulated in embodied, as opposed to verbal, ways.

In Chapter 4, "Dangerous Articulations," I read "The Erl-King" and "The Snow Child" as another pair of mirrored tales. Although the two stories hail from significantly different traditions and Carter writes them in dramatically different styles, I interpret the two together as Carter's way of simultaneously animating and challenging the precepts underlying psychoanalytic theories of language, first through familiar tropes of nineteenth-century Romantic poetry in "The Erl-King" and then through a stark reversal in "The Snow Child." As Margaret Homans (1986) has so convincingly argued, the Romantic poets enact Lacan's theory of language as desire—a theory based on the Law of the Father, represented by the phallus as privileged signifier and predicated on the mother's absence—through their figuration of nature as feminine and their desire for a sublime that often entails the annihilation of the Other. By gendering nature male in "The Erl-King" and introducing a heroine who shifts from seduced prey to virginal lover to murderous mother, Carter invigorates the Oedipal conflicts that underpin both Lacan's theories of language and much Romantic poetry before introducing a female subjectivity that challenges both with its multiplicity and presence.

In "The Snow Child" Carter continues to play with the idea of the Romantic aesthetic as an exemplar of Lacanian desire, and the story's Count literally speaks the child of his desires into being from the natural landscape. The story opens, however, with a decidedly sharp contrast between adult woman (the Countess) and nature, a distinction that forecloses the possibility of reading the Countess figuratively and thus unravels the jealousy plot that gives meaning to the "Snow White" tale tradition in the patriarchal imaginary. By denying the jealousy plot, Carter exposes the phallogocentric logic that structures the relationship of gender and desire to language. When the Count sexually penetrates the dead Snow Child, she simply melts away, and his fleeting articulation of his idealized woman is revealed as nothing more than a fantastic longing for the death-like girl. In presenting "The Erl-King" and "The Snow Child" as mirrored tales, I argue that Carter delves into the complexities of the patriarchal Romantic aesthetic—with its profound relationship to psychoanalytic theories of language—and lays bare the ways that such a tradition entraps both men and women in dangerous articulations.

In Chapter 5, "A Desire for Death," I elaborate on the pedophilic and necrophiliac fantasies of a pornographic culture introduced in Chapter 4 with the Count's desire for the Snow Child. In "The Lady of the House of Love," Carter recasts "Sleeping Beauty" as a vampire tale of deadly desires: the patriarchal desire for passive or dead women, on the one hand, and the Countess's literal desire for death as the only possible liberation from the confines of these conjoined narrative traditions on the other. Haunted by the narrative legacies of Charles Perrault, Jacob and Wilhelm Grimm, and Bram Stoker, "The Lady of the House of Love" exposes the dark allure of their misogynist imaginings. In this chapter I read the symbols and stylistics of Carter's story with and against dominant classical literary versions of "Sleeping Beauty" as well as with and against Gothic vampire narratives, especially Stoker's *Dracula*, to explore the ways that Carter metaphorizes narrative itself, particularly through her use of the ancestral portraits and (imagined) voices that perpetually haunt the vampire Countess, representations of patriarchal narrative inheritances and their lasting legacies. Through such layered and specific intertextualities, Carter transforms a patriarchal sexual desire for death into a feminist libratory one and encourages us to acknowledge the deadly cultural power that such narrative traditions exert over women.

In the final chapter, "Erotic Infidelities," I begin by situating Carter's three concluding stories—her wolf trilogy—within the context of feminist psychoanalytic understandings of *infidelity* as that which destabilizes patriarchal hegemonies and constructs. Considering these stories specifically as a trilogy, I read "The Werewolf," "The Company of Wolves," and "Wolf-Alice" as a set of "Little Red Riding Hood" tales that set in motion a nearly infinite set of betrayals—of literary antecedents, erotic retellings, even Carter's own transformations—that lead to productive ontological slippages for both women and wolves. As each of the three "Little Red Riding Hood" stories strays further and further from the canonical path and further and further from the "civilization" Carter invokes in "The Bloody Chamber," her women and wolves move away from language, speech, and articulation, inspiring us to consider the possibilities for a truly alternate erotics.

Textual Pleasures

> She is just not the kind of writer whose fiction abides interpretation with docility.
>
> Lorna Sage, "Introduction," *Essays on the Art of Angela Carter* (2007: 37)

If Carter's fiction—with its "'metafictional' critical reflection" (Sage, 2007: 37) and its self-conscious narrative arguments—courts interpretation, it also resists it, as Sage points out. The truth of this seeming paradox is that Carter's texts do both: inviting critical engagement at every turn while also frustrating tidy, singular meanings. Her refusal to "[abide] interpretation with docility" is precisely the pleasure of her work, and *The Bloody Chamber* perhaps exemplifies this best with its perpetual return to the collection's central concerns. Lucie Armitt sees in this return "the compulsive fascination it [*The Bloody Chamber*] holds for Carter's critics" and argues that "we appear driven by what Leo Bersani calls the masochistic pleasure of *unpleasure*, a dynamic functioning akin to an itch that seeks nothing better than its own prolongation" (1997: 90). As critics, we return again and again to *The Bloody Chamber*, enticed by the lure of its vast intertextual secrets and drawn by the masochistic pleasure of its multiple meanings that seem, always, just beyond reach.

Describing her attraction to writing radio plays, Carter wrote that she liked "to create complex, many-layered narratives that play tricks with time" (1985: 7), and this characterization certainly applies to the *Bloody Chamber* stories as well. Indeed, it is this complexity, this multiplicity, that performs one of the collection's own theoretical premises by challenging the phallogocentrism of singularity. In many ways, then, it is no surprise that a book-length critical reading of *The Bloody Chamber* in its entirety does not yet exist, because such projects often tend toward closure. Although I undertake such a study here, I offer *Erotic Infidelities* in the spirit of a Carteresque multiplicity, just one exploration of *The Bloody Chamber*'s many pleasures.

2

Labyrinthine Structures
"The Bloody Chamber"

"The Bloody Chamber" opens the door to an enticing and seductively dizzying maze, a labyrinthine structure of Carter's own making. Replete with her characteristic intertextual play and prolific allusions, the titular and privileged first story of the collection reworks Charles Perrault's "Bluebeard"[1] with the libertine spirit of the Marquis de Sade and the decadence of Charles Baudelaire and J. K. Huysmans, and in so doing, magnifies the classic tale's themes of male power and violence in relation to female curiosity and sexuality. The story's intertextual and referential richness extends well beyond the libertine and the decadent, however. Carter's intertexts build fascinating connections among themselves as well as to other texts and allusions—the story of Eve, the martyrdom of Saint Cecilia, eighteenth- and nineteenth-century pornographic art and literature, Symbolist and Surrealist visual art, Freudian psychoanalytic theory—all of which return to questions of female sexuality in a patriarchal culture. Although "The Bloody Chamber" seems to promise an exit (if only one could track all the references, map the connections among them, and navigate their allusive, and elusive, meanings), it quickly becomes evident that the paths Carter has set cross and cross again; her labyrinth is as complex and confusing as the social constructions of gender, sexuality, and power that similarly foil most attempts at escape.

The Sadeian Man

Although "The Bloody Chamber" follows Perrault's "Bluebeard" plot fairly closely, Carter's longtime interest in the writings of the Marquis de Sade and their lasting cultural influence ensure that they also figure prominently in her story. Carter herself acknowledged the centrality of Sade to the underlying themes of both "The Bloody Chamber" and "Bluebeard" in an interview with Les Bedford, saying that her story "did actually manage to get in most of de Sade, which pleased me" (Gamble 2008: 21).[2] Lacking a proper name, Carter's Bluebeard character is referred to only as the Marquis, and this title immediately forges a connection to the Marquis de Sade (Sheets, 1991: 647; Simpson, 2006). Of course, the two share much more than a title: Both are devoted libertines who take sexual pleasure in the pain, corruption, and torture of others, particularly innocent others, like Sade's virtuous Justine and Carter's naïve 17-year-old heroine.

Sade's frequent scenes of eroticized whippings, for instance, surface in an illustrated book of pornography that the heroine comes across in the Marquis's library: "the girl with tears hanging on her cheeks like stuck pearls, her cunt a split fig below the great globes of her buttocks on which the knotted tails of the cat were about to descend, while a man in a black mask fingered with his free hand his prick, that curved upwards like the scimitar he held. The picture had a caption: 'Reproof of curiosity'" (Carter, 1993: 16–17).[3] Robin Ann Sheets points out that through the illustration's title, "Reproof of Curiosity," Carter "links the flagellation scene, a staple of nineteenth-century pornography, to the Bluebeard tale" (1991: 646). Such scenes may be a staple of nineteenth-century pornography, but they are also quite commonly associated with Sade's writings, although literary examples certainly predate Sade as well. The pornographic illustrations do more than simply heighten the Marquis's arousal by anticipating the scenes he will stage with his virginal bride, so like the young girls depicted in his collection; they also provoke the heroine's shock and horror, the promise of her initiation into the Marquis's fantasies, so central to his sexual stimulation. Thus it is only after the Marquis finds her stunned by the images that he desires and deflowers her: "'My little nun has found the prayerbooks, has she?' he demanded, with a curious mixture of mockery and relish; then, seeing my painful, furious bewilderment, he laughed at me aloud, snatched the book from my hands and put it down on the sofa. . . . Then he kissed me. And with, this time, no reticence" (Carter, 1993: 17).

Earlier in the story, while the Marquis is giving the heroine a tour of the castle, he reproduces two other pornographic tableaux in their bedroom, which features "the grand, hereditary matrimonial bed . . . surrounded by so many mirrors! Mirrors on all the walls" (Carter, 1993: 14). As the Marquis watches the heroine notice her multiplication in the mirrors, he says, "See . . . I have acquired a whole harem for myself!" (14), hinting at *The Adventures of Eulalie at the Harem of the Grand Turk*, "the rare collector's piece" (17) he knows she will find in his library. Moments later, he begins to undress her until they become "the living image of an etching by Rops" (15): "the child with her sticklike limbs, naked but for her button boots, her gloves, shielding her face with her hand as though her face were the last repository of her modesty; and the old monocled lecher who examined her, limb by limb. He in his London tailoring; she, bare as a lamb chop. Most pornographic of all confrontations" (15). If the heroine perceives this to be the "most pornographic of all confrontations," she is also surprised—indeed, "aghast"—to find herself "stirring" (15), but the Marquis's re-enactment of the Rops etching does little to pique his desire, although he smiles at the possibility of delaying hers. "Clos[ing] [her] legs like a book," the Marquis quotes Baudelaire: "Anticipation is the greater part of pleasure" (15). Even though Baudelaire's sentiment is not sadistic, the Marquis's complete control of the scene, of the relationship, of the very terms of the heroine's sexual initiation, suggest that the pleasures they anticipate diverge dramatically. The heroine knows only enough to anticipate something from a romance novel, precisely the sort of book she was hoping to find in the Marquis's library ("I should have liked, best of all, a novel in yellow paper," 16) when she happened upon his collection of pornography. On their wedding night journey from Paris to the Marquis's castle in Brittany, her fantasies of a sensuous consummation reveal the fairy tale sensibilities of a teenaged bride.

> My satin nightdress had ... slipped over my young girl's pointed breasts and shoulders, supple as a garment of heavy water, and now teasingly caressed me, egregious, insinuating, nudging between my thighs. ... His kiss, his kiss with tongue and teeth in it and a rasp of beard, had hinted to me ... of the wedding night, which would be voluptuously deferred until we lay in his great ancestral bed in the sea-girt ... that magic place, the fairy castle. (Carter, 1993: 8)

For the Marquis it is precisely in his bride's limited and hegemonic romantic imagination that he sees the potential for corruption and torture, an entirely Sadeian perspective. Within this context, then, Baudelaire's sentiment becomes a sadistic one because anticipation is not intended to heighten the bride's pleasure; rather, the Marquis's pleasure is derived from forcing her to anticipate something she both desires and fears.

If the Marquis is a sadist, he is also a decadent aesthete with a particularly strong admiration for Baudelaire, his "favourite poet" (Carter, 1993: 27), and J. K. Huysmans. His passion for Wagner's operas—he takes his betrothed to see *Tristan und Isolde* on the eve of their marriage—further identifies him with Baudelaire, as does his "taste for the Symbolists" (20). He owns Gustave Moreau's fictitious "great portrait of his first wife, the famous *Sacrificial Victim*" (20), and his second wife was the barmaid discovered by Puvis de Chavannes and later portrayed in Odilon Redon's fictitious etching *The Evening Star Walking on the Rim of Night* (10). Even more, the Marquis's bloody chamber contains the fetishized remains of his wives, along with "an armful of the same lilies with which he had filled [the heroine's] bedroom" (28) such that it resembles an "embalming parlour" (14); the Marquis's three wives inhabit the story like Jeanne Duval, Marie Daubrun, and Madame Apollonie Sabatier, the three women whom Baudelaire both desires and disavows and who inspire his *Les fleurs du mal* (Pichois, 1989), a title that Carter seems to literalize with the Marquis's lilies.

Although the Marquis repeatedly recites lines from Baudelaire's poetry, the book that enjoys pride of place in his library is Huysmans's

Là-bas: "from some over-exquisite private press; it had been bound like a missal, in brass, with gems of coloured glass," and it is displayed on a "lectern, carved like a spread eagle" (Carter, 1993: 16). Huysmans was, of course, heavily influenced by Baudelaire, and Carter is undoubtedly developing her labyrinth with such interconnections. More significant in this regard, however, is the content of Huysmans's lesser-known work: *Là-bas* revolves around the protagonist's research into the life of Gilles de Rais, a fifteenth-century murderer who is commonly associated with Bluebeard in the French tradition (Hennard Dutheil, 2006: 196; Sheets, 1991: 645).[4] Gilles de Rais, like the Marquis, was known both for being a serial killer and for his "aesthetic sensibilities," and Sheets argues that by "locating [the Marquis's castle] in Brittany and by describing the villagers' fears of the bloodthirsty Marquis, Carter also evokes the brutal feudalism of the historical Gilles de Rais" (1991: 645).

As though describing Rais, Sade, Baudelaire, and Huysmans all, Carter's characterization of the Marquis as having a "leonine"-shaped head with a "dark mane" (Carter, 1993: 8), together with the Marquis's description of the bloody chamber as a "den" (21), makes explicit the beastly[5] side of both libertine sexuality with its implicit dehumanization and decadent culture with its gendered representational practices. At the same time, Carter suggests that such proclivities and tastes are further intensified by the Marquis's extreme wealth—he is the "richest man in France" (12), as "rich as Croesus" (10)—and she integrates detailed references to his artistic and literary pornography collection into a specific, extensive, almost exaggerated accounting of the named possessions and delicacies that convey his elite status: the bride's trousseau full of dresses from Poiret and Worth; a Bechstein piano; Isfahan carpets and Bokhara rugs; paintings by Ensor, Gauguin, Watteau, Poussin, and Fragonard and a wedding gift of "an early Flemish primitive of Saint Cecilia at her celestial organ" (14); Limoges and Sèvres china; Krug champagne; boxes of *marrons glacés*; "pheasant with hazelnuts and chocolate" (18); hothouse flowers; furs; and magnificent family jewels, such as the wedding ring, featuring "a fire opal the size of a pigeon's egg" (9), and the "choker of rubies, two inches wide, like an extraordinarily precious slit throat" (11). By writing the Marquis's pornographic and decadent library holdings into the other markers of his highbrow culture, Carter articulates some of the patriarchal specular practices implicit in much of the European art now canonized by our historical and cultural remove. In her reading of visual and narrative art in "The Bloody Chamber," Martine Hennard Dutheil argues that Carter invokes visual art to "[pursue] and [radicalize] the central argument made by John Berger in *Ways of Seeing*," specifically that European painting is dominated by "the visual convention whereby '*men act* and *women appear*'" (2006: 184–85; emphasis in original). Thus Carter implies that the beastliness of the Marquis's libertine sexuality and decadent culture might just as well lurk in nineteenth-century highbrow art and literature more generally.

The Ruby Wound

The Marquis is perhaps his most Sadeian and his most Baudelairean in the moment immediately preceding his young bride's defloration. Excited by her "painful, furious bewilderment" (Carter, 1993: 17), he rushes her to the bedroom where he demands that she put on her ruby choker, the fetishized wedding gift that conjures his future plans for her.

Aroused as much by the "blazing rubies" as by his wife's earlier horror, he kisses her neck and the jeweled promise of an impending wound before kissing her mouth. He then recites a line from "Les Bijoux," one of Baudelaire's "condemned" poems: "Of her apparel she retains / Only her sonorous jewelry" (17). Then, he "impales" her.

In contrast to her earlier fantasy of their wedding night "in his great ancestral bed in the sea-girt . . . that magic place, the fairy castle" (Carter, 1993: 8), the heroine's sexual initiation is a quick daytime affair after which the Marquis "lay beside [her], felled like an oak, breathing stertorously, as if he had been fighting with [her]" (17–18); she is left "cradling [her] spent body in [her] arms" (18). After he wakes and takes a business call, he turns to her and "stroke[s] the ruby necklace that bit into [her] neck, but with such tenderness now, that [she] ceased flinching" (18); he apologizes with sweeping platitudes about his "impetuousness" and his love, which brings her to tears and "[she] clung to him as though only the one who had inflicted the pain could comfort [her] for suffering it" (18). Later, having barely crossed the threshold of the bloody chamber, she recites another of Baudelaire's lines—"There is a striking resemblance between the act of love and the ministrations of a torturer" (27)—which she explicitly associates with this first sexual experience: "I had learned something of the nature of that similarity on my marriage bed" (27–28). Here, then, the heroine draws together the two bloody chambers, the two rooms where he "can go . . . to savour the rare pleasure of imagining [himself] wifeless" (21): their bedroom, with its bloody sheets and the jeweled promise of her eventual murder, and the forbidden chamber, with the bodies and bones of his previous wives. Both are redolent with the "lush, insolent incense reminiscent of pampered flesh" (18) from the Marquis's fetishized flowers, the white arum lilies that also call to mind death—the "undertakers' lilies" (15), the "funereal lilies" (9), signs of "an embalming parlour" (18). Connecting the two bloody chambers,[6] the mutual sites of both death and "pampered flesh," of the "ministrations of a torturer" and "the act of love," the heroine begins to understand her inevitable place in the Marquis's sadistic script.

With the heroine's dawning understanding, Carter casts "The Bloody Chamber" in the tradition of "Bluebeard" as a doubly told tale, a his-and-hers story with two distinct plots. Cristina Bacchilega distinguishes the two plots by the central motifs used to characterize them. On the one hand, the hegemonic plot—Bluebeard's plot—privileges the bloody key as the central motif, and the story revolves around his punishment of female curiosity and disobedience. On the other hand, the "slant" plot—the wife's plot—foregrounds the forbidden chamber as the dominant motif, and the story is motivated by "a process of initiation which *requires* entering the forbidden chamber" (Bacchilega, 1997: 107; emphasis in original).

In related work on "Bluebeard" as paradigmatic of feminist intertextuality, Casie Hermansson extends the tale's implicit doubling to articulate its two interrelated narratives: "Bluebeard's plot" and "Bluebeard's story" (unfortunately, this title erases the heroine's significance to its definition) (2001: 6). According to Hermansson, Bluebeard's plot is "endlessly self-perpetuating, endlessly self-justifying" and "based on unvaried repetition" (5), whereas Bluebeard's story includes the final wife's interruption of his tyrannical repetition and "thus transcends Bluebeard's plot" (6); as a result, "Bluebeard" always already contains a feminist critique of the misogynist logic behind Bluebeard's serial killing.

Not surprisingly, Carter takes up the tale's double nature but refuses a simple rewriting that celebrates the heroine's empowering initiation into the bloody chamber. Instead, she exploits and complicates the narrative doubling of "Bluebeard" in order to investigate the complexities of gender and desire in a patriarchal culture: sadism *and* masochism, women's complicity *and* resistance, the potential women have for pleasure *and* horror in their objectification. Thus, if throughout their courtship and into the first days of their marriage the Marquis has purchased his bride with his astounding wealth, gazed upon her with "the assessing eye of a connoisseur inspecting horseflesh, or even of a housewife in the market, inspecting cuts on the slab" (Carter, 1993: 11), and projected her into his pornographic illustrations and sadistic fantasies, it is through the bride's retrospective narration that she confesses her complicity in the Marquis's script. As first-person narrator, the heroine can inflect the story with the nuances of her conflicted emotions and experiences: arousal and anxiety, craving and disgust, knowing and naïveté. Because it is her story, she need not explain away the contradictions implicit in her emotional turmoil and emergent self-reflections. She can hint at her salvation even as she invests her story with the fatalism and inevitability of all "Bluebeard" tales, even as she confesses the ways in which she actively plays out the Marquis's script, the complicit nature of their competing—and interlocking—stories.

Within this context, then, the ruby choker is doubly significant. Not only is it the Marquis's prized fetish object—he forces her to wear it for her defloration, kisses it before kissing her mouth, strokes it as it "bit[es] into [her] neck" (Carter, 1993: 18), refuses to let her remove it "although it was growing very uncomfortable" (19), insists she wear it for her decapitation, slices away her shift so the choker alone remains when her head is on the chopping block—but it is also the mark of her survival. Thus, although the ruby choker has been widely read as foretelling the Marquis's intent to decapitate his wife[7] and even though he himself calls it "the necklace that prefigures your end" (36), in the defloration scene where its fetishization for the Marquis is most explicit, the heroine refers to it as "the family heirloom of one woman who had escaped the blade" (17). That woman was the Marquis's aristocratic grandmother, who survived the French Revolution and later commissioned the ruby choker in a shared celebration with other women of her class "who'd escaped the guillotine [and] had an ironic fad of tying a red ribbon round their necks at just the point where the blade would have sliced it through, a red ribbon like the memory of a wound" (11). In the end, the jeweled wound is the memory of a sentence never delivered: The heroine, like both the Marquis's grandmother and Saint Cecilia, survives the decapitation to which she is sentenced.

Yet, when the heroine first wears the ruby choker to the opera on the eve of their marriage, "everyone stared at [her]. And at his wedding gift . . . an extraordinarily precious slit throat" as well as a "gesture of luxurious defiance!" (Carter, 1993: 11). It is on this same evening that she demurely glances away from his lustful gaze and, in so doing, catches her own reflection in the mirror: "I saw how much that cruel necklace became me. And, for the first time in my innocent and confined life, I sensed in myself a potentiality for corruption that took my breath away" (11). From this moment the heroine is enticed by her objectification in the gaze of the crowd and in the Marquis's voracious look, and as Aidan Day points out, the first-person retrospective narration emphasizes her subsequent self-objectification, particularly when she refers to herself in the third person, multiply reflected as the "chic" and "elegant" girls in the bedroom's mirrors (1998: 154). The "cruel necklace" and the fashionable wardrobe are critical to her seduction and to her complicity in the Marquis's script. She herself sees that he has bought her—with her "potentiality for corruption," her "promise of debauchery only a connoisseur could detect" (Carter, 1993: 20), her "dark newborn curiosity" (22)—with "a handful of coloured stones and the pelts of dead beasts" (18).

At the same time, she also confesses her longing and desire for him, even as she registers her simultaneous revulsion. Recognizing their reproduction of the Rops etching and the Marquis's objectification of her, the heroine reveals the familiar seduction of his gaze: "As at the opera, when I had first seen my flesh in his eyes, I was aghast to feel myself stirring" (Carter, 1993: 15). When he defers her sexual initiation, she recalls that "I felt both a strange, impersonal arousal at the thought of love and at the same time a repugnance I could not stifle for his white, heavy flesh" (15). "I longed for him. And he disgusted me," she admits (22).

It is the heroine, not the Marquis, who characterizes their relationship with Baudelaire's equation of love and torture, an indication that she is not too innocent to understand its sadomasochistic nature: "He turned to me and stroked the ruby necklace that bit into my neck, but with such tenderness now, that I ceased flinching and he caressed my breasts" (18). According to Carter, for the Marquis as "for Sade, all tenderness is false, a deceit, a trap; all pleasure contains within itself the seeds of atrocities; all beds are minefields" (2006: 28). For the Marquis and the heroine, pleasure and pain, tenderness and deceit are thoroughly imbricated. Throughout their relationship the ruby collar—both privileged wedding gift and prized fetish—condenses the competing drives and desires of the heroine and the Marquis, the ways that love and torture, sadism and masochism, subjectivity and objectivity crosscut their relationship, and Carter seems to suggest that the line between women's complicity with and acquiescence to violent male oppression is a fine one drawn in blood on the bodies of women.

Dead-Ends: Pornography, Religion, Myth

Carter's exploration of women's potential to enjoy their objectification, particularly in relation to pornography and sadomasochism, is a reminder that "victimhood often carries with it the dangerously seductive companions of 'willingness' and 'virtue'" (Bacchilega, 1997: 122–23). Carter's nuanced treatment of gender, desire, and power in "The Bloody Chamber" (and in her other stories) has led some feminist critics to read the collection as ultimately conservative and reactionary. For instance, Patricia Duncker maintains that Carter's transformations of the fairy tale ultimately fall victim to the patriarchal ideologies that structure the genre itself; as a result, each tale "merely explains, amplifies and reproduces rather than alters the original, deeply, rigidly sexist psychology of the erotic" (1984: 6). Along similar lines, Robert Clark contends that Carter's representations of women "enjoying [their] own sexuality . . . are achieved at the cost of accepting patriarchal limits to women's power" (1987: 149). Avis Lewallen rightly points out that Duncker "overlooks the use of irony . . . which both acknowledges patriarchal structure and provides a form of critique against it" (1988: 147), but then she offers a similarly limited reading of "The Bloody Chamber" and its attention to sadomasochism and pornography, which she finds personally discomforting.

> Of all the tales in the volume I found "The Bloody Chamber" most troubling in terms of female sexuality, largely because of the very seductive quality of the writing itself. As readers we are asked to place ourselves imaginatively as masochistic victims in a pornographic scenario and to sympathise in some way with the ambivalent feelings this produces. The heroine's own subsequent recognition of total manipulation does not allay my unease at being manipulated by the narrative to sympathise with masochism. (Lewallen, 1988: 151)

Here, Lewallen draws on her own unease with masochism to justify her determination that the story is "troubling in terms of female sexuality," which further prevents her from considering the possibility that Carter might want to provoke readers into reflecting on their own collusion with the gendered representational practices that align European high art and literature with pornography.[8]

Many later feminist critics have challenged Clark, Duncker, Lewallen, and others who have contested Carter's representations of gender and desire, pointing out the various ways that Carter's fairy tales complicate the investment in the binary oppositions underlying their arguments, even when their arguments level the same critique against Carter.[9] In one of the most thorough engagements with Carter's critics, Merja Makinen articulates the point that a limited view of women's sexuality—one that fails to imagine that women "can be violent as well as active sexually, that women can choose to be perverse," as Duncker's and Lewallen's perspectives do—does little more than "incarcerate women back within a partial, sanitized image only slightly less constricted than the Victorian angel in the house" (1992: 9). In relation to the heroine's masochism more specifically, Bacchilega contests Lewallen's sense of having been manipulated into a sympathetic identification with the young bride as she narrates her experiences; instead, she reads the narration as "a painful recognition from within of masochism's presence in sexual and economic exploitation" (1997: 123). Sheets locates a similar awareness and a potential for agency in the heroine's masochism: "Masochism may have served her interests during the courtship and the initial sexual encounter: perhaps she assumed a passive role as a way to disguise her curiosity about sex and her desire for wealth" (1991: 652). Clearly, for Carter and readers willing to grant her "complex vision of female psycho-sexuality, through her [invocation] of violence as well as the erotic" (Makinen, 1991: 9), women are never only oppressed victims of male sexual desires, aggression, and violence; rather, they are active participants in "the dangerous pleasures of sexuality" (12).

But, as Carter has argued in *The Sadeian Woman*, sexuality and desire are always constrained by their social contexts. In her oft-quoted polemic, she shatters any pretenses to the contrary.

> We may believe we fuck stripped of social artifice; in bed, we even feel we touch the bedrock of human nature itself. But we are deceived. Flesh is not an irreducible human universal. Although the erotic relationship may seem to exist freely ... it is, in fact, the most self-conscious of all human relationships, a direct confrontation of two beings whose actions in bed are wholly determined by their acts when they are out of it. (2006: 9–10)

For Carter, sexuality in a phallocentric culture is always already determined by dominant myths of gender, and she sees in fairy tales, romantic fiction, religion, pornography, and marriage some of the most prominent social means for advancing patriarchal definitions of both women and men. If Carter's heroine escapes the internalized myth of women's virtue that so captivates Sade's Justine, she is nonetheless influenced and shaped by discourses of women's victimhood, as her resemblance to Saint Cecilia makes clear. The Marquis installs the "early Flemish primitive of Saint Cecilia" (Carter, 1993: 14) in his wife's music room to highlight their similarities. The "celestial" organ player and patron saint of music was also sentenced to death by decapitation, which she miraculously survived. Later, as the Marquis calls his wife to the chopping block, he addresses her directly as Saint Cecilia (38). At times, even the heroine—whose hair is "martyrized" (19) by the Marquis, who is commanded by him to "prepare [herself] for martyrdom" (36)—begins to wonder at her relation to Saint Cecilia: "In the prim charm of this saint, with her plump, sallow cheeks and crinkled brown hair, I saw myself as I could have wished to be" (14). In Saint Cecilia the heroine identifies a victimhood that seems to differ markedly from the torturous love she experiences in sadomasochism. As "a lifelong atheist and stringent opponent of the Judeo-Christian apparatus of belief" (Gamble, 2008: 42), Carter's invocation of Saint Cecilia in "The Bloody Chamber" only extends the labyrinthine nature of gendered identity, pointing out "religion's status as a readily available ideological refuge or mask which still seduces women into victimhood" (Bacchilega, 1997: 126).

Even more powerful than religious narratives and pornography for constructing and maintaining hegemonic gender ideologies, however, are the two cultural myths that Carter sees undergirding Western society: the biblical story of Eve and the psychoanalytic theory of the Oedipal complex. After a colorful summary of Freud's theory of female development during the Oedipal phase in *The Sadeian Woman*, Carter makes explicit the cultural influence of both myths: "Freud's account of this process has such extraordinary poetic force that, however false it might be, it remains important as an account of what seemed, at one point in history, a possible progression. It retains a cultural importance analogous, though less far-reaching, to the myth of the crime of Eve in the Old Testament" (2006: 146). It cannot be surprising, then, that Carter turns to "Bluebeard"—a tale that thematizes women's curiosity as motivating their disobedience and sexual knowing while also causing their punishment—as the primary intertext for the eponymous opening story of *The Bloody Chamber*.

Perrault concludes his widely known "Bluebeard" tale with two morals, one of which he titles "Moral" and the other "Another Moral." The "Moral" comments on female curiosity, whereas "Another Moral" reflects on male violence and women's verbosity.

Moral

Curiosity, in spite of its appeal, often leads to deep regret. To the displeasure of many a maiden, its enjoyment is short lived. Once satisfied, it ceases to exist, and always costs dearly.

Another Moral

Apply logic to this grim story, and you will ascertain that it took place many years ago. No husband of our age would be so terrible as to demand the impossible of his wife, nor would he be such a jealous malcontent. For, whatever the color of her husband's beard, the wife of today will let him know who the master is. (Lang, 1889: 295)[10]

In ranking the two morals through their differential titles, Perrault privileges the first, thereby forwarding it as the more accurate meta-interpretive guide of the two. Whereas the "Moral" thoroughly encapsulates the tale's biblical underpinnings, forever projecting Eve's transgression into the "Bluebeard" tradition, "Another Moral" allows "the feminine 'vice' of talk" (Bacchilega, 1997: 105) to overshadow the husband's violence. On first read, "Another Moral" seems to be a condemnation of male violence, but closer reflection undermines such a reading. After all, Perrault seems to suggest in what he has already marked as the lesser meta-interpretive guide, "No husband of our age would be so terrible." Male violence is a thing of the past, but the dangers of feminine curiosity and the oppressive nature of feminine verbosity endure. Bacchilega puts it bluntly in her characterization of the two morals: "Whether in a more crudely sexist translation or in the original, Perrault's two morals still uphold absolute patriarchy as a 'paradise,' lost when women's curiosity opened the door to the bloody chamber" (1997: 105). Although Perrault's classic version of the tale with its two morals consolidates the association between "Bluebeard" and the myth of Eve's temptation and transgression, the affiliation between Eve and the story's heroine extends well beyond, as Maria Tatar's documentation of the tale's illustrated history reveals (1987, 2004).[11]

Carter makes explicit the heroine's likeness to Eve when, after having entered the bloody chamber and subsequently been commanded by the

Marquis to prepare for her decapitation, the young bride contemplates her situation with her lover, Jean-Yves, the blind piano tuner. Their conversation cuts to the heart of Eve's story as the two seek to figure the ethical parameters of interdiction, temptation, disobedience, and punishment.

> "You do not deserve this," he said.
> "Who can say what I deserve or no?" I said. "I've done nothing; but that may be sufficient reason for condemning me."
> "You disobeyed him," he said. "That is sufficient reason for him to punish you."
> "I only did what he knew I would."
> "Like Eve," he said. (Carter, 1993: 37–38)

While Jean-Yves's comparison of the heroine to Eve might "[reveal] that his attitudes have been shaped by myths of feminine evil," as Sheets contends (1991: 654), I want to suggest that his analogy is much more complicated. As the heroine and Jean-Yves go back and forth, their positions alternate and shift at every turn in a way that productively exacerbates the complexities of Eve's story. Can Eve's transgression ever be disentangled from God's entrapment of her? Is Jean-Yves expressing his belief in the "myths of feminine evil," or is he revealing a sympathy for Eve's inevitable fall to God's manipulation? By amplifying these ambiguities in both "Bluebeard" and Eve's story, Carter destabilizes its preeminence in Western culture, foregrounding instead the patriarchal blind spot that validates the bloody key as the tale's central motif, a motif that obscures the husband's violence while emphasizing instead the wife's curiosity, transgression, and disobedience to God and the Law (of the Father). But, as the heroine realizes in the bloody chamber, Eve's story is inadequate for the job it has been accorded. In the center of the room on an ornate catafalque surrounded by candles, "the opera singer lay. . . . She was cool, he had embalmed her. On her throat I could see the blue imprint of his strangler's fingers" (Carter, 1993: 28). While the "blue imprint of his strangler's fingers" is clear on the first wife's neck, her transgression is not. At the time of her murder, the bloody chamber is not yet full of dead bodies; there is no infinite regression of murdered wives. Thus for the first wife there was not yet a bloody chamber, not yet an interdiction against her curiosity and eventual knowing. Here, then, at the center of the bloody chamber, Carter seems to reiterate the idea that power, dominance, control, and violence are in themselves sexually stimulating, an idea that puts the lie to Eve's story as foundational to contemporary relations between the sexes, a dead end.

Beyond God, the Father, the Marquis, and Freud

As noted earlier, Carter understands Freud's theory of the Oedipal phase to be almost as significant as the story of Eve in its cultural reach and force. I quote Carter's somewhat lengthy account, in *The Sadeian Woman*, of the Oedipal conflict as it pertains to girls because Freud's psychoanalytic narrative—and what Carter prioritizes in it—ultimately serves as one of her primary intertexts in "The Bloody Chamber."

> In the Freudian orchestration, now father enters the nursery and interposes his phallic presence between his daughter and her mother; his arrival in the psychic theatre, bearing his irreplaceable prick before him like a wand of office, a conductor's baton, a sword of severance, signifies the end of the mother's role as seducer and beloved. "The turning away from the mother is accompanied by a hostility; the attachment to the mother ends in hate," hypothesises Freud in his essay on femininity in the *New Introductory Lectures in Psychoanalysis*. The primary passion was incapable of the consummation of a child. The girl now turns to the father in the expectation he will give her the object that he possesses which she lacks, the phallus that is a substitute child and also makes children, that weapon which is a symbol of authority, of power, and will pierce the opacity of the world. (Carter, 2006: 145–46)

Freud's narrative drives the plot of "The Bloody Chamber," but not through Carter's fidelity to it. The heroine begins her story not with her courtship or wedding, as one might expect of a young woman just married, but with the journey away from her mother. Amid her excitement as the train conveys her from "the enclosed quietude of [her] mother's apartment, into the unguessable country of marriage," she experiences "a pang of loss as if, when he put the gold band on my finger, I had, in some way, ceased to be her child in becoming his wife" (Carter, 1993: 7). Almost immediately, then, Carter questions Freud's contention that a girl's successful gender development depends on her turning away from her mother in hate; here, newly married—what Freud would certainly deem a successful gender development—the daughter registers her separation from her mother as a loss, one so deep as to be felt in the body, a "pang." Later in the journey, after reflecting on her utter seduction by the Marquis's wealth and status, she claims, "I could not say I felt one single twinge of regret for the world of tartines and maman that now receded from me as if drawn away on a string, like a child's toy" (12), like Ernst Freud's *fort/da* game, in fact.

Freud saw in his grandson's game a masochistic attempt to exert control over the pain of his mother's absence, and Carter seems to suggest the heroine's similar attempt at control—as the "world of tartines and maman" is "drawn away on a string," the heroine no longer feels the "pang of loss," much less a "single twinge of regret"—while also hinting at her proclivity for masochism. By continuing the heroine's *fort/da* game beyond the pre-Oedipal phase and into young adulthood, Carter further interrogates the viability of Freud's theory of feminine sexuality, "challenging the Oedipal models of development which privilege separation over dependence" (Sheets, 1991: 654). Instead, she asserts the possibility of an enduring bond between mother and daughter against the "Western European context of competition and rivalry between women that devalues women," a rivalry she identifies in both Sade and Freud (Carter, 2006: 143).

While Carter's depiction of the heroine's relationship to her mother reimagines Freudian theories of femininity, her portrayal of the girl's relationship to the Marquis is much more Lacanian.[12] That the Marquis is the phallic presence in "The Bloody Chamber" is obvious, and the heroine exaggerates this point by collapsing God and her father into his characterization.[13] Early in the story, she describes the Marquis as "older . . . much older" (Carter, 1993: 8), and his fragrant cigar reminds her of the scent of her father; in another parallel, she recalls her father taking her to a performance of *Tristan und Isolde* (with the Marquis's first wife singing the part of Isolde), the same opera the Marquis takes her to see on the eve of their wedding. Later in the story, after the heroine uncovers all the horrors of the bloody chamber, she sees him as God: "The light caught the fire opal on my hand so that it flashed, once, with a baleful light, as if to tell me the eye of God—his eye—was upon me" (29). Here, the Marquis's omniscient eye articulates the relationship between masochism and the male gaze.

Sheets references Ann Kaplan's Lacanian theory of the male gaze to explain why the heroine might be aroused by her own objectification. According to Kaplan, when girls enter the Symbolic Order and succumb to the Law of the Father, they are "assigned to the place of the object" and become "the recipient of male desire, the passive recipient of his gaze"; as a result, Kaplan contends, they "[learn] to associate their sexuality with domination by the male gaze, a position involving a degree of masochism in finding their objectification erotic" (quoted in Sheets, 1991: 651). With the Marquis's God-like eye fixing the heroine in the bloody chamber, Carter implies that the masochism associated with the potential erotics of the male gaze also leads to the violent murders of the Marquis's wives. Moreover, in moving from Freud's masochistic *fort/da* game to Kaplan's Lacanian theory of masochism in relation to the male gaze, Carter contests the individualism of Freud's masochism, positing instead a social basis for masochism, one rooted in language and thus ideology. Carter seems to suggest that in a heterosexual economy women may be masochistic, but their masochism is produced and perpetuated by cultural forces.

In questioning the individual basis of masochism, Carter also interrogates the belief in the male eye as all powerful. Endowing the Marquis—as God, father, and husband—with the surveillant and knowing eye and the seeming right to decree the heroine's sentence, Carter literalizes the Law of the Father in a move that also caricatures him with its excessive phallicism. Brandishing his "great-grandfather's ceremonial sword" (Carter, 1993: 36) to execute the heroine, the Marquis cannot help but call to mind the phallic presence that Carter describes in *The Sadeian Woman*, the one who "[bears] his irreplaceable prick before him like . . . a sword of severance" (2006: 146). Placing the "sword of severance" in the Marquis's murderous hands, Carter mocks the cultural mythology of the all-powerful phallus that not only objectifies and oppresses women but also separates mother and daughter.

Of course, in Carter's story it is the mother (and not the brothers, as in Perrault's tale) who saves the young bride from decapitation. The phallic mother arrives on horseback, equipped with her husband's service revolver, and literally interrupts the Law of the Father in action: "The Marquis stood transfixed, utterly dazed, at a loss.... The puppet master, open-mouthed, wide-eyed, impotent at the last, saw his dolls break free of their strings, abandon the rituals he had ordained for them since time began" (Carter, 1993: 39). After his momentary paralysis—"sword still raised over his head as in those clockwork tableaux of Bluebeard" (40)—brought on by the shock of the *mother's* "arrival in the psychic theatre" (Carter, 2006: 146), the Marquis roars to life and, "without a moment's hesitation," the mother "put[s] a single, irreproachable bullet through [his] head" (Carter, 1993: 40). Carter's reversal of the daughter's hostile break from the mother at the center of Freud's Oedipal complex allows the mother to avenge the daughter in both "The Bloody Chamber" and in Freud's story of feminine sexuality.

Although the mother exerts a phallic power in this particular scene, Carter is careful to avoid reinscribing the cultural authority of the Oedipal complex by simply reinstalling the phallic mother to her earlier place of prominence. Instead, the avenging mother undercuts the importance of both vision (Freud) and language (Lacan) to psychoanalytic theories of the Oedipal phase, castration anxiety, and subjectivity. Thus, although the Marquis's eye (like God's) and his word (like the Law's) may be all powerful in a phallocratic culture, in Carter's story the mother relies on other ways of knowing and communicating to disrupt the seeming inevitability of the Marquis's plot. She is prompted to action by what the heroine refers to as her *"maternal telepathy"* (Carter, 1993: 40; emphasis in original), her ability to understand the mysterious phone call, a call that moves the daughter to tears, although all she can say is, "No, nothing [is] the matter. Mother, I have gold bath taps" (24), provided such a call ever transpired in the first place. After all, the Marquis informs her shortly before she is to be decapitated, "One may call inside the castle just as much as one please; but, outside—never" (37). Whether the maternal telepathy connects mother to daughter through the phone or through another more magical means, it does not depend on the language of the Symbolic Order; indeed, it falls entirely outside language and the symbolic, perhaps Carter's testamentto a bond that might precede *and* survive the daughter's concession to language and her submission to the Law of the Father.

In the end, the decidedly nonphallic prevails over the Marquis's violent and exaggerated phallicism. Jean-Yves, the heroine's lover, is a blind piano tuner, and his obvious symbolic castration results in his privileging of different sensory paradigms, particularly aurality and scent. As one would expect of a blind piano tuner, he has excellent pitch, a fine appreciation of music, and acute hearing; his sense of smell is sharp enough to detect the blood on the key the heroine offers as proof of the horrors she has found in the forbidden chamber. Despite her masochistic seduction by the male gaze, even the heroine seems more attuned to a range of sensory channels: She experiences "a tender, delicious ecstasy of excitement" (Carter, 1993: 7); her "excited senses [tell her] he was awake and gazing at [her]" (12); she knows "by some tingling of the fingertips" (16) that the untitled book she is about to open contains the pornographic images that will shock her. With the heroine's attention to a full range of sensations, her mother's telepathy, and Jean-Yves's attention to sound and scent, Carter offers an alternative to the implicitly gendered hegemonies of vision and language, an alternative that also begins to open up the phallocentric ideologies that sustain the oppressive force of marriage as thematized in the Marquis's attitudes.

At the end of "The Bloody Chamber," the heroine converts the castle to a school for the blind and donates the vast majority of her inheritance to charities, keeping only enough to open a small music school. She and Jean-Yves never marry but instead "[set] up house" with her mother, and the three "lead a quiet life" together (Carter, 1993: 40–41). If marriage holds together the power of patriarchy, the scopophilic objectification of women, their exchange as commodities, and the false universalizing of its romantic overlays, as Carter suggests, then her dramatic turn from the conclusion of Perrault's "Bluebeard"—when the heroine simply reproduces the patriarchal economies of marriage by using her inheritance to marry off both her sister and herself—may also be her most radical.

Seeking an Exit

The heroine's description of the quiet life that she, Jean-Yves, and her mother lead may resolve the plot, but it is certainly not the end of the story. In typical Carter fashion "The Bloody Chamber" concludes with the red mark on the heroine's forehead and, even more significantly, with her relief that Jean-Yves's blindness "spares [her] shame" (Carter, 1993: 41). The ambiguity of the heroine's shame, like the opacity of her sexuality and desire, is interpreted in different ways by those who see Carter's work as reactionary and reductive and by those who see it as more productive in its complexity. On the conservative side, for instance, Duncker and Lewallen locate the heroine's shame in her sexual collusion with patriarchy, "the complicity of women . . . who have desired to be possessed" (Duncker 1984: 11). Both critics condemn Carter for perpetuating gender binaries through the heroine's shame. Lewallen complains that "to be branded as guilty, despite recognition of the manipulation to which she has been subject, seems somewhat unfair" (1988: 152). However, as Day argues in response, the heroine's mark of shame "is not entirely unfair" because it registers the "responsibility on the girl's part for having been taken in by, at least, the Marquis' money" (1998: 158).[14] Suzette Henke similarly reads it as "the shame of youthful indiscretion in a tattoo of defilement" (2013: 50). Regardless of how it is interpreted, the heroine's red mark of shame forecloses the possibility of an easy feminist reversal in which the heroic mother conquers the sadistic father.[15]

Ironically, given the conservative interpretations of the heroine's enduring shame and the vitriolic response to *The Sadeian Woman* by Anglo-American antipornography feminists,[16] "The Bloody Chamber" ultimately stands against pornography. As Sheets makes clear in her analysis of the story in relation to the second-wave feminist debates over pornography, Carter "assumes that pornography encourages violence against women and that the association of sex, power, and sadomasochism in pornography is part of society's common prescription for heterosexual relations" (1991: 655). Unlike her antipornography critics, however, Carter does not begin with these assumptions. Rather than reject pornography out of hand in "The Bloody Chamber," she provides a nuanced exploration of the varied, often competing, drives and desires that underlie all sexuality as well as the cultural practices and productions that circumscribe them.

For Carter pornography supplies a ready paradigm for heterosexual relations, and as such it oppresses men as well as women through its false universalizing and "abstraction of human intercourse" (Carter, 2006: 4). Although men like Sade and his libertines are endowed with subjectivity and power in the pornographic script and in cultural myths of gender, Carter contends that they must nonetheless (or, perhaps, consequently) search in perpetuity for a phallus adequate enough to appease their castration anxiety and to satisfy the mother's insatiable desire: "He [Sade] wants a bigger, a yet bigger one and rummages around in the chest in which he keeps his dildos . . . to find one that will be big enough to console him for his fear of castration. . . . There is no solace for the libertine's insatiability because access to the object of love is always denied him" (2006: 151–52). Here, in the *Sadeian Woman*, Carter conflates Freud's fetish and Lacan's phallus and connects them with sadism and pornography, a connection she brings to life through the Marquis, his collection of pornography, his lilies, the bloody key, and the ruby choker in "The Bloody Chamber." Even as she plays up the Marquis's extreme fetishism—and his related denial of an other's subjectivity—Carter also hints at his underlying trauma. A passing reference to the housekeeper as his foster mother suggests the early absence of his biological mother (Carter, 1993: 14), and his initial response to the heroine's accepting his marriage proposal—"not one muscle in his face stirred, but he let out a long, extinguished sigh" (9)—implies that he himself recognizes, and perhaps regrets, the inevitability of the scripts he is compelled to enact. Connecting the sigh more directly with his sadistic fetishism and his entrapment in the pornographic scripts of his own making, the Marquis later "[emits] that same, heavy sigh as he had done when [she] said that [she] would marry him" after transferring the blood from the key to the heroine's forehead (36). Cognizant of the Marquis's trauma, Carter insists that in his moment of greatest control and knowing, the moment the heroine hands over the bloody key, his face "contained a sombre delirium that seemed to [the heroine] compounded of a ghastly, yes, shame but also of a terrible, guilty joy as he slowly ascertained how [she] had sinned" (36). Here, the Marquis's emotions—his simultaneous shame, guilt, and joy—capture the complicated nature of his sadism, fetishism, and pornographic imagination.

In its nonpathological and less extreme forms, "fetishism may indeed be instrumental in constructing an autonomous subjectivity" by facilitating a control over the self (McCallum, 1995: 30). The significance of self-mastery for subjectivity is, of course, gendered in a patriarchal society, with men, as the universal subjects, assumed to be self-controlled, self-contained, rational. For Carter the perpetuation of this cultural myth of masculinity is one of pornography's greatest dangers because it renders impossible a true sexual reciprocity. The libertine's penchant for the orgy, for sex with accomplices as opposed to lovers or partners, underscores the threat that reciprocity poses for patriarchal subjectivity.

> The libertine would not trust a partner, who would rob him of pleasure by causing him to feel rather than to experience.
>
> The presence of his accomplices preserves his ego from the singular confrontation with the object of a reciprocal desire which is, in itself, both passive object and active subject. Such a partner acts on us as we act on it; both partners are changed by the exchange. (Carter, 2006: 171–72)

To "feel rather than to experience," to be "changed by the exchange," necessarily entails a loss of control and the possibility of a momentary shattering of subjectivity. Within this context the Marquis's orgasm, which demands the briefest loss of control, is ruinous: "In the course of that one-sided struggle, [the heroine] had seen his deathly composure shatter like a porcelain vase flung against a wall; [she] had heard him shriek and blaspheme at the orgasm" (Carter, 1993: 18). As part of the heroine's description of her painful defloration, in which she figures her husband as having been "fighting with [her]" (18), "that one-sided struggle" seems at first to refer to the Marquis's dominance over her; however, the phrase is productively ambiguous, and the "one-sided struggle" might just as well apply to the Marquis's own internal struggle for release and control in his moment of orgasm. It inspires blasphemy because it challenges the boundaries of the self, and it almost instantaneously moves the Marquis from godly realm of complete mastery to the depths of hell with its completion. As such, the Marquis's orgasm reverberates with Carter's description of the explicit loss implicit in the Sadeian orgasm: "During the irreducible timelessness of the moment of orgasm, the hole in the world through which we fall, he has been as a god, but this state is as fearful as it is pleasurable.... He has burst into the Utopia of desire.... And, just as immediately, he has been expelled from it, a fall like Lucifer's, from heaven to hell" (2006: 175–76).

Such an orgasm, according to Carter, "is never the instrument of love" (2006: 176), because love requires the reciprocity that so frightens the Marquis and the libertine; instead, he, like Sade's libertines, chooses "diabolical solitude" (2006: 176), despite his simultaneous yearning to vanquish it through sadistic fetishism and pornographic fantasy. Indeed, the Marquis endeavors to live up to his favorite poet's Sadeian declaration: "When I have inspired universal disgust and horror, then I will have conquered solitude" (quoted in Carter, 2006: 38).

Thus, even at the height of her fear, the heroine notices the Marquis's "stench of absolute despair" and "[feels] a terrified pity for him, for this man who lived in such strange, secret places that, if I loved him enough to follow him, I should have to die. The atrocious loneliness of that monster!" (Carter, 1993: 35). With the heroine's "terrified pity" and the Marquis's "strange, secret places" that would lead to her death, Carter reiterates the damage that pornography and other cultural myths of gender wreak on both men and women. For Carter one possible exit from this oppressive labyrinth involves love—not a pseudo-romantic fairy-tale love but rather its radical counterpart, a love she finds in Emma Goldman's treatise on women's emancipation and with which she concludes *The Sadeian Woman*: "A true conception of the relation of the sexes will not admit of conqueror and conquered; it knows of but one great thing: to give of one's self boundlessly, in order to find one's self richer, deeper, better" (quoted in Carter, 2006: 177–78).

"The Bloody Chamber" remains as labyrinthine as the cultural and theoretical discourses that Carter engages throughout the story. Her complex rendering of both the Marquis and the heroine, with their equally complicated drives and their interlocking desires, denies all hope for a clear and easy path to the exit, and it may be this very refusal to provide directions through the labyrinth that Carter's feminist critics most resent about *The Bloody Chamber*. Not surprisingly, reductive readings structured by a logic of binary gender, such as Duncker's (1984) and Lewallen's (1988), only lead to dead-ends. Not deterred by dead-ends and misleading paths, however, Carter takes readers along with her as she herself explores the dark and dizzying corridors of "civilization": phallogocentric language, psychoanalytic theory, the aesthetics of gendered representational practices, the false universalizing of pornography.

In defending Jean-Yves as more than a dephallicized and thus inadequate partner for the heroine, Sheets speculates that "perhaps if Carter were to continue the story, she would develop a male sexuality centered on smell, touch, and sound" (1991: 655); even more, Sheets imagines that such a sexuality might help facilitate a "tradition of mutual gazing" (655) that expresses what Jackie Byars identifies as "a 'different voice' and a different kind of gaze that we've not heard or seen because our theories have discouraged such 'hearing' and 'seeing'" (quoted in Sheets, 1991: 655). Although Carter does not extend "The Bloody Chamber" beyond the quiet life shared by the heroine, her mother, and Jean-Yves, she nonetheless continues to explore the possibilities for an alternate erotics throughout the collection. In the feline stories Carter imagines a mutual gaze outside the confines of the Symbolic Order, and in the wolf trilogy she writes erotic possibilities that challenge dominant understandings of desire. Thus, although none of the stories in *The Bloody Chamber* forge a path out of the labyrinth, each suggests a possible course worth exploring, the light of a possible exit urging us on.

3

Beastly Subjects
The Feline Stories

Haunted by the specter of the leonine Marquis, Carter's two "Beauty and the Beast" stories unsettle the animal desires so well obscured by the mythologies of gender and romance that drive the classic versions of the tale. The pair of stories opens with "The Courtship of Mr. Lyon," a fairly conventional retelling set in and around early-twentieth-century London, and follows with "The Tiger's Bride," a much more fantastic transformation that holds past and future together in southern Italy. Read jointly as mirrored tales that are intertextually connected to each other and to classic versions of "Beauty and the Beast," Carter's transformations first draw out and condense the gendered ideologies at the heart of the tale and then critically reimagine the phallocentric systems of power and privilege that determine and define their beastly subjects.[1] "Puss-in-Boots," the third feline story, while not a "Beauty and the Beast" tale, proposes a different material reality in response to the problematics of gender and subjectivity that drive the first two stories, ultimately gesturing toward a utopian alternative to their conclusions.

The most widely known version of "Beauty and the Beast" is Madame Le Prince de Beaumont's 1756 story. Beaumont's tale, explicitly intended for young women by their self-identified "sage gouvernante" (Hearne, 1989: 2), was heavily influenced by Madame Gabrielle de Villeneuve's 1740 novelistic treatment of the same story written for an adult audience of "court and salon friends" (2). As an instructional tale, Beaumont's "Beauty and the Beast"[2] is a moral lesson about the value and reward of looking beyond superficial appearances in order to appreciate another's inner qualities; or, as Carter puts it in her review of Betsy Hearne's *Beauty and the Beast: Visions and Revisions of an Old Tale*, "A man should be loved for his inner qualities alone, especially if he has an outwardly repulsive appearance but pots of cash" (Carter, 1991: 124). Beaumont's tale is, of course, rooted in its cultural and historical context, and given its almost immediate translation into English, the story's characterization of Beauty and its explicit and implicit lessons clearly index eighteenth-century French and English ideals of femininity.

Earlier examples of the tale type (ATU 425C) feature dramatically different heroines based on their particular social contexts.[3] Thus, for instance, in Apuleius's second-century (CE) Roman story of "Cupid and Psyche," sexuality and desire are much more overt than in Beaumont's "Beauty and the Beast." With a typically incisive gloss, Carter characterizes the heroine as going from Psyche, who is "silly and sexy, pregnant by her invisible, possibly monstrous husband" and "so overcome with enthusiasm that she throws herself upon his sleeping body" (Carter, 1991: 124), to Beauty, who is "clean, tidy, a good housekeeper, prone to self-sacrifice and susceptible to moral blackmail" (124). Even more, because "Beauty and the Beast" has remained in print continuously since the eighteenth century and has rarely deviated from its literary source, Beaumont's tale has been granted a certain cultural authority and authenticity. As a result, the dominant myths of femininity and the associated moral lessons that originally gave meaning to her story continue to inhabit the tale, and it is precisely these meanings and their underlying precepts that Carter exposes, challenges, and rethinks in her own transformed tales.

In the Eye of the Beast: "The Courtship of Mr. Lyon"

"The Courtship of Mr. Lyon" stands out in *The Bloody Chamber* for its relative fidelity to its literary ancestor, the timidity of its retelling, and its uncharacteristically traditional fairy-tale ending. Anny Crunelle-Vanrigh describes it as "the least unsettling" of all the tales in the collection and suggests that in "closely following the plot of Madame Leprince de Beaumont's story, Carter also seems to endorse this eighteenth-century writer's moral point" (2001: 128). Although Crunelle-Vanrigh goes on to complicate this initial observation, her point opens up an important question: Why does Carter's "Courtship of Mr. Lyon" track Beaumont's "Beauty and the Beast" so carefully?

Beaumont's "Beauty and the Beast" is frequently characterized as a romance in which a young woman finds that love blossoms when she can learn to look beyond surface appearances to see the true nature of her physically repugnant suitor. Yet, in an ironic reversal, just below the appealing surface of the story lies its true nature: "The classic fable *Beauty and the Beast* is simply the story of an arranged marriage," proclaims the "Greatest Living Poet" in Salman Rushdie's *Shame* (quoted in Teverson, 1999: 215). Thus, whereas "Beauty and the Beast" seems to foreground romantic love over arranged marriage, Carter's updated retelling, set in early-twentieth-century London and the surrounding countryside, discounts any such distinctions. Like Rushdie's Greatest Living Poet, Carter lays bare the reality of exchange with her description of the daughter's transfer from father to Beast.

> When, as they sipped their brandy, the Beast, in the diffuse, rumbling purr with which he conversed, suggested, with a hint of shyness, of fear of refusal, that she should stay here, with him, in comfort, while her father returned to London to take up the legal cudgels again, she forced a smile. For she knew with a pang of dread, as soon as he spoke, that it would be so and her visit to the Beast must be, on some magically reciprocal scale, the price of her father's good fortune. (Carter, 1993: 45)

Regardless of the circumstances, for Carter marriage always reveals a woman's status as object of exchange within a patriarchal culture and highlights the foundational myths that imagine this exchange as critical to the origin and maintenance of human society.

Carter's faithfulness to Beaumont's version underscores not the timelessness of the tale (and its moral lesson) but rather the timelessness of the oppressive institution underlying it.[4] The historical specificity and material detail of "The Courtship of Mr. Lyon"—"the old car stuck fast in a rut" (Carter, 1993: 41), "the Palladian house" (42), "the telephone" (43), "the card of a garage that advertised a twenty-four-hour rescue service" (43)—firmly situate men's exchange of women in the modern era. Through these particularities of time and place Carter calls attention to "the archaic social systems still at work in [the] contemporary world" (Bryant, 1989: 446) and denies the easy tendency to imagine away such systems as part of a distant historical past or a fairy-tale realm. If marriage, pornography, and idealized romantic love all contribute to what Carter calls "false universalizing" and if their "excesses belong to that timeless, locationless area outside history, outside geography, where fascist art is born" (Carter, 2006: 13), then Carter takes an especially clever turn by locating "The Courtship of Mr. Lyon" *within* history and *within* geography. With the story's historical and geographic particularities, Carter establishes an ironic continuity with Beaumont's "Beauty and the Beast," a continuity that underscores the fact that marriage—as idealized romantic love, as system of exchange—is little more than a "false [universal], to dull the pain of particular circumstances" (6). "To be a wife is to act out a masochistic fantasy," Carter writes in "The Marriage Hearse," a section she ultimately omitted from *The Sadeian Woman*. For Carter the romanticization of marriage only naturalizes women's oppression: "The institutionalized bond legislates inequality. It reifies the oppression of the weak by the strong until it looks like a natural law."[5] Moreover, although women are certainly complicit in upholding this cultural myth, it is nonetheless one created by men: "So the wife embraces the fate she herself has constructed for herself in a state of unknowing.... And although she has herself to blame for her suffering, she has not only herself to blame.... Men invented the fiction of the good wife."[6]

Within this context women are necessarily presumed to be objects, and Carter plays up the heroine's objectness. First portrayed as though "made all of snow" (Carter, 1993: 41), Beauty, her father's "pet" (41), is most frequently described in language that recalls fine decorative objects: "carved out of a single pearl" (46), her face taking on the "lacquer of the invincible prettiness that characterizes certain pampered, exquisite, expensive cats" (49). In terms of exchange, though, Beauty is worth exactly the price of a single rose; her value is clearly articulated in the Beast's simple command to her father: "'Take her the rose, then, but bring her to dinner,' he growled; and what else was there to be done?" (45). As Aidan Day so astutely points out, Beauty's object status and her exchange value are never questioned by the story's male powers (nor, for that matter, by her), although Carter certainly implies an outside to this patriarchal system: "Beauty's father accedes to an agreement based on the idea of an impersonal, unalterable law of contract. Carter's sly question emphasizes his accession and questions its grounds. Outside of this system, quite a number of things might be done" (1998: 137).

Even though the flower-loving Beast and the thieving father set in motion the conditions for the daughter's exchange in both Beaumont's and Carter's stories, Carter's modern retelling allows for a critical embellishment in the form of Beauty's photograph.

> The Beast rudely snatched the photograph her father drew from his wallet and inspected it, first brusquely, then with a strange kind of wonder, almost the dawning of surmise. The camera had captured a certain look she had, sometimes, of absolute sweetness and absolute gravity, as if her eyes might pierce appearances and see your soul. (Carter, 1993: 44)

By slipping a photo into her otherwise shiny, almost material, characterizations of Beauty as pearly and lacquered decorative object, Carter makes explicit the patriarchal mechanisms—scopophilia, voyeurism, the male gaze[7]—that naturalize women's objectification, even when exaggerated, as it is in her story. In so doing, she also exposes the controlling logic of the "Beauty and the Beast" tradition, a logic structured by the double standard of desire and its relation to the gaze. The Beast looks freely at Beauty; indeed, he is essentially compelled by the terms of the fairy's curse to do so because her beauty is the key to his disenchantment, as the transformed prince later explains: "A wicked fairy condemned me to remain under that shape, till a *beautiful* virgin should consent to marry me" (Beaumont, 1783: 66; emphasis mine).[8]

It can be no surprise that in Beaumont's tale the first words the Beast speaks to Beauty after her father leaves concern his watching her: "Beauty, said the monster, will you give me leave to see you sup?" (Beaumont, 1783: 58). The question is, of course, a disingenuous one, as the very premise of the story grants him the permission to do so; even Beauty recognizes that as the case: "That is as you please, answered Beauty, trembling" (58). Beauty, on the other hand, is essentially prevented from gazing at the Beast by his frightening physical appearance, an appearance that enforces the explicit injunction against *women's* gazing at men in the earlier cognate tales such as "Cupid and Psyche" and other invisible bridegroom stories. Instead, she is encouraged to "see" in more metaphoric fashion by looking beyond the Beast's physical body to his inner being.

The ideology of masculine desire and the associated privileging of the male gaze that structure "Beauty and the Beast" come to the fore in Jean Cocteau's 1946 film *La Belle et la Bête*. As Sylvia Bryant writes in her compelling reading of Carter's "Beauty and the Beast" stories alongside Cocteau's film, "*La Belle et La Bête* very much solicits looking" and "the most pervasive and compelling visual lure, of course, is Beauty herself" (1989: 442). Cocteau, even more than Carter, remains faithful to Beaumont's story, and the filmic medium allows him to amplify the Beast's gazing at Beauty.

> He stands behind her chair, peeping over her shoulder, seeing her—as the spectator sees her—while she sees nothing but the table before her. . . . He "sees" her, even, when she is absent from the line of his vision, for as omnipotent master, his omniscient eye frames her to physical advantage in doorways and on staircases as she moves through his house. (Bryant, 1989: 444)

Although Bryant does not address Cocteau's film as one of Carter's likely intertexts (she simply reads them together), Carter herself characterized *La Belle et La Bête* as "Jean Cocteau's enormously influential 1946 film, which gave a fresh lease of life to the whole genre of the art fairy tale," suggesting that "it is this film, which gave the old tale an impressive stamp of intellectual respectability, that has helped make the story so popular today" (Carter, 1991: 123). Others have argued that Carter found inspiration for the leonine Beast of "The Courtship of Mr. Lyon" in Cocteau's own lion-headed Beast (Barchilon, 1993: 271; Crunelle-Vanrigh, 2001: 130). More important than Carter's inspiration for the beastly Mr. Lyon, however, is the way that she subtly and only slightly reworks the gendered dynamics of gazing that inform both Beaumont's tale and Cocteau's film.

Initially, it seems that Carter is simply reproducing Beaumont's description of Beauty's first encounter with the Beast. Beaumont's phrase "Beauty herself could not help trembling at the awful apparition" (1783: 105) is clearly echoed in Carter's "she could not control an instinctual shudder of fear when she saw him" (1993: 45). Both reiterate the bias against women gazing on men, even in their beastly forms. Later in "The Courtship of Mr. Lyon," however, when the Beast looks up at Beauty after kissing her hands, Carter has Beauty return his look: "He drew back his head and gazed at her with his green, inscrutable eyes, in which she saw her face repeated twice, as small as if it were in bud" (47). This scene, which on the surface is not so very different from Beaumont's nightly proposal scenes, opens up into Carter's cutting critique. Here, as Beauty returns the Beast's gaze, she—like the Beast, like Cocteau's viewers, like Beaumont's readers—sees only herself, the ideal-I of Lacan's mirror phase, the reflected perfection she has been taught by her phallocentric culture to seek in all her relationships. Her objectification within the story, within the tale tradition, within the filmic tradition, denies her a subject position from which to see the Beast; instead, she is confined to object status, and she sees herself in (and through) the eyes of the Other.

Back in London with her father, Beauty remains the object of the gaze, but now she herself is among her most active viewers as she finds herself drawn to mirrors: "She took off her earrings in front of the mirror; Beauty. She smiled at herself with satisfaction. . . . She smiled at herself in mirrors a little too often, these days" (Carter, 1993: 48–49). As is always the case for Carter, women are not simply oppressed by patriarchal institutions, and Beauty's incessant mirror gazing—"her trance before the mirror" (49)—reflects Beauty's internalization and perpetuation of women's object status. Thus Carter reminds us that this particular fairy tale features a double enchantment, a double curse: the prince's transformation into beastly form and Beauty's transformation into object status. Yet at the end of Beaumont's tale and Cocteau's film, there is only one clear disenchantment. In Carter's story Beauty's trance before the mirror is broken when the Beast's spaniel arrives to remind her that she has forgotten her promise to the Beast, and Carter seems to hint at the possibility of Beauty's potential as viewing subject when she returns to him: "How was it she had never noticed before that his agate eyes were equipped with lids, like those of a man? Was it because she had only looked at her own face, reflected there?" (50). This glimpse of Beauty's potential subjectivity recalls the scene of the Beast's disenchantment in the classic versions of the tale, the one fleeting moment in all "Beauty and the Beast" stories when the heroine searches the transformed prince's face for signs of the beast she has come to love; however, the immediacy with which she is convinced that the prince is, indeed, her beast ensures that she not gaze too long upon him, that she quickly slip back into her place beside his side, object of his desire.

In "The Courtship of Mr. Lyon," Carter follows the scene of Beauty's seeing the Beast anew with his explanation of his dying condition.

> "I'm dying, Beauty," he said in a cracked whisper of his former purr. "Since you left me, I have been sick. I could not go hunting, I found I had not the stomach to kill the gentle beasts, I could not eat. I am sick and I must die; but I shall die happy because you have come to say good-bye to me." (Carter, 1993: 50)

With her slight variation to the Beast's dying words—in Beaumont's version the Beast is so "afflicted" by Beauty's absence that he "resolves to starve [himself]" (1783: 65)—Carter emphasizes the emotional blackmail that motivates Beauty's actions in both stories. For Carter the story of "Beauty and the Beast" revolves around this guilt-induced pressure, and she calls the tale "an advertisement for moral blackmail: when the Beast says that he is dying because of Beauty, the only morally correct thing for her to have said at that point would be, 'Die, then'" (Haffenden, 1985: 83). Of course, Beauty does not tell the Beast to die in either version of the story. Thus, while maintaining her overall fidelity to Beaumont's story, Carter rearranges and diminishes the narrative moment of Beauty's gazing upon the Beast. By shifting the nature of her own Beauty's gaze—reducing it from an active look to a passing observation—and by altering its placement in the narrative sequence so that it occurs *before* his emotional blackmail, *before* her disenchanting him, Carter forecloses the potential for subjectivity inherent in the traditional Beauty's gazing in wonder at the prince as she asks after her beloved Beast.

The thought of telling the Beast to "Die, then" never occurs to Beauty. She is too much the good girl for such a sentiment, and that—for Carter—signals both her oppression and her complicity in her oppression. Having internalized the Oedipal myth of the father's power, the good girl is obedient, proper, polite; she believes in her innocence and her virginity as her greatest virtues. Carter's Beauty is by definition the perfect daughter, the perfect good girl: "She stayed, and smiled, because her father wanted her to do so; and when the Beast told her how he would aid her father's appeal against the judgement, she smiled with both her mouth and her eyes" (Carter, 1993: 45). Later, despite her wishes, Beauty forces another smile and agrees to stay with the Beast while her father leaves to address his legal concerns. At this point, underlining the question of Beauty's subjectivity, the narrator addresses the reader directly with the imperative, "Do not think she had no will of her own" (45). What follows, however, seems to call that claim into question; indeed, the imperative is punctuated with a semicolon, thus suggesting an intimately confused or ambiguous relationship between the two parts of the sentence: "Do not think she had no will of her own; only, she was possessed by a sense of obligation to an unusual degree and, besides, she would gladly have gone to the ends of the earth for her father, whom she loved dearly" (45–46). Here again Carter emphasizes women's and girls' active participation in the patriarchal systems that oppress them. Being the good daughter, the good girl will only ever limit women's autonomy, as Carter makes clear in her description of Sade's Justine: "She is a child who knows how to be good to please daddy; but the existence of daddy, her god, the abstract virtue to which she constantly refers, prevents her from acting for herself" (2006: 63).

The production of the good girl is, of course, Beaumont's goal. As the *sage gouvernante* with a passion for instilling in young women the values that would allow them to please daddy, that would make them ideal good girls and, ultimately, marriageable women, Beaumont is an especially pertinent target for Carter's critique. For Carter Beaumont exemplifies women's internalization of patriarchal values and cultural narratives and is complicit in further inculcating these controlling ideologies in girls and young women. Thus Carter's almost faithful rendering of Beaumont's "Beauty and the Beast"—atypical among Carter's transformed fairy tales for exactly this fidelity—functions like a subtle satire to undermine the lessons driving Beaumont's tale. As far as Carter is concerned, Beaumont's tale produces women as victims who not only self-identify as such but also locate their virtue in their victimization, thereby underscoring its worthlessness and its meaninglessness except as consolatory myth: "If there is no virtue in her suffering, then there is none, it turns out, in her virtue itself; it does nobody any good, least of all herself" (Carter, 2006: 45).

Carter has little patience for the woman-as-victim paradigm, especially when figured as virtue, and she brings her Beauty and Sade's Justine together in the language of herbivores, helpless prey in a system they do not quite understand: "The lamb does not understand why it is led to the slaughter and so it goes willingly, because it is in ignorance . . . it is hampered by the natural ignorance of the herbivore, who does not even know it is possible to eat meat" (Carter, 2006: 163). In one of the story's rare passages in which Carter offers insight into Beauty's interiority, Beauty herself takes on this identification: "When she saw the great paws lying on the arm of his chair, she thought: they are the death of any tender herbivore. And such a one she felt herself to be, Miss Lamb, spotless, sacrificial" (Carter, 1993: 45).

In *The Sadeian Woman* Carter argues that in a patriarchal culture the ambiguous and gendered distinction between *flesh* and *meat* indexes structural and sexual relations between men and women: "The relations between men and women are often distorted by the reluctance of both parties to acknowledge that the function of flesh is meat to the carnivore but not grass to the herbivore" (2006: 163). Although her reading of Sade's novels suggests that both men and women line up under the signs of carnivore and herbivore, Carter also identifies the strong cultural inclination for men to occupy the position of predatory carnivore with women as their prey, a cultural mythology that women like Beauty willingly accept and endorse through their good behavior, decorum, and virtue. By maintaining the similarities between her Beauty and the heroine of Beaumont's tale, Carter shows the path by which the *sage gouvernante* leads her little lambs to slaughter.

In true Carter style, however, she cannot help but hint at an outside to the patriarchal systems that constrain women's subjectivity. The not-so-rhetorical question appended to the Beast's terms for her exchange—"and what else was there to be done?" (Carter, 1993: 45)—offers one example, which was discussed earlier. The very title of her story offers another. The ambiguity of "The Courtship of Mr. Lyon"—is it his courting of Beauty, or is it her courting of him?—can be interpreted in ways that resonate with the critique Carter forwards by adhering so closely to Beaumont's text. That is, the title might be understood as condensing another of Beaumont's lessons, specifically, how young women ought to embody and perform femininity so as to be courted; implicit in the potential to be courted is the young woman's priming the suitor to court her, a type of courting in itself. For Carter, then, "The Courtship of Mr. Lyon"—Beauty's courtship of him by making herself properly available to his courting—might provide yet another example of women's complicity in male systems of power and privilege. But the ambiguity of the subject position in the title might also point to the possibility of women approaching an Other from a subject position, a courting in which she might invite him into a beastly sexual relationship on her own terms.

Carter seems to raise this possibility a second time when she describes Beauty browsing a "collection of courtly and elegant French fairy tales about white cats who were transformed princesses and fairies who were birds" (1993: 46). The passage clearly refers to Marie Catherine d'Aulnoy's "White Cat," one of the most well-known stories from her late-seventeenth-century fairy-tale collections. Although frequently considered alongside "Beauty and the Beast" because of the animal(esque) lovers, "The White Cat" revolves around a princess who chooses to live as a cat rather than accept the marriage that her fairy guardians have arranged for her; then, having met a prince who falls in love with her as a cat, she orchestrates her disenchantment, ensures an audience with the prince's father, seeks the king's approval of her marriage to his son, and confers kingdoms on the king and the prince's brothers. In an insightful analysis, Andrew Teverson reads Carter's reference to d'Aulnoy's "White Cat" as a clever metacommentary on, and reversal of, the lessons at the heart of Beaumont's didactic tale.

> "The White Cat" operates more as a parable of feminine independence. It is this sleight of hand on Carter's part—the introduction of a tale that is radically opposed to enforced unions into the rewrite of one that is meant to recommend them—that is her most ingenious revisionary stroke, and constitutes a subtle subversion of de Beaumont's narrative. (Teverson, 1999: 215–16)

Carter's reference to "The White Cat" (which preceded Beaumont's "Beauty and the Beast" by more than fifty years), together with the modern setting of "The Courtship of Mr. Lyon," forces an awareness of marriage as a historically and culturally specific patriarchal construct, not a timeless inevitability. As such, it also suggests an outside to the extensive social world so naturalized by dominant and oppressive ideologies of gender.

At one point, even Beauty experiences a fleeting, incomprehensible sense of that outside. Happily ensconced in her London life of "the opera, theatres; a whole new wardrobe" (Carter, 1993: 48), Beauty visits a florist to send the Beast some white roses. Upon leaving the florist, "she experienced a sudden sense of perfect freedom, as if she had just escaped from an unknown danger, had been grazed by the possibility of some change but, finally, left intact. Yet, with this exhilaration, a desolating emptiness" (48). Here, Carter's ambiguity is especially productive. Beauty may, of course, feel liberated by having discharged a final debt: her white roses for the one her father initially stole from the Beast. But, it is also possible to read Beauty's "exhilaration" and "desolating emptiness" as her (largely unconscious) response to being "grazed by the possibility of some change." The possibility of an outside to the patriarchal systems and bourgeois institutions that enclose her would certainly provoke a sense of both "perfect freedom" and "unknown danger" in the good girl. Even as she is overcome by this utterly strange set of sensations, she distracts herself with (or is distracted by) her father, who has "planned a delicious expedition to buy her furs and she was as eager for the treat as any girl might be" (48). Thus, just as Beauty might begin to ponder the possibility of an outside, she pulls back, enthusiastically reincorporated into the safety of a world in which she knows how to be daddy's good girl.

Seeing the Beast Within: "The Tiger's Bride"

If Carter abandons Beauty to her father, her furs, and her leonine husband in "The Courtship of Mr. Lyon," she fosters other possibilities for the heroine of "The Tiger's Bride," her second, more radically reimagined telling of "Beauty and the Beast." Before exploring those possibilities, however, Carter begins with extended opening scenes that magnify, indeed almost parody, the themes that drive the "Beauty and the Beast" tradition explored in the previous section. Thus "The Tiger's Bride" also concerns the male exchange of women, but in this story Carter immediately cuts to the heart of the matter: "My father lost me to The Beast at cards" (1993: 51), the heroine recounts at the start of her story. This frank testament reveals two significant features of the "The Tiger's Bride": First, women's status as objects within patriarchal systems of exchange will not be nestled within the typically consolatory myths of romantic love invoked to promote marriage, and, second, this will be the heroine's story. Throughout, Carter relies on similar imagery and language as relays between the two stories, drawing out the potential for each to comment on and critique the other and ultimately allowing the heroine of "The Tiger's Bride" to inhabit the possible outside that only grazes Beauty in "The Courtship of Mr. Lyon."

That women are commodities to be exchanged among men is made abundantly clear in the almost exaggerated terms of the wager between the father and The Beast; the stakes are set when, at the end of the night, the father is left with nothing "except the girl" (Carter, 1993: 54), as The Beast reminds him. Once the bet is established between the men and the cards are being played, the heroine addresses the reader directly: "You must not think my father valued me at less than a king's ransom; but, at *no more* than a king's ransom" (54; emphasis in original). In Carter's stories the imperative seems to force the reader into confronting the irony implicit in the cultural discourses and mythologies she engages throughout her narrative arguments. Here, then, as in the case of the imperative about Beauty's having a will of her own in "The Courtship of Mr. Lyon," what the narrators are telling us we "must not think" is exactly what we soon discover to be true; in this case the heroine makes this explicit by adding, "but, at *no more* than a king's ransom," thereby calling attention to the specific, quantifiable value of a daughter, ordinarily thought to be beyond a literal price, although that is, of course, the cultural myth that Carter pushes us to interrogate.

Upon losing the hand—losing his daughter—the heroine's father quotes *Othello* to convey his sense of loss: "'Like the base Indian,' he said; he loved rhetoric. 'One whose hand, / Like the base Indian, threw a pearl away / Richer than all his tribe . . .' I have lost my pearl, my pearl beyond price" (Carter, 1993: 55).[9] The daughter's comparison to a pearl in the father's melodramatic and regretful tribute recalls descriptions of Beauty from the previous story: "a young girl who looked as if she had been carved out of a single pearl" (46), "that pearly skin of hers" (48). By uniting the two young women in this way, Carter underscores the fact that even a woman capable of narrating her own story, a woman who cannot be guilted into accepting responsibility for her objectness, her exchange value, is nonetheless circumscribed by the patriarchal system in which she remains a commodity to be traded. In another convergence of the two stories, when The Beast first meets the heroine, he presents her with the white rose from his buttonhole in a gesture that emphasizes the fact that this daughter is not even remotely to blame for the coming transaction; unlike Beaumont's Beauty and the future Mrs. Lyon, this heroine never asks for the rose and is thus free from the emotional blackmail and guilt that motivate the traditional tale, made explicit when the merchant in Beaumont's story returns from the Beast's castle with the stolen roses: "'Here, Beauty,' said he, 'take these roses; but little do you think how dear they are like to cost your unhappy father'" (1783: 53). Nonetheless, the heroine shares their fate, a point Carter accentuates through the white roses in each of her stories.

The lines from *Othello* also incite The Beast, who roars and growls in response; his simian valet translates The Beast's frank quip to the father's performative mourning: "If you are so careless of your treasures, you should expect them to be taken from you" (Carter, 1993: 55). The Beast may condemn the father's carelessness, but he too sees the daughter only as "treasure," one of the father's possessions. In this scene the daughter's exchange between The Beast and the father is reduced to its most basic mechanics; it simply indexes the economics of status, debt, and obligation implicit in the institution of marriage. As "pearl beyond price" and a "treasure," the heroine is little more than phallus to her father and The Beast, the ultimate signifier of male power. The Beast's and the father's straightforward wager strips away the social niceties of the clubby masculinity motivating Beauty's exchange in "The Courtship of Mr. Lyon": the garage service, the invitation to dinner, the brandy, the legal advice. Carter continues to flay Beaumont's story by cutting away at one of her own.

If, as discussed earlier, women's objectification and exchange value are predicated on a patriarchal "scopic economy" (Irigaray, 1985: 26), then Carter imagines an alternative economy in "The Tiger's Bride." However, she first stages an exaggerated scene of male scopophilia to create the background against which her alternative might stand in high relief. Here, then, The Beast expresses his desire to view the heroine; as always, his simian valet translates his request.

> My master's sole desire is to see the pretty young lady unclothed nude without her dress and that only for the one time after which she will be returned to her father undamaged with bankers' orders for the sum which he lost to my master at cards and also a number of fine presents such as furs, jewels, and horses—. (Carter, 1993: 58)

The repetitive stutter that focuses attention on the heroine's naked body—"unclothed nude without her dress"—foregrounds the fetishistic nature of The Beast's desire, and Carter plays up the ways in which such a fetish can be predatory and carnivorous by literalizing the beastliness of the male gaze in relation to masculine desire and power. The heroine also recognizes the potential danger in The Beast's scopophilic fantasy, and she protects herself by responding with a "raucous guffaw" (58); as she points out, "No young lady laughs like that!" (58).

Not one to seek daddy's approval or to be enticed—or distracted—by furs and jewels, this heroine laughs in the face of The Beast's desire to see her virginal flesh and counters his offer with one of her own.

> You may put me in a windowless room, sir, and I promise you I will pull my skirt up to my waist, ready for you. But there must be a sheet over my face, to hide it; though the sheet must be laid over me so lightly that it will not choke me. So I shall be covered completely from the waist upwards, and no lights. There you can visit me once, sir, and only the once.... If you wish to give me money, then I should be pleased to receive it. But I must stress that you should give me only the same amount of money that you would give to any other woman in such circumstances. However, if you choose not to give me a present, then that is your right.
> (Carter, 1993: 59)

Even though the two offers seem entirely opposed in terms of the heroine's exposure to The Beast's gaze—"unclothed nude without her dress" versus "completely covered from the waist upwards, and no lights"—the heroine's frank counteroffer articulates the essential sameness of the proposals. Her explicit and detailed directions lay bare the economics of the transaction at the center of The Beast's request; stripped of its seeming gentility—the crass "skirt [pulled] up to [her] waist" as opposed to "unclothed nude without her dress," "money you would give to any other woman in such circumstances" as opposed to "fine presents such as furs, jewels, and horses"—The Beast's offer is no different from the one she makes in response, an offer that elicits a single tear-turned-diamond,[10] a sign, she hopes, of his shame.

Carter is invested in more than simple critique, however, and her commitment to the possibility of an outside to the Symbolic Order and the Law of the Father inspires another scene of looking. Pausing along a river bank while out riding horses, the valet informs the heroine that if she will not allow The Beast to gaze at her nude body, she must look upon his; as The Beast removes his mask (painted with the face of a man) and his cape, the heroine realizes that "the tiger will never lie down with the lamb; he acknowledges no pact that is not reciprocal. The lamb must learn to run with the tigers" (Carter, 1993: 64). In a reversal of the tale's traditional injunction against female gazing at male subjects, the heroine is forced to take in The Beast's tigerly form: his feline shape, his coloring and striping, his head, his musculature. She studies him and in his face sees "the annihilating vehemence of his eyes, like twin suns" (64); at that, she feels her "breast ripped apart as if [she] suffered a marvellous wound" (64). Unlike Beauty, who sees only herself reflected in the Beast's eyes in "The Courtship of Mr. Lyon," the heroine of this tale finds nothing reflected in The Beast's eyes. There is no Lacanian ideal-I to be found in the gaze of this Other. In fact, there is nothing to see, a nothing-to-see that leads to a "marvellous wound" in the heroine's chest, perhaps an opening of her heart and certainly a reimagining of woman's other, more notorious wound, the wound that defines her, that problematizes her, Irigaray's "nothing-to-see" (1985: 26) in the phallocentric logic of psychoanalysis that undergirds Western culture.[11] Thus Carter's implicit critique of Lacan's theory of subjectivity in relation to the mirror stage, her exceedingly clever invocation of Irigaray's "nothing-to-see" (itself a condemnation of the very premise upon which Freud develops his theory of sexual difference), and her differently figured "marvellous wound" all begin to destabilize the primacy of the phallus, the primacy of the Law of the Father, and to suggest an outside to the Symbolic Order.

Not surprisingly, then, when the valet moves to cover The Beast, the heroine stops him. She is no lamb; or, if she is, she wants to run with the tiger. She seeks reciprocity. She chooses, at this point, to undress: "I showed his grave silence my white skin, my red nipples, and the horses turned their heads to watch me, also, as if they, too, were courteously curious as to the fleshly nature of women" (Carter, 1993: 64). Although The Beast, referred to simply as "the tiger" in this one instance, runs off to hunt with his valet after the heroine has exposed herself, it is this moment of reciprocity and mutuality that frees her: "I felt I was at liberty for the first time in my life" (64). She fully embraces the possibility that only grazes Beauty in "The Courtship of Mr. Lyon."

The Beast, however, is yet to be so liberated. Back from the hunt, he has donned his mask and cloak, "to all appearances, a man" (65). Even more, he continues to see the heroine as an object of exchange, now one who has fulfilled the terms of his request; she sees in the magic mirror that The Beast has "paid cash on the nail for his glimpse of my bosom" and, along with the money, he has sent a note indicating that "the young lady will arrive immediately" (65). But, having moved into the realm of a new possibility, she refuses to comply, not because of her pride or even her shame, but because of her desire. She knows she is not "some harlot with whom he'd briskly negotiated a liaison on the strength of his spoils" (65).

When the heroine first glances in the magic mirror and sees her father, she thinks for a moment that he is smiling at her, that he is returning her gaze, but he is smiling only at his newfound wealth. When she turns to the mirror a few moments later, he is gone and all she finds is "a pale, hollow-eyed girl whom [she] scarcely recognized" (Carter, 1993: 65). Carter cannot stop playing with mirrors, or with theories of gender and the gaze. In this mirror scene Carter seems to suggest that the heroine is now done with the father, disgusted that his avarice blinds him to her, done too with the Law of the Father, blind to her subjectivity. Although she barely recognizes herself, it is not the misrecognition of the ideal-I but rather a near misrecognition that continues to move her outside the Symbolic Order and into the perfect freedom she experienced in the aftermath of her naked interchange with The Beast, a freedom heralded by her decision to send her mechanical twin to her father in her place.

At this point in a traditional "Beauty and the Beast" story, the heroine's only remaining task would be to disenchant the beast; of course, Carter wants none of that, and this is where her story really moves into the fantastic. Alone in her room, the heroine affixes The Beast's diamond-tear earrings to her ears and begins to strip; she finds the task harder than anticipated, especially considering she has already exposed herself to The Beast. However, that initial stripping occurred outside, whereas the heroine is now ensconced in her new room, what appears to be the only room in the palazzo suitable for human habitation (and a luxurious habitation at that). Surrounded by the trappings of human culture—brocade sofas, Oriental carpets, cut-glass chandeliers—she becomes self-conscious: "I was unaccustomed to nakedness. I was so unused to my own skin that to take off all my clothes involved a kind of flaying. . . . I felt as much atrocious pain as if I was stripping off my own underpelt" (Carter, 1993: 66). Nonetheless, wearing only the fur coat The Beast has delivered for her return to her father, she makes her way to The Beast's room, where the valet takes her coat, now transformed into a "pack of black, squeaking rats" that quickly scurry away (66).[12] Like the heroine, The Beast has shed his gown, his mask, his wig; he paces the floor "between the gnawed and bloody bones" (66)—as though awaiting her arrival? as though dejected by her presumed departure for her father's house? Regardless, her naked rush to him and his anxious pacing hint at their mutual desire. Upon entering his room, she begins to seduce him, "approaching him as if offering, in [herself], the key to a peaceable kingdom in which his appetite need not be [her] extinction" (67). She squats and extends her hand, ensuring that she is within "the field of force of his golden eyes" (67); she is entirely still as he growls, sinks to his forepaws, lowers his head, bares his teeth, sniffs the air. And then, his own slow approach leads to an inverted disenchantment.

> He dragged himself closer and closer to me, until I felt the harsh velvet of his head against my hand, then a tongue, abrasive as sandpaper....
>
> And each stroke of his tongue ripped off skin after successive skin, all the skins of a life in the world, and left behind a nascent patina of shining hairs. My earrings turned back to water and trickled down my shoulders; I shrugged the drops off my beautiful fur. (67)

As many critics have noted, "The Tiger's Bride" is a tale of reciprocity that can only develop between two subjects.[13] In being forced to see each other in ways other than they expect, in recognizing but not reflecting each other, The Beast and the heroine usher each other into being, into an autonomous subjectivity that falls well outside the Symbolic Order, outside a phallogocentric language, outside a sexual desire overdetermined by the privileging of the male gaze and the objectification of women. Dani Cavallaro similarly reads the scene as one of escape from the Symbolic Order: "At this point, the heroine's entire being is transformed into a fluid site of *jouissance*, as all of its senses, limbs, organs and nerves appear to be working together toward a symphony of unnamable bliss" (2011: 125).

They inhabit a fantastic realm where the tongue serves other purposes, among them an alternate erotics.

Carter's fairy tales regularly couple women and nonhuman animals[14] as desiring subjects, and their relationships prove provocative and alluring because of the animals' ambiguous status in her stories—never entirely metaphor, never entirely material. But, then, women are also ambiguous in the same way; defined by cultural myths of gender, they too are never entirely material, never entirely metaphor. In addition, both are obviously Other to man, and Carter stages their fantastic meetings and extraordinary attractions as a critique of the hierarchical ontologies that similarly oppress them. The heroine of "The Tiger's Bride" calls attention to their mutual othering as she reflects on their unusual riding party.

> I was a young girl, a virgin, and therefore men denied me rationality just as they denied it to all those who were not exactly like themselves . . . the six of us—mounts and riders, both—could boast amongst us not one soul, either, since all the best religions in the world state categorically that not beasts nor women were equipped with the flimsy, insubstantial things. (Carter, 1993: 63)[15]

The heroine's metaphysical reflection highlights the social construction of both gender and animal nature, an idea Carter explores and deconstructs in much of her fiction and nonfiction (see, e.g., Pollock, 2000). Yet, by carefully negotiating the fine line between productive similarity and reductive overidentification, Carter remains keen to the shifting differences in power between women and animals, differences exacerbated by the fact that all the fairy-tale animals in *The Bloody Chamber* are male.[16] Girls and women are advantaged by virtue of their being human, whereas the beasts they encounter are advantaged by virtue of their being predators.

In his lectures on the nature of the beast and the sovereign, Jacques Derrida argues that both are outside the law, the beast because he is "ignorant of right" (2009: 32) and so at a distance from the law and the sovereign because he need not respect the laws that he has the right to make (17). Being outside the law, being outlaws, "they call on each other and recall each other, from one to the other," and they share "a sort of obscure and fascinating complicity, or even a worrying mutual attraction"

(17). Derrida tends to align women with animals because both are subjected to the sovereign, but his theorization of how a mutual outlawness attracts and links beast and sovereign might lend insight into Carter's female-animal couplings, particularly as she situates both women and animals beyond the law (of the father). For Carter women can be outside the law in two senses: On the one hand, based on psychoanalytic theory, women are outside the Law of the Father because of their inability to identify fully with the phallus as the privileged signifier, thus troubling their complete entry into the Symbolic Order and rendering them incomprehensible, unrepresentable, or nonexistent; on the other hand, Carter wants to believe that women might escape from the inscription in and by the Law of the Father to inhabit a realm of greater possibility, such as she describes in "The Tiger's Bride." Derrida's suggestion that the beast and the sovereign make demands of each other, that they are held together by their complicities and their mutual attraction outside the law, helps articulate the ever-shifting meanings, desires, powers, and theories implicit in Carter's woman-animal couplings. Outside the law, in both senses, Carter's women and beasts similarly call on and recall each other to enlarge the realm of possibility where alternative subjectivities and desires might flourish.

The subjects of Carter's animal-human transformations and mutual becomings—in "The Tiger's Bride" and in the wolf trilogy (discussed in Chapter 6)—are held in the "identificatory metamorphosis" that Derrida attributes to the beast and the sovereign (2009: 32). Playing, as always, with language, Derrida theorizes from the homonym *et/est*—the beast *et* the sovereign, the beast *est* the sovereign—that the two are always "becoming the other, being the other," locked by the *et* in a "passage from the one to the other, the analogy, the resemblance, the alliance" represented by the *est* (32). In *The Bloody Chamber*, Derrida's identificatory metamorphosis is also a paradoxically permanent state of transition, a process, a perpetual becoming-Other that calls to mind Mary Pollock's reading of the collection as "situat[ing] both human and animal characters in a borderland between human consciousness and the consciousness of other species, the realm of the almost/not quite human" (2000: 48).

Furthering the ideas of a reciprocal becoming and a liminal human-animal consciousness, Carter rewrites devourment, so frequently associated with the beastly boogeyman intent on gobbling up misbehaving children, an association given concrete form in the heroine's early memory of the lurking tiger-man with which her nurse threatens her into good behavior. The tiger-man's threat of devourment is like the sovereign's "power of devourment (mouth, teeth, tongue, violent rush to bite, engulf, swallow the other, to take the other into oneself too, to kill it or mourn it)" (Derrida, 2009: 23), but what the heroine finds in The Beast once she braves her "earliest and most archaic of fears, fear of devourment" (Carter, 1993: 67) is something entirely different. Rather than being devoured (both literally and metaphorically), the heroine elicits from The Beast, from the tiger, the "tremendous throbbing" (67) of his purr. As Derrida points out, because the sites of devourment—"the mouth, the maw, teeth, throat, glottis, and tongue" (2009: 23)—are also the sites of speech, they affect the ears—hearing, listening—as well, such that "the place of devourment is also the place of what carries the voice . . . in a word, the place of vociferation" (23). The Beast's purr—his animal vociferation—signals the move away from a hegemonic devourment that threatens to engulf and internalize the Other, to subsume the Other in a phallogocentric and sovereign language; instead, "the sweet thunder of this purr" constitutes a different mode of communication, an alternative language of desire in which The Beast's tongue licks away "all the skins of a life in the world" (Carter, 1993: 67). In "becoming the other, being the other," in the borderland of a double consciousness, Carter's metamorphosing characters thus contribute to an imagined world in which autonomous subjects are free to come into being, where they might be brought into being by an outlaw(ed) Other, outside the Symbolic Order.

Yet The Beast's purr is more than subversive vociferation. It literally disturbs the foundations of patriarchal civilization emblematized by the Marquis's castle in "The Bloody Chamber."

> The sweet thunder of this purr shook the old walls, made the shutters batter the windows until they burst apart and let in the white light of the snowy moon. Tiles came crashing down from the roof.

> ... The reverberations of his purring rocked the foundations of the house, the walls began to dance. I thought: "It will all fall, everything will disintegrate." (Carter, 1993: 67)

Immediately preceding The Beast's licking away her worldly skins, the heroine's wonderfully ambiguous "it"—the palazzo? patriarchal culture? the Symbolic Order?—provides an apt conclusion to a story that seeks to dismantle the gendered literary and theoretical structures which Carter interrogates in the collection's first two stories. The Beast's "throbbing" (67) and thunderous purr replaces the soul-shattering orgasm so feared by hegemonic masculinity; in place of the male orgasm as the "annihilation of the self" (Carter, 2006: 176), The Beast's purr meets the heroine's *jouissance* in a different kind of shattering. On a more literal level and even before this point of potential disintegration, The Beast's palazzo suggests a crumbling of the structures of "civilization" so critical to patriarchal power. Although clearly evoking the labyrinthine nature of the Marquis's castle—"suites of vaulted chambers opening one out of another like systems of Chinese boxes into the infinite complexity of the innards of the place" (Carter, 1993: 57)—The Beast's dilapidated palazzo, with its sheet-covered furniture, its dining room used to stable horses, its roof beams marked with old swallows' nests, does not index his power. Distanced from the Marquis's castle, from Mr. Lyon's Palladian house, The Beast's palazzo, what at first glance seems to be his "megalomaniac citadel" (57), materializes Carter's desire to discard the trappings of "civilization" as she strips away the layers of a human "life in the world" to imagine what might exist outside.

What the Cat Saw: "Puss-in-Boots"

Although "Puss-in-Boots" is obviously not a "Beauty and the Beast" tale, I read it alongside "The Courtship of Mr. Lyon" and "The Tiger's Bride" to suggest that Carter's three feline stories are best understood in dialogue with each other. The feline stories cohere around animal-human relations and the questions of gender, subjectivity, and desire that they address. Collectively, they emphasize "the economic underpinnings to fairy tale marriage" (Tiffin,

2009: 78) that Carter troubles in this particular set of stories as well as in "The Bloody Chamber." As a rollicking and randy first-"person" (first-"cat"?) account of sexual exploits, ardent desire, and even love, "Puss-in-Boots" attempts to provide an alternative material reality for the problematics of gender and desire that Carter first exposes and then explodes in "The Courtship of Mr. Lyon" and "The Tiger's Bride," a material reality that might live up to the utopian fantasy of "The Tiger's Bride."

"Puss-in-Boots" opens with the cat's self-naming, a naming that anticipates the story's attention to class as a key determinant in marriage and in the very conceptualization of sexual possibility: "Figaro here; Figaro, there, I tell you! Figaro upstairs, Figaro downstairs and—oh, my goodness me, this little Figaro can slip into my lady's chamber smart as you like at any time whatsoever" (Carter, 1993: 68). In Beaumarchais's comic play, bedroom politics result from a chaotic mix of aggressive pursuit, intricate subterfuge, mistaken identity, and general misunderstanding, all of which are scripted by the proprieties of gender and class. Carter's own reference to *The Marriage of Figaro* in *The Sadeian Woman* further articulates the ways that love and sexual attraction are circumscribed by a range of material forces.

> Considerations of social class censored the possibility of sexual attraction between the Countess and Figaro before it could have begun to exist, and if this convention restricted the Countess's activities, it did not affect those of her husband.... Our literature is full, as are our lives, of men and women, but especially women, who deny the reality of sexual attraction and of love because of considerations of class, religion, race, and of gender itself. (Carter, 2006: 10–11)

Although "Puss-in-Boots" clearly engages the themes of Beaumarchais's play and even relies on similar sexual antics and comedic subterfuge for its plot structure, Carter is careful to liberate her characters from the prohibitions, both explicit and implicit, that interfere with love and desire. Indeed, true to her fashion, Carter imagines subjectivity and sexual autonomy through perpetual becomings, Derrida's identificatory metamorphoses, and an alternative economy of desire, all of which she locates in an everyday material reality that is quite different from the façade of reality in "The Tiger Bride."

Given the prominence of naming in the story's opening scene, it might seem surprising that only one human character receives a name: Signor Panteleone. What should be less surprising, of course, is that in keeping with the commedia dell'arte tradition, Signor Panteleone is the rich and greedy patriarch. In granting only Signore Panteleone a name, Carter literalizes Lacan's name of the father, and in rendering him impotent, both literally and metaphorically, she immediately undermines his power and questions the Lacanian model of subjectivity as determined by entry into the Symbolic Order. In contrast to the human characters, however, the two cats are given proper names: Tabs and Puss. Puss is even named twice, beginning the story as Figaro and then becoming Puss when he receives his boots and meets his "master" and "boon companion" (Carter, 1993: 70). Puss's referring to his human mate as "Master" throughout the story (and Carter's capitalizing it as though it were a proper name) is ironic on at least two levels. First, Puss's master remains nameless and is thus never aligned with the name of the father, although he bears a title that would seem to suggest such a correlation; second, the title of "Master" foregrounds the anthropocentric and thus hierarchical conceptualization of human-animal relationships even as Puss undermines it by taking on the role himself.

With these ironies of naming, Carter refuses a blunt critique of the phallogocentric patriarchal order; rather, she insists on its nuances by drawing out the complexities that emerge with class and species distinctions. Thus, for instance, despite his hegemonic-sounding title, Master is socially marginalized and essentially powerless in relation to the named Signor Panteleone, a point Carter stresses with her opening reference to Figaro. Even though Figaro is initially Puss's name and even though he serves as his master's "valet de chambre" (Carter, 1993: 69) just as Beaumarchais's Figaro serves as the Count's valet, the name also fits Master, who occupies a somewhat analogous role in the story; like Beaumarchais's Figaro, Master must rely on wit and subterfuge to keep his lover from the clutches of the rich patriarch (or, more precisely in this case, to clutch his lover from the rich patriarch's keep). For Carter, then, "Figaro" is a shifting signifier, slipping back and forth between cat and human, highlighting the failure of language to define them and reiterating the impotence of the name and the Law of the Father.

Carter's play with names, naming, and the name of the father—her implicit critique of the Lacanian theory of subjectivity—recalls the significance of reciprocity so critical to the ideas about subjectivity and desire that she advances in "The Tiger's Bride." In contrast to that story's fantastic and profound tone, "Puss-in-Boots" maintains the comedic tone of *The Marriage of Figaro*. As a result, Carter relies on minor mishaps and lighthearted misunderstandings to interrogate the phallocentric privileging of seeing and speaking and to set the stage for the final ruse that results in Signor Panteleone's death. Neither seeing nor speaking are particularly effective for human communication in this story. After catching only a fleeting glimpse of Signor Panteleone's veiled wife, Master falls in love with her, a common trope and typical use of the male gaze to drive the narrative. After that passing glance, however, Carter frustrates Master's ability to gaze upon this woman as beautiful object, although she is clearly an object for Signor Panteleone, his most prized possession. Keeping her like a princess locked away in a tower, Signor Panteleone "unlocks the shutters and lets his wife look out" for an hour each day, "and while she breathes the air of evening, why, he checks up on his chest of gems, his bales of silk, all those treasures he loves too much to share with daylight" (Carter, 1993: 81). Carter's exaggerated characterization of how Signor Panteleone views his wife—equivalent to gems, silk, treasures—resonates with her similar descriptions of the treasured beauties, the pearly daughters, of "The Courtship of Mr. Lyon" and "The Tiger's Bride."

Against this intertextual background and with Master unable to see his beloved, Puss and Tabs conspire to pass a love note from him to the lovely lady, but language also proves difficult: "He spent three hours over his letter.... He tears up half a quire of paper, splays five pen-nibs with the force of his adoration" (Carter, 1993: 73).[17] Having finally succeeded with what Puss deems a "masterpiece" (74)—and what Carter conveys as platitudes (perhaps in her own version of Irigaray's mournful complaint about the impossibility for the words "I love you" to mean anything [1985: 206–208])—the lady responds that she cannot "usefully discuss his passion further without a glimpse of his person" (Carter, 1993: 74). Even before the real action begins, she challenges gender norms by insisting on seeing *him*. Puss and Tabs again take care of the arrangements, but the general cacophony of the square where Master goes to serenade the lady is too crowded; she fails to see him, fails to hear him. In Carter's "Puss-in-Boots" the trope of heterosexual romantic love falters with the ineffectiveness of sight and language.

Puss intervenes with his daring scaling of the early Palladian building ("If rococo's a piece of cake, that chaste, tasteful, early Palladian stumped many a better cat than I in its time," Carter, 1993: 74–75). Once inside the lady's room, he directs her gaze to Master and, as though by magic, the square quiets for his enchanting song.

> I would never have said, in the normal course of things, his voice would charm the birds out of the trees, like mine; and yet the bustle died for him, the homeward-turning costers paused in their tracks to hearken, the preening street girls forgot their hard-edged smiles as they turned to him and some of the old ones wept, they did. (75)

Here, by creating an opportunity in which Master and Signor Panteleone's wife recognize each other, Carter seems to suggest that song and music might accomplish what phallogocentric language cannot: "And now the lady lowers her eyes to him and smiles, as once she smiled at me" (75). In Puss's comparing the way the wife smiles at Master to the way she previously smiled at him, he hints at the possibility of a look free from the "cultural impedimenta of our social class, our parents' lives, our bank balances, our sexual and emotional experiences, our whole biographies" (Carter, 2006: 10). That is, the wife sees Puss as an extraordinary cat. When she first glimpses him, he "rears briefly on his high-heeled boots; jig with joy and pirouette with glee" (Carter, 1993: 71) and she "draws her veil aside" (71) to see and smile at him. Later, when he climbs into her bedroom, she exclaims, "Puss in boots!" (75), thus essentially naming him. He is an individual cat, an autonomous subject, not simply an animal that she categorizes generally as *cat*. Puss's direction, together with Master's music and song, elicits the same gaze, the same smile, suggesting that the wife also sees Master as an individual, an autonomous subject. Her request to see Master and her holding his look indicate her own subjectivity, because she is able to transgress the previously discussed fairy-tale injunction preventing women from gazing at men. For Carter, then, music seems to work—like (and with) Puss and Tabs—to enable what the humans cannot bring about on their own. Master and Signor Pantaleone's wife are too distracted and constrained by the social conventions and social constructions of the Symbolic Order to see each other freely, and Carter brings these distractions and constraints to life in order to end the fleeting nature of their mutual gaze: the "creaking of carts in the square . . . an ululation of ballad-singers and oration of nostrum peddlers" (74) and "Then, bang! a stern hand pulls the shutters to" (75).

In their reciprocal seeing, Carter also expands the possibilities for sexual agency, granting Signor Panteleone's wife an autonomous desire that Carter finds unimaginable for the wife's counterpart in Beaumarchais's tale: "It was impossible for the Countess in Beaumarchais's *The Marriage of Figaro* to contemplate sleeping with her husband's valet, even though he was clearly the best man available" (Carter, 2006: 10). Unlike the Countess, Signor Panteleone's wife welcomes the liaison with the poor and socially marginal Master, and Carter's colorful description of their sexual activity disrupts the universalizing conventions of pornography she so forcefully opposes in *The Sadeian Woman*. Puss's bawdy account forecloses what Carter identifies as the "gap left in [the pornographic text] on purpose so that the reader may, in imagination, step inside it" (16); focalized through a randy tomcat's eyes, articulated in a cat tongue, the humans' sexual encounter is stripped of the usual romantic and pornographic tropes.

> As if the whirlwind got into their fingers, they strip each other bare in a twinkling and she falls back on the bed, shows him the target, he displays the dart, scores an instant bullseye. Bravo! Never can that old bed have shook with such a storm before. And their sweet, choked mutterings, poor things: 'I never . . .' 'My darling . . .' 'More . . .' And etc. etc. (Carter, 1993: 78)

As Puss makes clear with his ellipses and "etc. etc.," the clichéd "language of love"—part of the social fantasy that structures sex itself—is so familiar that it need not even be articulated. Indeed, from Puss's perspective, the humans' perceived need for the "choked mutterings" is both pitiable and irrelevant. In a later scene Puss captures their well-matched gusto in equally candid style: "Up and down, up and down his arse; in and out, in and out her legs. Then she heaves him up and throws him on his back, her turn at the grind, now, and you'd think she'll never stop" (82). Through Puss's frank cat narration and refusal to indulge the language of pornography, Carter imagines sexual encounters that directly subvert the cultural fantasies yoking gender identity to sexual scripts: "(She, of course, rarely approaches him; that is not part of the fantasy of fulfillment.) She is most immediately and dramatically a woman when she lies beneath a man, and her submission is the apex of his malehood" (Carter, 2006: 8). Instead of "the fantasy love-play of the archetypes" (7), Carter grants both Master and Signor Panteleone's wife a subjectivity and sexual agency that begins to make conscious the historical, social, and economic trappings—the hegemonic discourses, the enduring narratives—that limit and bind sexual desire with myths of universality.

Among the hegemonic discourses of gender and sexuality that Carter finds most troubling is the insistence on a separation between reproduction and sexual pleasure, and it is precisely in Sade's refusal to allow Eugenie's mother's orgasm in *Philosophy in the Boudoir* that Carter locates Sade's failure to write a liberatory pornography.

> Were Madame de Mistival to have come, then all the dykes would be breached at once . . . pleasure would have asserted itself triumphantly over pain and the necessity for the existence of repression as a sexual stimulant would have ceased to exist. . . . Instead of constructing a machine for liberation, he substitutes instead a masturbatory device. He is on the point of becoming a revolutionary pornography; but he, finally, lacks the courage. (Carter, 2006: 153–54)

Not surprisingly, Carter ventures where Sade lacked the courage to go, and Signor Panteleone's wife's capacity for sexual pleasure and her resulting pregnancy intervene in the most repressive discourse of gender and sexuality. In addition, after Tabs and Puss have arranged Signor Panteleone's deadly fall down the stairs, his wife—caught in flagrante delicto with Master by the old hag, the undertaker, and his assistants—removes the key ring from her husband's lifeless grip and declares that Master will be her second husband. Now controlling the wealth, she refuses her social place as exchange object between and among men. With such an ending—which Carter extends to the happy domesticity of the wife's pregnancy and Tabs's "three fine, new-minted ginger kittens" (Carter, 1993: 83)—"Puss-in-Boots" pointedly addresses and redresses the patriarchal discourses she engages, explores, and even explodes in the other two feline stories.

And yet even Carter's seemingly straightforward happy ending resists the hegemonic fantasy of heterosexual romance and marriage. Although the kittens certainly share Puss's coloring, Tabs and Puss's catness leaves open the possibility of multiple paternity, a point Carter not only underscores but also maps onto human relationships in her revision of Perrault's moral: "So may all your wives, if you need them, be rich and pretty; and all your husbands, if you want them, be young and virile; and all your cats as wily, perspicacious and resourceful as: PUSS-IN-BOOTS" (Carter, 1993: 84).[18] The ambiguity introduced by the second-person voice is a productive one for Carter, and the plural "wives" and "husbands," together with the use of the conditional, decouples her happy ending from the compulsory heterosexuality and universalization of traditional fairy-tale happy endings.

In the end, Carter's "Puss-in-Boots" is a story of sexual desire and love, and, especially, the possibility that the two might come together for liberating ends outside the patriarchal confines of the Law of the Father. Early in the story, when Master falls so hard for Signor Panteleone's wife that he neglects everything, Puss believes that a single sexual encounter will cure him of his longing. Echoing Lacan's theory of desire, Puss proclaims, "Love is desire sustained by unfulfilment" (Carter, 1993: 72). Puss, of course, turns out to be wrong, and his error, Carter seems to suggest, is also Lacan's. For Master, both love and desire can be satisfied, but this love depends on a willingness to understand orgasm not as the Sadeian "annihilation of the self" (Carter, 2006: 176) but rather as an opening of the self to another, as "the instrument of love" (176). That such a love is possible is Carter's most radical claim, both in *The Sadeian Woman* and in her feline stories.

Carter's feline stories embrace and foster a multidimensional multiplicity—in terms of tales and themes, voices and felines—that resists the phallocentric logic of the singular. Her two versions of "Beauty and the Beast" and her "Puss-in-Boots" generate themes and tropes that reverberate between them. Her felines range from beastly to helperly, from wild to domesticated, sometimes slipping from animal to human and human to animal, but never in any clear or programmatic progression and never with any clear sense of categorical distinctions. The feline stories move among and between first-, second-, and third-"person" voices; they resonate with disembodied voices, with women's voices, animal voices, animal languages, animal sounds, from the discordant cat music of "The White Cat" that haunts "The Courtship of Mr. Lyon" to the tiger's earth-shaking purr that reverberates through "The Tiger's Bride." In some cases Carter's human characters fail to understand the animal sounds, these other languages, but those who do enjoy the identificatory metamorphosis and continuous becoming-Other that might usher in an autonomous subjectivity and an alternate erotics.

4

Dangerous Articulations
"The Erl-King" and "The Snow Child"

If the transformative power of the Tiger's alfresco strip show and his later licking away the heroine's skins "of a life in the world" (Carter, 1993: 67) perhaps tempt us into imagining "nature" as an untroubled escape from the socially constructed and intricately gendered trappings of patriarchal culture, Carter quickly disabuses us of such folly with "The Erl-King" and "The Snow Child." Lest we forget that nature and culture are equally socially constructed and sexed, "The Erl-King" opens with a description of the woods that immediately conjures the labyrinthine structures of the Marquis's castle and The Beast's palazzo: The woods are a "subtle labyrinth" (84) that "enclose and then enclose again, like a system of Chinese boxes opening one into another" (85). By repeating and recontextualizing the metaphor of the Chinese boxes—which was first used to describe The Beast's palazzo where "suites of vaulted chambers [open] one out of another like systems of Chinese boxes into the infinite complexity of the innards of the place" (57)—and by explicitly affixing that metaphor to the labyrinth,[1] Carter draws out the elaborately constructed foundations of both the social world and the natural world and creates the backdrop against which "The Erl-King" and "The Snow Child" unfold.

Although "The Erl-King" and "The Snow Child" differ radically in terms of style and literary genealogy, the two stories come together in the spirited grip of their desolate natural settings. Reading them together magnifies Carter's critical examination of women's subjugation in and through metaphors of nature. From rich autumnal decay to bleak winter austerity, Carter's narrative environments engage the Romantic ethos and thus compel a return to questions of gender, language, and desire. Both "The Erl-King" and "The Snow Child" amplify the texture of the natural world, thereby encouraging Carter's simultaneous animation and critique of the psychoanalytic theories that structure such questions, theories embedded in familiar tropes of nineteenth-century Romantic poetry and its gendered idealization of the natural landscape.

Romantic Longing: "The Erl-King"

As Harriet Linkin (1994) so beautifully demonstrates, Carter's version of "The Erl-King" is saturated with the British Romantic aesthetic. Both the story and Linkin's reading of it explore the feminine subject position in, and in relation to, Romantic poetry and its underlying ideologies. No longer the silent or silenced object of desire, Carter's Romantic heroine narrates a story that exposes the legacy of male oppression and "the ways in which female desire colludes in erecting the bars of the golden cage for the Romantic as well as the contemporary writer" (Linkin, 1994: 306). Linkin's thorough and attentive reading identifies and interprets Carter's broad array of Romantic intertexts and their relation to structures of desire; the most inspired aspect of Linkin's analysis, however, emerges in her characterization of Carter's heroine as herself a savvy reader of these Romantic traditions and allusions. For Linkin the heroine has become a characteristically postmodern metafiction (though she does not label her as such) whose "allusive language reveals a knowledge of Romantic fictions that will write her role in the story she expects to enact" (314). Moving in parallel with Carter, Linkin endows the heroine with a powerful subjectivity that allows her to express her agency relative to the patriarchal logic of the Romantic tradition and to her interpellation in its enduring legacy.

This doubled feminine subjectivity—Carter's fiction, Linkin's metafiction—contributes to the ultimate tragedy of "The Erl-King," at least according to Linkin's reading: "In seizing on death as the answer, the protagonist writes herself out of one master plot only to place herself in another, equally damning one" (1994: 310). Linkin's hope for the heroine is, of course, that her familiarity with the Romantic aesthetic will enable her to navigate a way through and, most important, out of its narrative constraints. This is why Linkin is so disappointed when she finds the heroine falling into the trap of inverted male and female roles. Linkin argues that the heroine has been seduced by the knowledge of the danger posed to her by the plots of Romantic poetry, and this in turn "shapes her expectations of the erl-king to induce a self-fulfilling prophecy" (319). In Linkin's reading it is only in the heroine's imagination, informed by the Romantic ethos, that the Erl-King actually threatens to do her harm. This assumption sadly forecloses the "possibilities for love to flesh out the Romantic model of the poet in her substitution fantasy" (322), even when she narrates her own story in an attempt to avoid expected Romantic figurations.

Throughout her analysis Linkin privileges the heroine's literary knowledge and narrative practices, clearly distinguishing her from Carter and her project of "literary criticism through fiction" (1994: 306). Carter's relationship to "The Erl-King" is referenced only in Linkin's opening and closing frame, which points to a more general relationship to the intertexts than the heroine's nuanced and layered engagements: "Carter tests the outlines of the Romantic ideology to see whether and how its contours might embody a female aesthetic form" (307). In so clearly divorcing the heroine from Carter, Linkin does more than grant the heroine an independent subjectivity, however; she also implies the possibility of a productive gap between them. Thus, although Linkin concludes by integrating the two perspectives—her final claim (that "Carter demonstrates the larger failure of a Romantic aesthetics whose master plot requires the subjugation of the other" [322]) echoes the heroine's failure to imagine the possibility of love in the Romantic mode—I want to read into the space between the two in order to consider the ways in which Carter's project might extend beyond the critique of Romantic aesthetics and ideology that Linkin has so compellingly established.

With abundant references to William Blake and William Wordsworth, Samuel Coleridge and John Keats, Percy Bysshe Shelley and Robert Browning, Christina Rossetti and Dorothy Wordsworth structuring "The Erl-King" (Linkin, 1994: 307, 313), Goethe's "Erlkönig" might seem to exist at an intertextual remove.[2] Yet Goethe's version of the Danish folk ballad, with its simultaneously tempting and terrifying Erlkönig, proves a particularly significant intertext for Carter's explorations of masculinized nature. In her notes for the story Carter references Frances Hodgson Burnett's *Secret Garden*,[3] and Dickon's ability to speak with birds, charm wild animals, and read the local flora and fauna resonates in the Erl-King's character. Inside the walls of the secret garden, the animals congregate around Dickon—"Dickon held his rabbit in his arm, and perhaps he made some charmer's signal no one heard, for when he sat down, cross-legged like the rest, the crow, the fox, the squirrels, and the lamb slowly drew near and made part of the circle, settling each into a place of rest as if of their own desire" (Burnett, 2010: 197)—just as they do around the Erl-King, who similarly captivates the birds and beasts.

> Ash-soft doves, diminutive wrens, freckled thrushes, robins in their tawny bibs, huge, helmeted crows that shone like patent leather, a blackbird with a yellow bill, voles, shrews, fieldfares, little brown bunnies with their ears laid together along their backs like spoons, crouching at his feet. A lean, tall, reddish hare, up on its great hind legs, nose a-twitch. The rusty fox, its muzzle sharpened to a point, laid its head upon his knee. On the trunk of a scarlet rowan a squirrel clung, to watch him; a cock pheasant delicately stretched his shimmering neck from a brake of thorn to peer at him. There was a goat of uncanny whiteness, gleaming like a goat of snow, who turned her mild eyes towards me and bleated softly, so that he knew I had arrived. (Carter, 1993: 85–86)

Animal charmers both, Dickon and the Erl-King also share the pipe music that attracts creatures, including girls and young women, to them; Dickon's "soft, strange little notes" (Burnett, 2010: 137) float through the Erl-King's "two notes of the song of a bird" that transform the heroine's "girlish and delicious loneliness" into sound (Carter, 1993: 85).

If both Dickon and the Erl-King represent the possibility of a masculinized nature, Carter ultimately abandons Dickon's childhood innocence in favor of the dark, predatory sexuality implicit in Goethe's "Erlkönig," a sexuality that her heroine finds captivating. Writing against the Romantic hegemony of a highly feminized nature and underscoring the centrality of the Erl-King's dark sexuality to his allure, Carter embraces Goethe's "Erlkönig" to explore the sexual and psychoanalytic implications of a masculinized nature. His presence thus haunts her story, and the father's attempts to comfort his son in Goethe's "Erlkönig" reverberate throughout "The Erl-King." When the boy asks his father whether he sees the Erlkönig, he replies, "My son, it is a streak of mist" (Law, n.d.), and this image is reproduced in the heroine's description of her initial foray into the wood: "There was a little tangled mist in the thickets, mimicking the tufts of old man's beard" (Carter, 1993: 85). When the boy asks his father whether he hears the Erlkönig, he replies, "It's the wind rustling in the dry leaves" (Law, n.d.), an image that appears on several occasions when the heroine describes the Erl-King's hair: "His hair that is the colour of dead leaves, dead leaves fall out of it; they rustle and drift to the ground" (Carter, 1993: 87). And the son's final words, "Erlking has done me harm!" (Law, n.d.), obviously provide the story's refrain, "Erl-King will do you grievous harm" (Carter, 1993: 85, 90).[4]

While the Erlkönig may be widely recognized as the "suitor and predator" (Dye, 2004: 2) whose "ghostly companionship . . . destroys as it cherishes, or which cherishes only in order to destroy" (Lawley, 2001: 258), few critics are willing to see in the child a reciprocal desire. Ignace Feuerlicht hesitantly registers such a reading by way of André Gide even as he calls it into question: "Such an authority on pederasty and expert on Goethe as André Gide could read in the 'Erlkönig,' though where is hard to tell, that the child is more charmed than terrified that he is yielding to the mysterious seduction in the beginning, and that only the father is frightened" (1959: 73). Despite the general resistance to such a reading, however, the Erlkönig offers a range of enticements—games, attention, flowers, a mother with many golden robes, daughters who will dance and sing for the boy, and his own love and desire for the child—and Carter translates this fact into the Erl-King's appeal, although the heroine is seduced not so much by his objects as by the promise of his embraces.

Carter's masculinization of nature, together with the desire it inspires, exacerbates the space that Linkin leaves between author and heroine and challenges the psychoanalytic myth of language that British Romantic poetry both exemplifies and perpetuates. Margaret Homans captures the essence of this myth of language when she writes that "the death or absence of the mother sorrowfully but fortunately makes possible the construction of language and culture" (1986: 2). The underlying logic of this foundational mythology, as Homans suggests, is rooted in another Western master narrative: the Oedipal complex, as described by Freud and elaborated, through semiotics, by Lacan. For Lacan the Oedipal stage assimilates language, desire, and gender based on the coincidence of the child's acquisition of language and his dawning awareness of sexual difference. That is, in associating the father's power to disrupt the bond between mother and child with the phallus, the child accedes to its status as both primary (all-powerful) signifier and the mark of difference from the mother.

This recognition of the power of the phallus motivates the child to enter the Symbolic Order and to comply with the Law of the Father, which entails an adherence to the incest prohibition (the *non* of the father), and to a sign system predicated on difference and absence (the *nom* of the father). Because "it is symbolic language alone that can approximate the bridging of the gap between child and mother opened up by the simultaneous arousal and prohibition of incest" (Homans, 1986: 7), language becomes desire in Lacan's theory. Premised as it is on language and consequently on language's dependence on the absent referent, desire remains forever unfulfilled, caught in an endless chain of substitutes that ultimately circle back to the child's prohibited desire for the mother. As Homans points out, such a conceptualization of desire in relation to language is specifically male: "The son's search for substitutes for the forbidden body of his mother will therefore constitute, not a universal human condition, but a specifically male desire, the desire of the son who must renounce his mother" (9).

Expanding on Lacan's inherently phallocentric theory of language and its sex-based logic,[5] Homans articulates the related process by which figuration and literalization are culturally defined through gendered understandings of desire rooted in the Oedipal complex.

> Figuration, then, and the definition of all language as figuration gain their hyperbolical cultural valuation from a specifically male standpoint because they allow the son, both as erotic being and as speaker, to flee from the mother as well as the lost referent with which she is primordially identified. Women must remain literal in order to ground the figurative substitutions sons generate and privilege. (1986: 9)

Of course, in a patriarchal culture, women and literal language are also epistemologically aligned with nature and the natural. Consequently, as Juliet Mitchell makes clear, in the Lacanian narrative of psychosexual development, the girl's "subjugation to the law of the father entails her becoming the representative of 'nature' and 'sexuality,' a chaos of spontaneous, intuitive creativity" (quoted in Gilbert and Gubar, 1979: 49). It is precisely this convergence of gender, the literal, nature, and sexuality that Romantic poetry obsessively stages and celebrates. In figuring nature as feminine and maternal and in writing women as forever unattainable and idealizing them as muse, dream, and fleeting inspiration, nineteenth-century male poets played out their simultaneous need for mother substitutes permissible under the Law of the Father while also absenting them in order to ensure the semiotic gap upon which their own textual production depended (Homans, 1986: 40–42).

This Romantic longing for the sublime, so often thematized as a desire to merge with a feminized nature, is a dangerous pursuit. Its attainment involves a blatant transgression of the Law of the Father because such a coupling necessarily sutures the semiotic gap; in addition, it results in the annihilation of the subject through the complete union of self and other. Nonetheless, this desire is at the heart of the romantic quest. Anticipating Homans's later interpretations, Helene Moglen's definition of the romantic quest foregrounds both its aesthetic and erotic dimensions: "to resolve aesthetically or erotically the subject-object conflict—obliterating the division between the 'I' and the 'not-I' by fusing the two in a redemptive state of feeling" (1976: 29). At the same time, Moglen also calls attention to the sadomasochistic nature of the romantic quest's goal: "Union is realized through a pattern of domination in which the ego masters and absorbs 'the other.' . . . That such a relationship will be sadomasochistic to varying degrees seems inevitable since they are defined by subjugation and the exercise of power" (29–30).

It is most likely the seductive power of this danger—with its heady and tangled swirl of aesthetics and erotics, with its probable domination that might yet hint at a possible subjectivity—that attracts Carter to the Romantic. As Linkin (1994) makes clear, Carter thoroughly understands the oppressive nature of the romantic quest, the perils of women's emplotment in such narratives, and even women's own collusion in the structures of desire that reproduce their victimization. What Linkin fails to address, however—what the space between Carter and her heroine reveals—is that Carter's "Erl-King" does more than explore the possibility of a feminist Romantic aesthetic. Carter's story, with its rich romantic tropes and vast allusions, also reworks the Lacanian subtexts of Romantic poetry to try, once again, to depose the Oedipal myth from its cultural prominence and to dispute a theory of language and desire that requires women's absence. Thus, even though Carter certainly entertains, critiques, and revises Lacan's theories of the mirror stage, the gaze, and the meaning of the phallus in "The Bloody Chamber" and in the feline stories, with "The Erl-King" she delves more deeply into the questions of gender, language, and desire that animate the collection as a whole.

Linkin's perceptive analysis identifies "The Erl-King" as a double narrative in which the first version demonstrates the heroine's command of the tropes of Romantic poetry while the second version attempts to recast her story in a more reflexive vein that might keep her from falling prey to the very dangers she identifies (with) in the first version. Reading from the space between the heroine and Carter, however, suggests another way of understanding the mirrored narratives: not simply the heroine's two versions of her story but rather Carter's playful appropriation of nineteenth-century *women's* writing practices in which mirrored plots, doubled tales, and shadow texts are embedded within the primary narrative (Gilbert and Gubar, 1979). Lorna Sage claims that Carter "never accepted the madwoman-in-the-attic school of thought about the woman writer" and certainly resisted women's interpellation into such a social construction of female authorship (1994: 31), but Carter's appropriation of the mirroring embodied by the mad or monstrous woman *as trope* articulates those interpellations by setting them against the Romantic aesthetic. In this way and consistent with Linkin's reading, the second version comments on the first while also interrogating the tropes it invokes. Locating the agency for the telling with Carter instead of with the heroine allows Carter's nuanced and layered critique to emerge most fully and liberates the second version of the tale from the reductive trap of inverted sex roles that Linkin laments.

"The Erl-King" opens with a vivid description of the woods that seems to exemplify the Romantic aesthetic even as it suggests a subtle parody. If an often feminized nature proves the scene of contemplation for the male Romantic poets, Carter's nature is itself the contemplative agent: "The year, in turning, turns in on itself. Introspective weather" (Carter, 1993: 84). If the sublime, in language and in life, is one of Romanticism's primary goals, Carter's Erl-King lives an especially mundane life full of daily chores (chopping the fire wood, fetching the water, milking his goat), and he resorts to rough language, such as "'bum-pipes' or 'piss-the-beds'" for the dandelions he picks for his salads (86). Carrying this restrained but sly parody throughout the first version of the story, Carter imagines the Erl-King as an instantiation of the Romantic desire for union with nature and thus a representation of the male poets, but his lessons for the heroine confuse literal and figurative: "He told me how the wise toad who squats among the kingcups by the stream in summer has a very precious jewel in his head. He said the owl was a baker's daughter" (86–87). By translating the figurative into the literal, the Erl-King himself literalizes the figurative message: nothing is as it seems, least of all, Carter seems to suggest with her gentle mocking, the Romantic poets' textual hierarchies.

The Erl-King's claim that "the owl was a baker's daughter" does much more than reveal his reading of the figurative as literal; its multiple intertextualities also lend insight into the logic of Carter's doubled narratives. "The owl was a baker's daughter" is perhaps most widely recognized as one of the lines Ophelia speaks at the height of her madness in Shakespeare's *Hamlet*. As a reference to the legend of the baker's daughter who was turned into an owl by Christ when she provided him, disguised as a beggar, with only a stingy bit of bread, the phrase encapsulates women's inability to see beyond the surface (their essential literal-mindedness) and their "true" nature (what lies beneath their outward appearances). In the context of Ophelia's madness, Robert Tracy (1966) argues that the two converge, and his nuanced historical interpretation indicates that the allusion refers specifically to the tension between appearance and reality as they pertain to gender and sexuality: Is the seemingly virtuous woman actually a whore?

For Carter, then, the line "the owl was a baker's daughter" parodies the male poetic investment in the figurative and gestures toward women's madness, especially in relation to their sexual desire as defined by both men and women in the hegemonic imaginary. The fact that the parody and the quotation occur in the first version of the story, whereas the themes of madness and women's sexuality that they index are explored much more thoroughly in the second version, is critical to an understanding of the tale's doubling. Whereas the first version largely adheres to the traditional Romantic aesthetic, the second version mirrors—reproduces, inverts, and refracts—it. This perverted twinning suggests that Carter is writing not only in the tradition of the male Romantic poets but also in the tradition of the nineteenth-century women writers who sought ways to voice their resistance to the patriarchal dominance of the hegemonic Romantic ethos.

In their classic work on nineteenth-century women writers' resistance to literary paternity, Sandra Gilbert and Susan Gubar (1979) theorize that women authors practiced various forms of duality—from male pseudonyms and doubled plots to monstrous alter egos and madwomen in the attic—as a way of voicing their anger and frustration with the social constraints that circumscribed their lives and impeded their writerly existence. Although Carter is not subject to the same sorts of social limitations as her nineteenth-century counterparts, she nevertheless plays with parody—"one of the key strategies through which this female duplicity reveals itself" (Gilbert and Gubar, 1979: 80)—and creates mirrored tales that feature young women who rub up against madness, young women who are made mad and who rescript that madness, in order to draw out her nuanced and complex critique of the Romantic ethos and, especially, the ways in which its dominant tropes reproduce hegemonic myths of gender, language, and desire.

In the first version of the story, Carter imagines the Erl-King as both father figure[6] and lover, and the seduction plot is consistent with both the conventions of Romantic poetry and the "Romantic fascination with incest" (Gilbert and Gubar, 1979: 207). The Erl-King's masculine command of an earthy domesticity—his diet from the "bounty of the woodland," his "rustic home," his "wood fire crackling in the grate, a sweet, acrid smoke, a bright, glancing flame" (Carter, 1993: 86–87)—together with his lessons for the heroine about the flora and fauna, about weaving baskets and cages, contributes to his fatherly persona. In addition, he exerts a patriarchal control over the plot, despite the fact that it is narrated from the heroine's perspective; in keeping with the traditional gendering of hegemonic Romantic poetry, even she minimizes her agency in this version of the tale. First drawn to the Erl-King by his enticing birdcall, a call "as desolate as if it came from the throat of the last bird left alive," a call that goes "directly to [her] heart" (85), the heroine repeatedly returns to the Erl-King; but he is always the one who directs their sexual rituals: "He lays me down on his bed of rustling straw where I lie at the mercy of his huge hands" (87). Even more, he establishes the terms of their exchange: "He is the tender butcher who showed me how the price of flesh is love" (87). And he literally dictates her domination: "Skin the rabbit, he says! Off come all my clothes" (87). For the Erl-King, to speak is to make happen. His metaphoric command—his command of language—instantiates his desire, and the heroine's clothes remove themselves at his behest. This exaggerated power of male articulation is, of course, part of Carter's understated parody and underscores the fact that the first version of the story does not simply reproduce the Romantic aesthetic but also works to unsettle its dominant tropes.

As the first version of the story progresses, the heroine becomes increasingly aware of the Erl-King's potential dangers: his "white, pointed teeth," his ability to lure and cage songbirds, his cold air that "crisps the hairs on the back of [her] neck" (Carter, 1993: 87). However, she is "not afraid of him; only, afraid of vertigo, of the vertigo with which he seizes me. Afraid of falling down" (87), afraid—in the patriarchal imagination—of her fall from grace, her fall from purity made manifest by her desire for the Erl-King. The extended scene of the heroine's fear of falling simultaneously conveys the depth of her fear and her assimilation of romantic love to the Romantic aesthetic.[7]

> Falling as a bird would fall through the air if the Erl-King tied up the winds in his handkerchief and knotted the ends together so they could not get out. Then the moving currents of the air would no longer sustain them and all the birds would fall at the imperative of gravity, as I fall down for him, and I know it is only because he is kind to me that I do not fall still further. (88)

When the heroine finds in the Erl-King's kindness a solution to the problem he has inspired, Carter exposes the heroine's containment within the typical nineteenth-century romantic plot that she herself has created. As this scene makes clear, the myth of a redemptive and romantic love—implicit in the Romantic pursuit of the sublime—may be structured by patriarchal ideologies, but it is sustained by both men's and women's commitment to it. Falling for this myth of romance, falling into the romantic plot, is the real danger, Carter seems to suggest.

At the close of the first version of the story, the heroine contemplates the Erl-King's ability to cast her in both the myth and the place of Persephone: "He could thrust me into the seed-bed of next year's generation and I would have to wait until he whistled me up from my darkness before I could come back again" (Carter, 1993: 88). In this speculative fantasy the heroine identifies with the myth of the rape of Persephone, and although the means of their victimization differ, both women are violently displaced to the darkness of the underworld. By writing Persephone's story into her tale, Carter gives vivid form to Romanticism's highly gendered system of sexuality, a system of extreme gendering that, Moglen argues, left little space for women's self-definition as other than victim.

> Male power was affirmed through an egoistic, aggressive, even violent sexuality. Female sexuality was passive and self-denying. The woman, by willfully defining herself as "the exploited," as "victim"; by seeing herself as she was reflected in the male's perception of her, achieved the only kind of control available to her. (1976: 30)

Here, then, Carter's heroine seeks in Persephone's story a way to imagine a self in light of her passive consent to the Erl-King's sexual dominance—her acquiescence to "lie at the mercy of his huge hands" (Carter, 1993: 87)—which ultimately leads to her vertigo, to her sense of losing control.

At the same time, however, Carter most likely invokes Persephone's story in the context of Romanticism because she knows it also raises the specter of Mary Shelley's early feminist dramatization, *Proserpine*, which centers on the Edenic mother-daughter bond and its disruption by male desire and violence. Susan Gubar argues that women writers such as Shelley and Elizabeth Barrett Browning, whose *Aurora Leigh* is also a retelling of Persephone's story, reframe the myth—despite feminist criticisms such as Simone de Beauvoir's claim that it perpetuates "destructive stereotypes of female passivity and masochism" (Gubar, 1979: 302)—in order to "re-define, to re-affirm and to celebrate female consciousness itself" (303). Although the content of Shelley's *Proserpine* offers a critique of "male domination in sexual relationships" and mourns the fact that "in a patriarchal society women are divided from each other and from themselves" (305), its formal structure replicates the gendered hierarchy of literary production during the Romantic period with Mary Shelley's blank verse drama and Percy Bysshe Shelley's two lyric poems.

As a typically female character in a typically Romantic tale, the heroine's identification with Persephone is run through with all these intertextual meanings. And yet, as Linkin has established, Carter's heroine is not confined to the Romantic plot she inhabits; rather, her fluency with the dominant tropes intended to contain her actually allows her to exceed the boundaries of Romanticism. By speculating about what the Erl-King *could* do to her, she also reflects on her narrative positionality. Thus, in entertaining the possibility that she *could* fall victim to the forceful and aggressive sexuality underlying Romantic poetry and its gendered articulations, Carter's heroine draws out the dangers of such articulations while also rejecting both the passive acceptance of a totalizing patriarchal oppression and the consolatory myth of an Edenic community of women. The heroine's final sentence in the first version of the story forecloses the possibility of her speculations: "Yet, when he shakes out those two clear notes from his bird call, I come, like any other trusting thing that perches on the crook of his wrist" (Carter, 1993: 88). The certainty of her testimony—when he calls, "I come"—overrides the speculative possibility that the Erl-King *could* "thrust [her] into the seed-bed of next year's generation." With the heroine's confession of her active desire, Carter insists that women are—and always have been—complicit in the narratives that subjugate them, a fact she exacerbates in the second version of her story.

In the second version of the story, Carter revisits the key scenes of the first version's seduction plot, but in this case the heroine narrates her agency as central to the mutual desire she shares with the Erl-King. Here, then, she is not drawn by the power of the Erl-King's song to initiate their story but rather joins of her own accord: "I found the Erl-King sitting on an ivy-covered stump winding all the birds in the wood to him on a diatonic spool of sound" (Carter, 1993: 88). The fact that their relationship originates in the heroine's discovery of the Erl-King and not in his efforts to enchant her with his musical call does not mean that she determines the course of their narrative, however. Thus, even though Carter's second version strays further from the Romantic aesthetic than the first version does, it still appropriates the textual practices through which nineteenth-century women writers engaged and resisted the hegemony of literary paternity and the cultural dominance of the masculine Romantic ethos. As a result, the heroine's choices and desires must still be contained; within this context, then, it is the rain that prompts the heroine to seek shelter in the Erl-King's cottage, thus mediating her desire and offsetting the complete agency inherent in her dangerous choice: "I walked into the bird-haunted solitude of the Erl-King, who keeps his feathered things in little cages he has woven out of osier twigs and there they sit and sing for him" (88).

Unlike the Erl-King's absolute sexual dominance in the first version, which is supported by his magisterial dictates and their disembodied responses, the choreography of the seduction in the second version depends on both characters' embodied subject positions. In this case the heroine does not wait for the Erl-King to "[lay her] down on his bed of rustling straw" (Carter, 1993: 87) but instead initiates their intimate liaisons: "I lie down on the Erl-King's creaking palliasse of straw" (88). Nor does the Erl-King undress her by virtue of metaphoric command: "He strips me to my last nakedness, that underskin of mauve, pearlized satin, like a skinned rabbit; then dresses me again in an embrace so lucid and encompassing it might be made of water" (89). Carter's doubled image of the skinned rabbit recasts the masculine Romantic figuration of desire in the literalized materiality of physical bodies that Homans associates with women's writing of the period. The act of being stripped to one's "last nakedness, that underskin of mauve, pearlized satin, like a skinned rabbit" challenges the male poets' articulation of desire as typified by the command to "skin the rabbit"; echoing the Erl-King's command in the first version, the heroine's "last nakedness" of the second version acknowledges women's vulnerability in the context of hegemonic Romanticism while also gesturing toward the possible freedom (the stripping away of "all the skins of a life in the world" experienced by the heroine of "The Tiger's Bride") and a certain sensuality (the "embrace so lucid and encompassing it might be made of water") afforded by desire.

And yet, as Carter demonstrates, the mutual desire of the story's second version is also consistent with the Erl-King's sexual dominance in the first version. Indeed, the second version exposes his predatory sexuality much more fully: "Ach! I feel your sharp teeth in the subaqueous depths of your kisses. . . . You sink your teeth into my throat and make me scream" (Carter, 1993: 88). Although these painful ministrations make the heroine scream, they are also exactly what she finds so enticing. Thus, even though she is initially immune to the lure of the Erl-King's call, after their sexual encounter she finds herself increasingly under his control: "How sweet I roamed, or, rather, used to roam . . . he drew me towards him on his magic lasso of inhuman music" (88–89). Even as the heroine recognizes the Erl-King's dominance over her and her affinity with the caged birds he has lured with his call, she entertains a fantasy in which such a sadomasochistic relationship might also be a traditionally romantic one.

> If I strung that old fiddle with your hair, we could waltz together to the music as the exhausted daylight founders among the trees; we should have better music than the shrill prothalamions of the larks stacked in their pretty cages as the roof creaks with the freight of birds you've lured to it while we engage in your profane mysteries under the leaves. (89)

Here, then, Carter's wry extension of the opening line of Blake's poem—"How sweet I roamed, or, rather, used to roam"—not only points to the heroine's sense of confinement, a recurrent trope in nineteenth-century women's fiction, but also mirrors the first heroine's assimilation of romantic love to the Romantic aesthetic.

For Carter, as for the women writers she invokes, such an assimilation poses a particular danger because it subsumes Romanticism's quest for the sublime—for the complete union of self and Other—under the sign of romantic love, thereby naturalizing the highly gendered impulse to dominate and annihilate the object of desire. In this way the heroine takes her sadomasochistic relationship with the Erl-King for a romantic one and longs to become one with him.

> His skin covers me entirely; we are like two halves of a seed, enclosed in the same integument. I should like to grow enormously small, so that you could swallow me, like those queens in fairy tales who conceive when they swallow a grain of corn or a sesame seed. Then I could lodge inside your body and you would bear me. (Carter, 1993: 89)

In posing an entirely feminine and corporeal way of overcoming the boundary between self and Other, however, Carter parodies the Romantic poets' transcendental goals. Instead of intense sexual union and meditative communion with nature as the means for merging self and Other, she privileges fairy tale enchantments—long associated with women and, during the Romantic period, with uneducated women in particular—in order to expose the masculinist underpinnings of the Romantic sublime. Within this context Carter's feminization of the Erl-King as pregnant fairy-tale queen also incarnates the male fantasy of procreation—"I could lodge inside your body and you would bear me"—and makes explicit the metaphor at the foundation of the myth of literary paternity. In coupling the heroine's desire for a sublime union with a literalization of the Erl-King's power to bear the female subject, Carter highlights the Romantic sublime as an especially trenchant manifestation of the myth of literary paternity by articulating the logic through which the sublime desire to annihilate the feminine Other gives rise to the need for the poet to bear her, repeatedly, in language. Even more, Carter's heroine suggests that her conflation of romantic love and the Romantic ethos makes her complicit in her own poetic interpellations; that is, by fantasizing a way for the Erl-King to bear her, the heroine facilitates her transition from subject to signifier, one in "a chain of substitutive signifiers" representing "language's search for substitutes for the object" (Homans, 1986: 10).

In the scene immediately following the heroine's fantasy of her annihilated subjectivity, Carter draws out the masochistic nature of the Romantic sublime and articulates it with women's madness: "His touch both consoles and devastates me.... Eat me, drink me; thirsty, cankered, goblin-ridden, I go back and back to him to have his fingers strip the tattered skin away and clothe me in his dress of water, this garment that drenches me, its slithering odour, its capacity for drowning" (Carter, 1993: 89). Here, the Erl-King's simultaneously consoling and devastating touch conjures intertextual madwomen—Laura and Lizzie from Christina Rossetti's "Goblin Market" and Ophelia from Shakespeare's *Hamlet*[8]—whose presence in the second version of the story reiterates nineteenth-century women writers' use of the mad or monstrous double to represent their "self-division, their desire both to accept the strictures of patriarchal society and to reject them" (Gilbert and Gubar, 1979: 78). In thematizing the heroine's masochism as exactly this type of doubling, Carter implies that male authors' compulsive need to bear women into language and women's complicity in that process are maddening.

For nineteenth-century women writers the trope of madness might have offered an outlet for expressing their anger and frustration at their subjugation to the patriarchal order, but their madness was nonetheless still defined by the male imaginary, as Carter makes clear in the specific intertextual cases of Laura, Lizzie, and particularly Ophelia.[9] Laura and Lizzie, the two sisters of Rossetti's "Goblin Market," exemplify the structural double so frequently used to figure "good" and "bad" women; the transgressive Laura goes mad with her desire for more goblin fruit after an initial, forbidden taste, whereas the obedient Lizzie resists the goblins' temptations and ultimately saves her sister from her mad desire. Carter, however, reduces the two sisters to a singular voice when she appropriates their words for her heroine: "Eat me, drink me; thirsty, cankered, goblin-ridden." Here, then, Laura's madness—in the poem she describes herself at the height of her delirium as "thirsty, cankered, goblin-ridden" (Rossetti, 1970: 107)—also incorporates Lizzie's plea to her sister: "Eat me, drink me, love me" (106), she cries in the poem after she returns covered in the smashed fruit with which the goblins have pelted her. In collapsing Laura's mad desire with Lizzie's fruit-covered body, Carter reimagines madness as women's pleasure, sensual joy, and embodied desire, a redefinition she extends to Ophelia at the end of the sentence: "I go back and back to him to have his fingers strip the tattered skin away and clothe me in his dress of water, this garment that drenches me, its slithering odour, its capacity for drowning." The image of the Erl-King stripping away the heroine's "tattered skin" and then clothing her in "his dress of water" harkens back to their earlier encounter in which he strips her to "her last nakedness" and "dresses" her in an "embrace so lucid and encompassing it might be made of water." Twice evoking the sensual feel of water on freshly naked skin, Carter recontextualizes Ophelia's "garments, heavy with their drink" (*Hamlet*, Act IV, Scene 7, line 206)—the symbol, in the play and in visual representations, of the madness that drives her to suicide—to again suggest that women's madness might be differently understood as a corporeal, joyful, and sensory pleasure.

As with the nineteenth-century women writers whose fictive doublings Carter imitates, the heroine is pulled between the potential freedom of a mad sensuality and the romantic illusions that sustain hegemonic myths of desire. In both of Carter's versions of "The Erl-King," an increasing wind and cold descend in the aftermath of their sexual encounter, and it is this shift in weather that the heroine reads as a sign of the Erl-King's detachment, a detachment that ultimately diminishes the heroine's sense of self. In the first version the heroine thus responds to her vertigo by fusing romantic love with the Romantic aesthetic. In the second version, however, the heroine's encounter with madness—regardless of whether experienced as self or through a double—disrupts the totalizing narratives and shifts the course of the story: "He spreads out a goblin feast of fruit for me, such appalling succulence; I lie above him and see the light from the fire sucked into the black vortex of his eye, the omission of light at the centre, there, that exerts on me such a tremendous pressure, it draws me inwards" (Carter, 1993: 89). As the Erl-King's eyes continue to enthrall her, she again finds herself caught in a fantasy of self-annihilation: "Your green eye is a reducing chamber. If I look into it long enough, I will become as small as my own reflection, I will diminish to a point and vanish. I will be drawn down into that black whirlpool and be consumed by you. I shall become so small you can keep me in one of your osier cages and mock my loss of liberty" (90). Sated with the Erl-King's feast of goblin fruit—with the taste of madness fresh on her tongue—the heroine now resists the myth of romance that she previously embraced: "I loved him with all my heart and yet I had no wish to join the whistling congregation he kept in his cages" (90). She no longer desires to "grow enormously small, so that you could swallow me." In fact, she knows that it is the Erl-King's gaze—the reflection that bears her into language, that transforms her from subject to signifier, that traps her in a chain of substitutes—that makes her small, so small he can keep her in a cage on his wall of imprisoned birds.

At this point the heroine is compelled by the logic of the Romantic aesthetic to become the monstrous woman if she is to resist the Erl-King's seductive threat: "I shall take two huge handfuls of his rustling hair as he lies half dreaming, half waking, and wind them into ropes, very softly, so he will not wake up, and, softly, with hands as gentle as rain, I shall strangle him with them" (Carter, 1993: 91). This is, of course, the ending that so disappoints Linkin with its inability to surmount Romanticism's "master plot [that requires] the subjugation of the other" (1994: 322); instead, it simply reimagines an inverted ending to Robert Browning's "Porphyria's Lover." Prioritizing Carter's perspective over that of the heroine, however, reveals the rich and nuanced complexity of the conclusion with its narrative shift in perspective from first person to third person and its productive slippage between mother and daughter.

After the heroine confesses her plan to strangle the Erl-King, the narrative assumes the third-person perspective even as it continues with the fantastic plot, describing first how *she* will free the caged birds and then how "she will carve off his great mane with the knife he uses to skin the rabbits" (Carter, 1993: 91).[10] Stringing the fiddle with his hair, she creates an enchanted instrument that "will play discordant music without a hand touching it. The bow will dance over the new strings of its own accord and they will cry out: 'Mother, mother, you have murdered me!'" (91). In moving from first-person to third-person narration, Carter reiterates the significance of the heroine's monstrous double—both "I" and "she"—and women's inherent multiplicity. As discussed in previous chapters and as Irigaray (1985) has convincingly argued, multiplicity, and women's multiplicity in particular, contests the logic of the singular that grants the phallus its status as privileged signifier. The doubling implicit in the shifting perspectives is further replicated in the slippage between mother and daughter at the story's close, and the specificity of mother and daughter, particularly in relation to the Erl-King as father and finally son, clearly indicates Carter's investment in challenging once again the Oedipal myth as the basis for Freud's theory of psychosexual development, Lacan's theory of language, and much of Western civilization.

With the elision of mother and daughter, Carter destabilizes the calculus of desire that structures Freud's account of familial sexual dynamics while also foregrounding Romanticism's tacit investment in his theory. If mother and daughter are one, then the son's desire for the mother is the father's desire for the daughter, just as the daughter's desire for the father is the mother's desire for the son. Freud's theory of the Oedipal complex, however, cannot accommodate these multiple and reciprocal lines of desire because they undermine the father's threat and, subsequently, the fear of castration fundamental to patriarchal civilization. Carter foreshadows this ambiguity in the first version of the story when the heroine describes the fatherly Erl-King as "the tender butcher who showed me how the price of flesh is love" (Carter, 1993: 87). Here, the intentionally ambiguous terms of their exchange[11]—her flesh for his love, his flesh for her love—suggest that the underlying logic of the Oedipal complex is based, at least in part, on a projection: Although the daughter may desire the father, the *theory* of her desire veils the father's desire for the daughter. This is obviously a precarious foundation for a theory as weighty as the Oedipal complex and its authorization of patriarchy. After all, as Jane Gallop points out, "Patriarchy is grounded in the uprightness of the father. If he were devious and unreliable, he could not have the power to legislate" (1982: 75). Even more, if "the price of flesh is love," then love and desire are not only deeply and infinitely entangled but also forced into systems of exchange that operate in different registers: not love for love and flesh for flesh, but love for flesh and flesh for love. Such misalignments, Carter seems to argue, drive the patriarchal impulse to contain women's sexual desire by coercing it into a relationship with love, thereby furthering the assimilation of the Romantic ethos to cultural discourses of romance.

Carter's critique of the Freudian Oedipal complex is necessarily also a critique of the Lacanian theory of language, gender, and desire, especially as manifested in hegemonic Romantic poetry. In addition to contesting the primacy of the singular phallus with women's multiplicity, Carter's doubled "Erl-King"—with its mother-daughter heroine and its productively imprecise lines of incestuous desire—confounds the Romantic poet's unconscious identification as the son who must banish the threatening mother to figuration within his texts where he can safely yearn for her even as he ensures her eventual death or absence. Within this context Carter's ultimate reversal of the Romantic master plot resists the idea that "the mother's absence is what makes possible and makes necessary the central projects of our culture" (Homans, 1986: 2). Playing with the stereotypically feminine practice of writing as literalization, Carter kills off the Romantic son—representative of the movement's highly patriarchal ethos—in order to retrieve the mother from her literary exile and death, the absence on which the Lacanian Symbolic Order absolutely depends. At the same time, Carter's monstrous female heroine takes on the Bloomian Oedipal struggle to destroy the poetic father whose influence inspires such anxiety. Consequently, the mother's survival also frees her, along with her symbolic substitutes, from their entrapment in masculine figuration, thereby transforming them all from signifiers back into subjects: "She will open all the cages and let the birds free; they will change back into young girls, every one" (Carter, 1993: 91). With the mother's life—a life among her substitute signifiers-turned-subjects, no less—Carter rejects the Law of the Father and unsettles the Lacanian theory of language, gender, and desire. Although this may not fully recuperate women's sexual subjectivity, or even the Romantic aesthetic, it at least gestures toward the possibility of women's comprehensibility in the enchanted language of the magical fiddle's song.

Coldhearted Desire: "The Snow Child"

Whereas Carter stages women's subordination to masculine articulation from the mother's perspective in "The Erl-King," in "The Snow Child" she dramatizes the dire consequences it has for the daughter. Condensing the same themes into this sparsely told tale, Carter also challenges German Romanticism's literary canonization of the fairy tale—Goethe's "Erlkönig," the Grimms' *Kinder- und Hausmärchen*—through male appropriation and authorship. Of all the tales in *The Bloody Chamber*, "The Snow Child" hews most closely to its fairy-tale intertext, a lesser-known version of "Snow White" collected but never published by the Grimms and later reproduced in Bruno Bettelheim's *Uses of Enchantment* (1989). Omitted from the Grimms' collection, which was intended to educate children in proper bourgeois ideology, the version Carter selects for her intertext centers on the father's wish for a daughter, thus emphasizing the way literary paternity obscures the daughter's vulnerability and subjugation to the father's deepest desires.

In this version of the tale, the wintry landscape—mounds of snow, pools of blood, ravens—inspires a count's desire for "a girl," who magically appears as Snow White as soon as he has finished uttering his wishes. Jealous of her husband's love for Snow White, the Countess conspires to be rid of her, ordering the coachman to drive off while Snow White is fetching the Countess's dropped glove or picking roses at her behest. Already a bare tale, especially compared to the Grimms' much more extensive anthologized version involving the magic mirror, the Huntsman, the dwarfs, the disguised Queen, the glass coffin, and the Prince, Carter strips the story even further by paradoxically amplifying the description of the frozen landscape and the Countess's attire while tightening the story's symbolically charged fairy-tale motifs ("So the girl picks a rose; pricks her finger on the thorn; bleeds; screams; falls" [Carter, 1993: 92]).[12]

Given the stark economy of "The Snow Child"—the story barely exceeds a single page—Carter's detailed opening description is significant: "Midwinter—invincible, immaculate. The Count and his wife go riding, he on a grey mare and she on a black one, she wrapped in the glittering pelts of black foxes; and she wore high, black, shining boots with scarlet heels, and spurs. Fresh snow fell on snow already fallen; when it ceased, the whole world was white" (Carter, 1993: 91). In a reversal of the Romantic aesthetic, Carter explicitly disarticulates the Countess from the snow-covered landscape—her black horse, black furs, black boots with scarlet heels against the whole white world—and thus forecloses the possibility of reading her as the stereotypically frigid woman to the ever-desirous man. In so doing, she writes woman and landscape together, but clearly distinct from each other, to provide a critical backdrop for the story and for her return to many of the questions she confronts in "The Erl-King."

Rejecting the misogynist discourse of women's frigidity from the outset, Carter focuses on the Countess's exteriority—as opposed to the interiority that reveals the Queen's vanity and jealousy in the Grimms' version—to highlight the fact that this culturally imposed narrative blames women for their sexual subjugation. Freud, for instance, attributes women's frigidity to their inability to transition successfully from infantile (clitoral) sexuality to mature (vaginal) femininity, often the result of pre-Oedipal anxieties such as guilt over desiring the father (Faulk, 1973: 259); Bettelheim generalizes this culpability in his psychoanalytic interpretation of Snow White when he contends that "we do not know why the queen in 'Snow White' cannot age gracefully and gain satisfaction from vicariously enjoying her daughter's blooming into a lovely girl, but something must have happened in her past to make her vulnerable so that she hates the child she should love" (1989: 195). With "The Snow Child" Carter suggests that we do, in fact, know what remains so mysterious to Bettelheim: Her austere story posits patriarchal desire, articulation, and power as likely sources of the Queen's difficulty in living up to idealized gender expectations.

Carter's claim that "some of the stories in *The Bloody Chamber* are the result of quarrelling furiously with Bettelheim" (Haffenden, 1985: 83) is particularly germane to "The Snow Child," with its piercing imitation of his opening Snow White story and its minimized plot capable of "extract[ing] the latent content from the traditional stories" (84). In rejecting the correspondence between women and landscape, Carter insists that the Countess cannot be blamed for behavior inspired by her inscription in oppressive patriarchal discourses; in so doing, Carter writes patriarchal power into the narrative to correct for Bettelheim's reading it out. Even when hinting at the father's desire for the daughter in the lesser-known version of "Snow White," Bettelheim ignores or overlooks the patriarchal ideologies that structure the Oedipal complex and motivate the other woman's behavior: "The oedipal desires of a father and daughter, and how these arouse the mother's jealousy which makes her wish to get rid of the daughter, are much more clearly stated here than in more common versions" (Bettelheim, 1989: 200). Bettelheim's failure to consider the gendered dynamics of Freudian psychoanalytic theory may not be exceptionally surprising, but Carter highlights this failure and continues to critique Freud's theory of psychosexual development, and the Oedipal complex in particular, with "The Snow Child."

In this context the story's frozen landscape also discloses the way in which the myth of women's frigidity rationalizes men's desire for the younger woman—"the girl," the daughter[13]—as both sexual and semiotic replacement for the mother figure, who supposedly grows to deny the father's sexual interest. That is, it is the wintry scene—stereotypically associated with women's frigidity insofar as women and nature are conflated in the Romantic aesthetic and the phallocentric imaginary—that gives rise to the Count's wish for "the girl," who materializes from his desire as well as from the landscape: "As soon as he completed her description, there she stood, beside the road, white skin, red mouth, black hair and stark naked; she was the child of his desire and the Countess hated her" (Carter, 1993: 91–92). Carter's seamless movement from the Count's articulation of his desire to the Snow Child's appearance to the Countess's hatred reiterates her critique of Lacan's theory of language, gender, and desire discussed in relation to "The Erl-King." Here, Carter actualizes Lacan's theory of language *as* desire predicated on the mother's absence in order to critique its implications for women's subjectivity. By incarnating the phallocentrism at the foundation of Lacan's theory, "The Snow Child" returns to the fact that under the Law of the Father "the speaking or writing subject is constitutively masculine while the silent object is feminine" (Homans, 1986: xii); as such, Carter seems to suggest in this story that women are entirely subject to male articulation in ways that undermine any potential for subjectivity and mutual identification.

Despite the fact that the Snow Child and the Countess are allied in their objectified and silenced figurations in the Symbolic Order, they are nevertheless locked in an eternal fairy-tale rivalry, which Carter both exaggerates and interrogates. Playing up both of the women's status as decorative objects reflecting the Count's power, Carter symbolizes their competition through the Countess's clothing, so crucial to her subjectivity at the start of the story. Twice the Countess attempts to dispatch the Snow Child, but the Count verbally intervenes each time; the first time, the "furs sprang off the Countess's shoulders and twined round the naked girl," and the second time, "her boots leapt off the Countess's feet and on to the girl's legs" (Carter, 1993: 92). Overstating the object status of both women, Carter ensures that neither the Countess nor the Snow Child is the agent in this scene—the clothes magically disappear and reappear at the Count's word, much as the heroine's clothes remove themselves at the Erl-King's command—and their lack of subjectivity evacuates the force of the jealousy assumed to structure their relationship. Instead, the Count's power to dictate its terms renders it simply pathetic. Thus, even though Carter certainly implies that the relationship between the Countess and the Snow Child, between mother and daughter, is always already overdetermined as one of female rivalry—"she was the child of his desire and the Countess hated her"—the Countess's utter lack of interiority also opens up the possibility that the assumed jealousy of the scene is just as likely to be socially ascribed as psychologically motivated.[14]

Underlying all of this, of course, is the father's desire for the daughter, and Carter translates this latent meaning into the story's most arresting scene.

> So the girl picks a rose; pricks her finger on the thorn; bleeds; screams; falls.
> Weeping, the Count got off his horse, unfastened his breeches and thrust his virile member into the dead girl. The Countess reined in her stamping mare and watched him narrowly; he was soon finished.
> Then the girl began to melt. Soon there was nothing left of her . . . (Carter, 1993: 92)

In rendering the Count's rape of the Snow Child in such frank and graphic terms, Carter makes explicit the unspoken desire—the father's desire for the daughter—that tacitly governs the Oedipal complex through projected fantasies of the child's desire for the parent of the opposite sex. Jane Gallop makes a similar point when she contends that "the Oedipal complex, the incest taboo, the law forbidding intercourse between father and daughter, covers over a seduction, masks it so it goes unrecognized" (1982: 75). Even as Carter and Gallop call attention to the way in which the daughter's seduction underpins the Oedipal complex and its significance for Lacan's theory of language, they also recognize the vast cultural investment in denying it. Such a denial is especially insidious, Carter seems to suggest, because it refuses the possibility of a female subject position, particularly for the daughter; in the end, girls are nothing more than overdetermined and thus meaningless signifiers: "a feather a bird might have dropped; a bloodstain, like the trace of a fox's kill on the snow; and the rose she had pulled off the bush" (Carter, 1993: 92).

For Carter, however, the rose proves a much more complex symbol: "The Count picked up the rose, bowed and handed it to his wife; when she touched it, she dropped it. 'It bites!' she said" (Carter, 1993: 92). Commonly read as a symbol of the Snow Child (e.g., Bacchilega, 1997; Barchilon, 1988; Chainani, 2003), the biting rose concludes the story with a rich and productive ambiguity. As a symbol it exceeds its likely referents: not entirely the girl, who has melted into a collection of signs; not entirely representative of the Countess, who first demands that the Snow Child pick it for her; not entirely a reflection of the Count, who authorizes her picking it and who later ceremoniously hands it to his wife. In multiplying the possible meanings of the biting rose, Carter plays with the traditional fairy-tale motif and the common Romantic trope that associates rose and girl, transforming Blake's sick rose into nature's mouthy assault. Resisting closure and containment, Carter's enchanted rose is also the *vagina dentata*, a paranoid male fantasy of women's supposed anger at their castration and an image Carter returns to in "The Lady of the House of Love." In both stories the biting and fanged rose outlives the girl it seems to signify, implying that the patriarchal fantasies through which she is constituted endure well beyond her living, material being.

When the Snow Child "picks a rose; pricks her finger on the thorn; bleeds; screams; falls," she becomes one of Carter's many sleeping beauties.[15] Indeed, in her notes and early drafts of "The Snow Child," Carter regularly titles the story "Sleeping Beauty,"[16] highlighting the centrality of the young woman in deathly repose to both the "Snow White" and "Sleeping Beauty" traditions. Cristina Bacchilega picks up on Carter's "Sleeping Beauty" allusions and reads the scene of the Snow Child's perverted initiation within that context to emphasize the fact that, even though "her death, rape, and fetishizing [become] painfully visible" (1997: 38), the rape itself brings no rebirth for the Snow Child as it does for Basile's sleeping beauty, Talia.

Thus, a murderous mother might entertain the fantasy of escaping her entrapment in the patriarchal imaginary, as does the heroine of "The Erl-King," but the daughter has no such luxury. After all, she is every father's secret desire, as Jacques Barchilon affirms when he characterizes "The Snow Child" as appealing to the "masculine erotic imagination" (1988: 221) and inspiring the question, "Which father has not dreamed of making love to his daughter?" (222).[17] In a pornographic and patriarchal culture—buttressed by the Freudian myth of the Oedipal complex as foundational to civilization—the father's repressed desire for the daughter re-emerges in pedophilic and necrophiliac fantasies like that enacted in the Count's rape of his dead Snow Child. Sadly, in the end, death provides neither solace nor escape for the Snow Child, forever only a set of signs and a sleeping beauty who incarnates her father's deepest desires.

5
A Desire for Death
"The Lady of the House of Love"

If Sleeping Beauty is patriarchy's dream girl, then the female vampire is its worst nightmare.

Sleeping Beauty is, of course, the virginal innocent to the female vampire's whorish aggressor. Deep in slumber, the enchanted princess is nothing but a pretty face, a supple body, there for the gazing, there for the taking. The female vampire, by contrast, awakens desires that threaten the very foundations of patriarchal order. Whether femme fatale or lesbian lover, she challenges heteronormativity, the boundaries of gender, and male control over the circulation of women.

In "The Lady of the House of Love" Carter disrupts the "two stereotypes of seductive femininity" (Hennard Dutheil de la Rochère, 2011: 340) by simultaneously writing a "Sleeping Beauty" tale and a Gothic vampire story. As a doubly told intertextual tale and metanarrative detailing the burdens of these literary traditions, "The Lady of the House of Love" is neither a simple retelling of "Sleeping Beauty" through the trope of the vampire nor a retelling of the vampire story through the idiom of "Sleeping Beauty." Rather, Carter's story brings both to life through the figure of the somnambulist vampire Countess, caught like her ancestral Sleeping

Beauties and her vampire forebears in the liminal state between sleeping and waking, between life and death, between fairy tale, Gothic novel, and metanarrative.

"The Lady of the House of Love" chronicles the lonely nights of a "young" vampire Countess, the sole "living" descendant of Nosferatu, who lives with a mute serving woman in a decaying castle above an abandoned village in Romania. Longing for an escape from her predestined life, the vampire Countess passes much of her time with a deck of tarot cards, forever hoping for an alternative future, an alternative life. This desire is satisfied when an English soldier, on leave and cycling through the forests of Romania, accepts the serving woman's invitation to dine at the castle. As the vampire Countess prepares to seduce—and feast upon—the soldier, she fumbles the ritual and, in the process, accidentally cuts her finger on a splinter of glass. Kissing her bleeding wound, the soldier thus frees her from her liminal state, helping her instead to a permanent death.

Sleeping Beauty in the House of Love

Donald Haase (2011) has highlighted the metafictional nature of the "Sleeping Beauty" tale tradition based on a reading of how storytelling, including the princess's in an early version, is thematized in Perrault, the Grimms, Disney, and the medieval *Roman de Perceforest*. Nonetheless, the tale type (ATU 410) is most widely known for its sleeping princess. If, as Haase convincingly argues, these versions "have an underlying preoccupation with the creative power of language and storytelling" (281) and the "Sleeping Beauty" tale is "a narrative that is driven by a fundamental concern with the agency of speech and the speaker, story and storyteller" (281), then it is especially significant that the tale type crystallizes around a princess who completely lacks that agency. In the classic literary versions of the tale, Sleeping Beauty is passive, yielding, available, and, most significantly, silent. She is enchantingly incapable of speaking her story, much less voicing any resistance to the hero's advances. Thus, although in the earliest literary version she may have participated actively in the tale's self-reflective meditation on orality and storytelling, by the later versions she has lost both the ability and the opportunity to do so.

Ruth Bottigheimer (1986) has carefully documented the Grimms' bias for silent girls and women, especially evident in the brothers' tendency to diminish female voice in *Kinder- und Hausmärchen* and overwrite female speech through their own edit(orializ)ing practices. In so doing, the Grimms altered the agency of women's words by casting them in the passive voice of narrators and limiting the range of verbs used to characterize women's speech acts. For Little Brier Rose, the Grimms' sleeping beauty, direct and active speech is confined to childhood, to the time when the princess still has the freedom of movement, the ability to roam the castle, to follow her curiosity in exploration. During one such exploration, she comes across an old woman spinning in a tower and asks her what the spindle is. This question is her only direct speech act in the entire story.

Whereas exegetically it is the slighted fairy's curse and the prick of Sleeping Beauty's finger that put her to sleep, in the Grimms' ideological narrative it is also this act of asking, combining as it does both curiosity and speech, that ushers in the princess's century of sleep. So critical is her silence to upholding the social structure that in the Grimms' version the princess's falling into sleep brings with it sleep for everyone. Her straightforward act of asking disturbs the underpinnings of her social world, and it is not until she wakes, silently, to the hero's kiss and to her rightfully passive place beside him that the inhabitants of the castle return to life, immediately resuming their normative roles as though there had been no interruption.

Marking the transition from child to adult, sleep transforms the young girl into the perfect woman: passive, silent, compliant, and sexually available. Little Brier Rose's womanly silence is particularly striking and especially socially significant compared with Charles Perrault's Sleeping Beauty, whose awakening is preordained and not dependent on the hero's kiss and whose slumber is solitary as opposed to social. In Perrault's 1697 "Sleeping Beauty in the Wood," Sleeping Beauty says to the approaching hero, "Is it you, my prince? . . . You have kept me waiting a long time!" (Perrault, 1977b: 64). Up to this point, the two versions are fairly closely aligned, but the princess's awakening signals their dramatic departure. In Perrault's version Sleeping Beauty engages the hero in conversation: "He was more tongue-tied than she, because she had had plenty of time to dream of what she would say to him" (66).[1] Little Brier Rose, on the other hand, awakens to the hero's kiss and simply "look[s] at him fondly" (Grimm, 1987: 189) before they descend from the tower, and their "wedding . . . was celebrated in great splendor" (189).[2]

Even more than her silence, Little Brier Rose's deathlike passivity is her most becoming feature, as it is for all the princesses in the "Sleeping Beauty" tradition. Beyond the reaches of a common waking, Sleeping Beauty highlights the necrophiliac desire for the beautiful corpse, the erotic fascination with dead women, so prevalent in a patriarchal and pornographic culture. In their deathlike repose they arouse an irresistible longing in the men who come across them. Even the Grimms' relatively chaste version hints at the sexual attraction of the beautiful, corpselike woman: "There she lay, and her beauty was so marvelous that he could not take his eyes off her. Then he leaned over and gave her a kiss" (Grimm, 1987: 189). More explicit is Giambattista Basile's 1634–1636 version in which the traveling King's "picking the fruits of love" results in the birth of twins to Talia, the sleeping beauty, who fails to wake even in childbirth: "He called to her, but no matter what he did and how loud he yelled, she did not wake up, and since her beauty had enflamed him, he carried her to a bed and picked the fruits of love" (Canepa, 2007: 414).[3] In Basile's version, "Sun, Moon, and Talia," the King's having sex with Talia despite his inability to wake her foregrounds the necrophiliac fantasy implicit in the "Sleeping Beauty" fairy tales, although subsequent versions, such as Perrault's "Sleeping Beauty in the Wood" and the Grimms' "Little Brier Rose," tend to shy away from such frank references to the hero's sexual acts with the sleeping princess. Nonetheless, the eroticization of the deathlike princess lurks beneath the surface of Sleeping Beauty's seemingly straightforward embodiment of the perfectly passive woman, especially in the Grimms' version, where Little Brier Rose remains silent even after her waking.

With "The Lady of the House of Love" Carter interrupts the confining legacy of the "Sleeping Beauty" tradition and highlights the burden of this fairy tale inheritance: its power to articulate and extend oppressive cultural constructions of *woman*. By importing the female vampire's Gothic sensibility into the "Sleeping Beauty" tradition, Carter foregrounds the essential interconnectedness of the two figures. Her ongoing fascination with sleeping beauties, female vampires, and living dolls—the alluring somnambulists who make their way through her fiction as well as her criticism[4]—lays bare the fantasy of necrophilia that drives the dominant cultural investment in women's passivity so perfectly exemplified by the "Sleeping Beauty" tradition and the Grimms' "Little Brier Rose" in particular.

Carter's seductive vampire Countess anticipates Sue-Ellen Case's well-known theorization of the female vampire's powerful ability to disrupt hegemonic gender ontologies. Case sees in the figure of the female vampire an "identification with the insult, the taking on of the transgressive" (1991: 2) that is constitutive of a queer theory and a queer desire "which seeks the living dead, producing a slippage at the ontological base and seducing through a gender inversion above" (3). With her vampiric Sleeping Beauty, Carter likewise celebrates the potential for slippage at the center of cultural constructions of gender, a slippage she exploits in "The Lady of the House of Love."

Embodying both the legacy of the female vampire and the "Sleeping Beauty" tradition, the beautiful somnambulist Countess is at once Sade's masochistic Justine and his sadistic Juliette, the sisters who offer up the only possible cultural signifiers for *woman* in their refracted images. Even more, Carter locates this exact conflation in Sade's potentially radical and transformative pornography:[5] "We see how the chaste kiss of the sentimental lover differs only in degree from the vampirish love-bite that draws blood" (Carter, 2006: 24–28). As both sadist and masochist, both "death and the maiden" (Carter, 1993: 93), Carter's beautiful somnambulist, her vampire Countess, bears all the weight of her narrative ancestors, the weight of the cultural desires for Sleeping Beauty's seeming innocence and the dark seduction and deadly sexuality of the Gothic vampire stories. Through such entwined ancestral legacies Carter exposes the fairy tale's grim underbelly.

As an intertextual tale, "The Lady of the House of Love" obviously depends on its patriarchal antecedents to provoke a discomfiting recognition. Although Carter has a translator's familiarity with Perrault's fairy tales and certainly gestures to his and Basile's versions of "Sleeping Beauty," "The Lady of the House of Love" seems to find its richest intertext in the Grimms' "Little Brier Rose," the version with the most passive heroine.[6] Like the castles belonging to these first sleeping beauties, the castle belonging to the beautiful somnambulist is abandoned and surrounded by roses that have "grown up into a huge, spiked wall that incarcerates her in the castle of her inheritance" (Carter, 1993: 95). Even in invoking the same imagery, Carter's slight shift in purpose is significant. Here, the "spiked wall" *incarcerates* the Countess, whereas the other thickets *protect* their sleeping princesses. As Carter's hero follows the mute crone from the village to the mansion, the literal sensuality of the Countess's roses—their scent, size, shape—overwhelm him and intimate the dangerous sexuality awaiting him.

> A great, intoxicated surge of the heavy scent of red roses blew into his face as soon as they left the village, inducing a sensuous vertigo; a blast of rich, faintly corrupt sweetness strong enough almost, to fell him. Too many roses. Too many roses bloomed on enormous thickets that lined the path, thickets bristling with thorns, and the flowers themselves were almost too luxuriant, their huge congregations of plush petals somehow obscene in their excess, their whorled, tightly budded cores outrageous in their implications. (Carter, 1993: 98)

Carter's elaboration of the "spiked wall" as full of "too many roses [blooming] on enormous thickets" calls to mind the Grimms' description of the thicket surrounding Little Brier Rose's castle on the day the successful prince comes to wake her; whereas Perrault's thorny bramble simply opens to the prince after the 100-year spell, the Grimms' previously dangerous hedge is in full bloom: "When the prince approached the brier hedge, he found nothing but beautiful flowers that opened of their own accord, let him through, and then closed again like a hedge" (Grimm, 1987: 188).

In establishing a particularly strong intertextual relationship between "The Lady of the House of Love" and the Grimms' "Little Brier Rose," Carter fully exploits the sexual imagery and clear metaphoric innuendo of the rose in the Grimms' fairy tale. Although the sexual symbolism of the rose *as* the sleeping princess is none too subtle in the Grimms' tale—not only is she named Little Brier Rose but the willing opening up of the protective thorn-hedge full of blooming roses also makes explicit such symbolic meanings—Carter exaggerates the sexual symbolism. Indeed, she almost fully translates it ("their huge congregations of plush petals somehow obscene in their excess, their whorled, tightly budded cores outrageous in their implications") in order to draw out the intoxicating and dangerous sexuality of both her own heroine and the Grimms' more passive and thus perhaps more alluring counterpart.

Carter further extends the symbolism of the rose beyond the opening thicket, beyond the heteronormative sexual meanings implicit in the Grimms' roses. For Carter the rose is much more literally the Countess's sexuality and her life. It is a magical and haunting souvenir of the Countess's enduring (cultural) legacy and the deadly consequences of embracing the doubled fantasy of her as both passive sexual object and active sexual subject. When the hero wakes in the morning—after the vampire Countess has been freed from her liminal existence—he finds only "a lace négligé lightly soiled with blood, as it might be from a woman's menses, and a rose that must have come from the fierce bushes nodding through the window" (Carter, 1993: 106). The rose is, of course, more than just a flower come through the window as the departed Countess's "voice-over" makes clear: "And I leave you as a souvenir the dark, fanged rose I plucked from between my thighs, like a flower laid on a grave" (107). No ordinary rose but a fanged rose—a *vagina dentata*, potent symbol of the fear of women's sexuality—the hero's souvenir of his night with the Countess survives, though barely, his journey from Romania to Britain, where he "resurrects" it in a glass of water until his "spartan quarters brimmed with the reeling odour of a glowing, velvet, monstrous flower whose petals had regained all their former bloom and elasticity, their corrupt, brilliant, baleful splendour" (107–108). Like Nosferatu's plague-infested rats, the Countess's rose travels from east to west and portends the widespread death of hundreds of thousands of young men, its scent wafting through the barracks on the eve of the hero's regiment's departure for France during World War I. Carter's roses are heady, intoxicating, and dangerous in their sensuality, their promise of death. As such, they force us to reimagine the seeming simplicity of the Grimms' roses, "nothing but beautiful flowers," nothing but the innocent Little Brier Rose.

Just as Carter gives the Grimms' rose fangs, so too does she equip her sleeping beauty: "She has no mouth with which to kiss, no hands with which to caress, only the fangs and talons of a beast of prey" (Carter, 1993: 104). Even though the vampire Countess might have the fangs and talons of a predatory animal, she is of course much more than simple "beast of prey"; her desire for "fresh meat"[7] is driven by sexual desire as well. Even as a little girl, when she could be satisfied by feasting on smaller animals, "she bit into their necks with a nauseated voluptuousness" (96). The beautiful somnambulist's "nauseated voluptuousness" reveals her simultaneous animal instinct and her enculturation, her internalized reluctance to fully succumb to her sensual gratification. As she grows older, both her reluctance and her desire deepen.

> But now she is a woman, she must have men. . . . She sinks her teeth into the [rabbit's] neck where an artery throbs with fear; she will drop the deflated skin from which she has extracted all the nourishment with a small cry of both pain and disgust. And it is the same with the shepherd boys and gipsy lads. (96)

In the vampire Countess's need for men, in her sexually charged but ambivalent ravishing of them ("It is dinner-time. It is bed-time," Carter, 1993: 104), Carter elaborates women's animal drives, women's dreams of sexual freedom, only to thwart them by raising the specter of Sade's Juliette. Like Juliette, the vampire Countess is confined by her social context, by the patriarchal culture that leaves no space for her as an autonomous sexual being, and Carter's description of Sade's "great women" might just as well apply to the Countess.

> A free woman in an unfree society will be a monster. Her freedom will be a condition of personal privilege that deprives those on which she exercises it of her own freedom. The most extreme kind of this deprivation is murder. These women murder.
>
> The sexual behavior of these women, like that of their men, is a mirror of their inhumanity. (Carter, 2006: 30)

As discussed in Chapter 2, Carter has been a controversial figure among feminist critics and literary scholars for precisely this type of complexity:[8] The Countess's expression of her animal drives, her seeming sexual autonomy and agency, are reduced to murder and monstrosity, the marks of her inhumanity. She is not an easy feminist heroine following her animal drives, luxuriating in her sexuality. Rather, she is dangerous because of the society that limits her, and Carter plays up the Countess's monstrosity by aligning her with the cannibalistic giant in "Jack and the Beanstalk." Transitioning from a description of the ritual tidying-up that follows the Countess's deadly seductions to the arrival of the hero, Carter offers two verses from the "Jack and the Beanstalk" nursery rhyme: "Fee fi fo fum / I smell the blood of an Englishman" (Carter, 1993: 96). Both the Countess and the giant are made monstrous by society's response to their insatiable, murderous appetites.

Yet the vampire Countess is not just an inhuman monster. Like her more traditional fairy-tale ancestors, she is also superlative in her beauty: "She is so beautiful she is unnatural; her beauty is an abnormality, a deformity, for none of her features exhibit any of those touching imperfections that reconcile us to the imperfection of the human condition" (Carter, 1993: 94). The heroine's perfect and unnatural beauty highlights the multiple ways in which she—as vampire, as fairy-tale princess, as "a free woman in an unfree society"—exceeds "the human condition." Even more, she is likewise at times the idealized passive sleeping princess, and like her fairy tale counterparts, she too has a special resting place: "In the centre [of her bedroom] is an elaborate catafalque, in ebony, surrounded by long candles in enormous silver candlesticks. In a white lace négligé stained a little with blood, the Countess climbs up on her catafalque at dawn each morning and lies down in an open coffin" (94). Although the Grimms' Little Brier Rose simply "fell down upon the bed that was standing there" (Grimm, 1987: 187), Perrault's and Basile's sleeping beauties are laid to rest in decorative splendor, as though for display and burial, much like the Marquis's murdered first wife in "The Bloody Chamber." In Perrault's tale the princess sleeps "on a bed covered with gold and silver embroidery" (Perrault, 1977b: 61), and in Basile's tale she is propped "upon a velvet chair under a brocade canopy"

(Canepa, 2007: 414). The image of the beautiful sleeping princess, on view as though in death, poised for the taking, satisfies the dark fantasy of necrophilia, and the Countess, at rest in her open coffin dressed only in her white negligee, makes this association more explicit.

As is the case for the fairy-tale sleeping beauties, the Countess's childlike innocence only heightens her allure. However, unlike her more traditional fairy-tale counterparts, whose passivity is their greatest attraction, the Countess is much more clearly *both* the beautiful and innocent child and the seductive and dangerous whore.

> He saw how beautiful and how very young the bedizened scarecrow was, and he thought of a child dressing up in her mother's clothes. . . . Her huge dark eyes almost broke his heart with their waiflike, lost look; yet he was disturbed, almost repelled, by her extraordinarily fleshy mouth, a mouth with wide, full, prominent lips of a vibrant purplish-crimson, a morbid mouth. Even—but he put the thought away from him immediately—a whore's mouth. (Carter, 1993: 100–101)

Sexual fantasies of pedophilia and necrophilia, so clearly entangled at the heart of the "Sleeping Beauty" tales, thus come to the fore in Carter's portrait of the vampire Countess. Even the naïve and virginal hero makes the connection upon entering the Countess's bedroom.

> His colonel, an old goat with jaded appetites, had given him the visiting card of a brothel in Paris where, the satyr assured him, ten louis would buy just such a lugubrious bedroom, with a naked girl upon a coffin; offstage, the brothel pianist played the *Dies Irae* on a harmonium and, amidst all the perfumes of the embalming parlour, the customer took his necrophiliac pleasure of a pretended corpse. (105)[9]

Carter further underscores the significance of the Countess's boudoir as brothel, the primal scene in which necrophiliac fantasies might be enacted, through the very title of her story, "The Lady of the House of Love," invoking as it does the common name for a brothel.[10]

Carter's earlier reference to the Countess's suite as "Juliet's tomb" (Carter, 1993: 100) is thus a particularly apt foreshadowing of what the bedroom promises: The vampire Countess embodies both Romeo's Juliet, the virginal and seemingly dead lover, an early sleeping beauty whose eternal waiting the Countess shares ("I've always been ready for you; I've been waiting for you in my wedding dress," 103), as well as Sade's Juliette, the sexually aggressive libertine. As such, the Countess's suite—"Juliet's tomb" (100), her "macabre bedroom" (105), "the Countess's larder" (96)—provides a perfect setting for Carter's tale, a different type of bloody chamber in which the sleeping beauty and the vampire seductress cannot be separated, where love and death are forever linked.

The Patrilineal Hauntings of Beautiful Somnambulists

While the "Sleeping Beauty" tale critically anchors Carter's reimagined fairy tale, "The Lady of the House of Love" finds a similarly rich intertext in Bram Stoker's *Dracula*, the quintessential Gothic vampire narrative. Portrayed through the iconic images of Sleeping Beauty, the vampire Countess also calls to mind Lucy Westenra, another beautiful somnambulist. For Lucy sleepwalking begins as an innocent habit, a holdover from childhood, until Dracula transforms her into a vampire whose somnambulism turns predatory. At once sleeping beauties and seductive vampire girls, the daughters of terrifying patriarchs, Lucy (metaphoric offspring of Dracula) and the vampire Countess (literal descendant of Nosferatu) are compelled to an aggressive and destructive sexuality. Lucy's final attempt to seduce her fiancé, Arthur Holmwood, articulates the implicit danger that all men face in the female vampire's blatant sexuality and transgressive gender.

> When she advanced to him with outstretched arms and a wanton smile, he fell back and hid his face in his hands.
>
> She still advanced, however, and with a languorous, voluptuous grace, said: "Come to me, Arthur. Leave these others and come to me. My arms are hungry for you. Come, and we can rest together. Come, my husband, come!"

> There was something diabolically sweet in her tones—something of the tingling of glass when struck—which rang through the brains even of us who heard the words addressed to another. (Stoker, 2011: 197)

Whereas Stoker violently punishes Lucy for her transgressions—both her series of blood transfusions and her brutal staking have been compared to gang rape[11]—Carter revives her spirit in the vampire Countess and, in so doing, challenges Stoker's domineering narrative legacy, a narrative legacy that obscures earlier vampire tales, particularly Sheridan Le Fanu's 1872 novella, "Carmilla."

As Elizabeth Signorotti (1996) convincingly argues, however, "Carmilla," which features the title character's vampiric seduction of Laura and their ensuing lesbian relationship, was not simply overshadowed by *Dracula*; rather, she contends, its unsettling and transgressive desires most likely contributed to Stoker's formulation of *Dracula* as a corrective to the novella's rejection of gender normativity and, especially, its "[defiance of] the traditional structures of kinship by which men regulate the exchange of women to promote male bonding" (607). Signorotti reads *Dracula* as Stoker's way of containing the female sexuality and desire at the heart of "Carmilla."

> *Dracula* is Stoker's response to Le Fanu's portrayal of female empowerment. If Le Fanu frees his female characters from subject positions in the male kinship system, Stoker decidedly returns his to exchange status and reinstates them in that system. . . . Rather than embrace sexually self-determining women such as Laura and Carmilla, Stoker placed the women of *Dracula* firmly under male control and subjected them to severe punishments for any sexual transgression. (619–20)

Like Signorotti, Carter seems to have read *Dracula* as a conservative response to the unfettered female desire in "Carmilla," and her vampire Countess both redeems Stoker's Lucy and recuperates Le Fanu's Carmilla. Indeed, Carter's fascination with the libratory potential of "Carmilla" is evident not only in the vampire Countess but also in "The Bloody Chamber," where Carter casts her as one of the Marquis's ex-wives.

> But the strangest of all these love letters was a postcard with a view of a village graveyard, among mountains, where some black-coated ghoul enthusiastically dug at a grave; this little scene, executed with the lurid exuberance of Grand Guignol, was captioned: "Typical Transylvanian Scene—Midnight, All Hallows." And, on the other side, the message: "On the occasion of this marriage to the descendent of Dracula—always remember, 'the supreme and unique pleasure of love is the certainty that one is doing evil.' Tout es amitiés, C."
>
> A joke. A joke in the worst possible taste; for had he not been married to a Romanian countess? And then I remembered her pretty, witty face, and her name—Carmilla. (Carter, 1993: 26)

Here, Carter's Carmilla—self-identified "descendent of Dracula"—gives herself freely in marriage, thus directly challenging the specific paternal legacy implicit in Stoker's attempts to keep Lucy, double of Le Fanu's Carmilla, from doing so.[12] Instead, Carter's Carmilla enters as a willing participant into an ostensibly sophisticated relationship, what the Marquis's most recent bride calls "grown-up games" (26), wherein love and desire seem to diverge from her much more naïve understanding of sex. This Carmilla, like her literary predecessor, has no ambivalence about her sexual appetites, although she does not yet know the Marquis's sadistic end to this particular grown-up game, and, like Le Fanu's Carmilla and Stoker's Lucy, she is ultimately killed off by the story's patriarchal force.[13] With "The Lady of the House of Love" Carter more fully stages and critiques this complex intertextual genealogy initiated by Le Fanu's "Carmilla," conjoining Carmilla and Lucy in the vampire Countess to reflect on the cultural implications of their deaths.

Opening her story with a description of the village below the Countess's chateau—"At last the revenants became so troublesome the peasants abandoned the village" (Carter, 1993: 93)—Carter immediately conjures the "ruined village" of "Carmilla" below an "equally-desolate château" (Le Fanu, 2003: 89), which we later learn to be "troubled by revenants" (138).

Against these backdrops the beautiful somnambulist vampire countesses—Countess Nosferatu and Countess Karnstein—dare to imagine the possibility of love within their compulsive hungers, an imagining that leaves them overcome by the hopelessness of their longing. Carmilla's emotional investment in her love and desire for Laura reveals an ambivalence and perhaps reluctance not found in vampire literature and lore up to that point.

> "I have been in love with no one, and never shall," she [Carmilla] whispered, "unless it should be with you."
> How beautiful she looked in the moonlight!
> Shy and strange was the look with which she quickly hid her face in my neck and hair, with tumultuous sighs, that seemed almost to sob, and pressed in mine a hand that trembled. (Le Fanu, 2003: 112)

With similar feeling, Carter's reluctant and lovelorn vampire Countess returns the complexities of Carmilla's desire to the figure of the female vampire whom Stoker reduced to nothing but compulsive and dangerous sexual aggression. With the popular and critical dominance of *Dracula*, Stoker's female vampires—not only Lucy but also the three who seduce Jonathan Harker at Dracula's castle—have effectively erased the female vampire's subversive potential, a subversive potential that Carter reinstates. Thus, where "Stoker imbues Lucy with Carmillaesque qualities" in an "attempt to redress Carmilla's defiant behavior" (Signorotti, 1996: 622), Carter invests her vampire Countess with the same traits to highlight Stoker's domineering narrative control and cruel punishment of women's sexuality and desire. At the same time, however, Carter constrains both her critique of Stoker and her recuperation of Carmilla with the vampire Countess's ultimate death. As she seems to suggest, for both Carmilla and the vampire Countess, in life there is little possibility for a female desire free from patriarchal construction and control, and with this Carter returns us to the fairy tale and its severely limited options. For both Carmilla and the vampire Countess, the happiest endings exist only in death, in escape.

For Carter, then, the twinning of Sleeping Beauty and the female vampire only reinforces the double limits on women's subjectivity, given the dominant cultural representations of *woman*. Consequently, the hero's kiss—his instinctive act of love, his kissing the cut on her finger from the splintered glass of her shattered dark eyeglasses—only momentarily frees her from the liminality of her somnambulism. As Carter makes clear, for the vampire Countess and for her more traditional "Sleeping Beauty" ancestors, "the end of exile is the end of being" (Carter, 1993: 106). The supposedly liberating kiss is not the harbinger of an alternative sexual freedom of the type Carter celebrates in *The Sadeian Woman* but rather a certain death; it is the symbol of fairy-tale love, a kiss that leads only to a conventional happily-ever-after, for Carter more of a happily-never-after. The fatality of the hero's kiss underscores the eternal liminality of women's position in a male-dominated society, caught forever between virgin and whore, between dead and deadening. Deadened in her current state by her lack of agency, the Countess's only escape is mortal death, which for Carter is a more satisfying option than the equally deadening future the hero imagines for her.

> We shall take her to Zurich, to a clinic; she will be treated for nervous hysteria. Then to an eye specialist, for her photophobia, and to a dentist to put her teeth into better shape. Any competent manicurist will deal with her claws. We shall turn her into the lovely girl she is; I shall cure her of all these nightmares. (Carter, 1993: 107)

Fairy-tale love—foretold by the Countess's tarot cards, enacted in the kiss, projected into the future by the hero—is the death of female animal drive, the death of female sexual desire, not the love that Carter believes to be a possible impetus to complete freedom. In *The Sadeian Woman* she contends that love might have a redemptive quality, that it might in fact be the only possible way of achieving women's emancipation on all levels: "Only the possibility of love could awake the libertine to perfect, immaculate terror. It is in this holy terror of love that we find, in both men and women themselves, the source of all opposition to the emancipation of women" (2006: 176). However, as Carter's vampiric sleeping beauty learns, this love is not the love of fairy tales, and female animal drives and sexual desires cannot be autonomous when circumscribed by the pornographic fantasies of a male-dominated culture, compelled as it were by numerous ancestral legacies. Thus in "The Lady of the House of Love" Carter exposes the misplaced cultural longing for, and faith in, a fairy-tale love, a romanticized love exemplified by the Grimms' immediate transition from the princess's waking and gazing up at her rescuer to their marriage and happily-ever-after. For Carter women are better off dead than dying a slow death in the stifling happily-ever-after of fairy tales where the happily-ever-after necessarily depends on the heroine's passivity and compliance, the killing off of her desire and sexual agency.[14]

A Metanarrative Tale of Literary Possession

If *The Bloody Chamber* is "a book of stories about fairy stories" (Carter, 1998c: 38), "The Lady of the House of Love" is perhaps the exemplar of Carter's metastorytelling. Running alongside her intertextual tale, Carter's metanarrative suggests that the literary and anthologized fairy tale is itself a cultural legacy that contributes to the deadly strictures on women's subjectivity and sexual agency. From such a metanarrative perspective, Carter's explicit vamp(ir)ing of "Sleeping Beauty" draws out the eternal power of its fairy-tale legacy, its power to incarcerate the heroine within its tradition, forever upholding the desirable, corpselike woman—the specter of the female vampire who, at rest in her coffin, is even lovelier than when alive—at the center of the tale.

Within this context the Gothic vampire narrative is foundational to Carter's metanarrative critique precisely because "the timeless Gothic eternity of the vampires, for whom all is as it has always been and will be, whose cards always fall in the same pattern" (Carter, 1993: 97) captures the timelessness of the "Sleeping Beauty" story, its constant return to the desire for a deathly, deadly sexuality. As a vampire, the beautiful somnambulist Countess is characterized by her never-ending life, by her being a "system of repetitions . . . a closed circuit" (93), by her frequent possession by ancestors whose very nature drives her to seek out fresh meat, fresh men. Her story is preordained and unfolds in its infinite repetition each night. She is narrative incarnate. As such, she and her story necessarily exceed their exegetical limits. Through her narrative the Countess is at once a Sleeping Beauty and a *story* about the fairy tale "Sleeping Beauty"; the narrative and the metanarrative are as permanently entwined as Sleeping Beauty and the vampire Countess. Thus, when Carter describes the beautiful somnambulist as "helplessly perpetuat[ing] her ancestral crimes" (93), she calls to mind both the crimes of the Countess's vampire forebears and the crimes of her patriarchal literary ancestors, canonized in the work of Basile, Perrault, the Grimms, Disney, and Stoker.

Throughout "The Lady of the House of Love" Carter cultivates the oppressive and tragic weight of such an ancestral burden: The Countess is unable to resist her voracious hunger ("All claws and teeth, she strikes, she gorges; but nothing can console her for the ghastliness of her condition, nothing," Carter, 1993: 95); she is incapable of dealing a different set of Tarot cards ("The Tarot always shows the same configuration: always she turns up La Papesse, La Mort, La Tour Abolie, wisdom, death, dissolution," 95); she is defenseless against possession by ancestral spirits ("She does not possess herself; her ancestors sometimes come and peer out of the windows of her eyes and that is very frightening," 103). The Countess's own "horrible reluctance for the role" (95), combined with her uneasy complicity in it, her futile imaginings of alternative possibilities, only compounds the oppressive nature of her inheritance: "She loathes the food she eats; she would have liked to take the rabbits home with her, feed them on lettuce, pet them and make them a nest in her red-and-black chinoiserie escritoire, but hunger always overcomes her" (96). She dreams of similar alternatives for the "shepherd boys and gipsy lads" who come to her as well: "A certain desolate stillness of her eyes indicates she is inconsolable. She would like to caress their lean brown cheeks and stroke their ragged hair" (96). Enacting the script of her patriarchal (narrative) inheritance, the Countess—"Nosferatu's sanguinary rosebud" (103)—is compelled by her ancestors, by the extent of their legacy and by their ongoing presence. In this way she perfectly embodies the fairy-tale tradition even as Carter's metanarrative strategy challenges it, a point that Case underscores in what could be a direct commentary on the Countess's "vampirish love-bite" (Carter, 2006: 25): "What the dominant discourse represents as an emptying out, a draining away, in contrast to the impregnating kiss of the heterosexual, becomes an activism in representation" (Case, 1991: 15).

Here, Case reads the female vampire against her usual interpellation as deadly monstrosity, suggesting instead that the dangers she poses for and to dominant culture might *also* challenge hegemonic representations of female, and especially queer, sexuality. Although Carter's vampire Countess is not queer in Case's sense, her "vampirish love-bite" nonetheless disturbs dominant discourses of love and romance.

Implicit in the Countess's life as narrative are questions of agency and alternatives that drive both the intertextual tale and the metanarrative, and Carter twice asks, "Can a bird sing only the song it knows or can it learn a new song?" (1993: 93, 103). It is a question asked through a metaphor with multiple referents—the Countess, the author, our gendered social scripts—and in "The Lady of the House of Love" Carter suggests that the answers might be tightly entangled. For instance, just as the Countess permits her ancestors to possess her, to "peer out the windows of her eyes," Carter invites other narrative legacies—the "Sleeping Beauty" fairy tale, Le Fanu's "Carmilla," Stoker's *Dracula*—to momentarily possess her heroine and thus her story. As the Countess wonders at the slim possibility of an alternative ending for the hero as well as for herself, an alternative borne of her desire and the extraordinary presence of Les Amoureux among the Tarot cards, she is nonetheless compelled to follow her regular rituals of seduction, the social niceties demanded of her gender and her class, the act she has performed innumerable times before: "attend[ing] to the coffee-making" (102), "offer[ing] him a sugar biscuit from a Limoges plate" (102), "keep[ing] up a front of inconsequential chatter in French" (103). For the hero, however, the social ritual of seduction, narrated in the third-person omniscient, is continually interrupted by the first-person internal script of the Countess's infinite story.

> I do not mean to hurt you. I shall wait for you in my bride's dress in the dark.
> The bridegroom is come, he will go into the chamber which has been prepared for him.
> I am condemned to solitude and dark; I do not mean to hurt you.
> I will be very gentle. (103)

> Embraces, kisses; your golden head, of a lion, although I have never seen a lion, only imagined one, of the sun, even if I've only seen the picture of the sun on the Tarot card, your golden head of the lover whom I dreamed would one day free me, this head will fall back, its eyes roll upwards in a spasm you will mistake for that of love and not of death. The bridegroom bleeds on my inverted marriage bed. (105)

Narrated in the future tense, the Countess's script succumbs to what has always come before. Both the Countess's and the hero's actions are simultaneously foretold and circumscribed by her narrative legacy, inspired not by their own power but by the weight of the narratives that lock them in place.

The Countess's story has its own overdeterminative power, and despite her longing for a way out of the "perpetual repetition of [her forebears'] passions" (Carter, 1993: 103), "she only knows of one kind of consummation" (103). During the tale's extended scene of seduction, Carter encourages the Countess's compulsive narrative to repeatedly disrupt the story she is telling, and the continual emergence of the Countess's story amid her own highlights its power, the enduring grip of the social scripts we inherit, the cultural legacies that maintain the seeming inevitability of our "nature," our identities, our gendering.

It is only when the Countess "has fumbled the ritual"—when she acts, when she *feels*—that her story "is no longer inexorable" (Carter, 1993: 105). The Countess's feelings for the hero, the unprecedented welling up of her tears at the thought of their fatal consummation, is the deviation from the script that breaks the spell of the narrative. In opening herself to the frightful possibility of love, she herself is responsible for setting in motion the events that ultimately free her, her tears doing as much to liberate her as the hero's tender kissing of her bleeding finger. In the Countess's resistance to the overwhelming force of her narrative inheritance, Carter seems to suggest that there is always a potential for agency, for the subject as well as for the author of a fairy tale with an enduring patriarchal ancestry, but acting on that potential is no small feat. Rather, it requires embracing the type of love that threatens the libertines, that threatens the patriarchal order.

For the Countess altering the script results in both freedom and death, an escape from the eternal oppression of her history and her social context, an escape from the oppressive compulsion to act on her animal drives and sexual desires, desires defined and limited by the male-dominated society that renders them foreign to her. For Carter, as author of a fairy tale with a strong patriarchal genealogy, revising the script opens up the "Sleeping Beauty" story even as it sustains its intertextual counterparts to make explicit the doubled meanings of "fairy tale," the doubled work such stories accomplish as both popular romance and cultural fiction that we too often (mis)take for reality. As metanarrative, "The Lady of the House of Love" argues for the possibility of another song, another tale, though not an entirely new one. In this "stor[y] about fairy stories," Carter details the weight of the fairy-tale tradition, a weight surprisingly easy to bear but nearly impossible to cast aside, as the Countess demonstrates. Even more, for Carter, both men and women are complicit in the fairy tale's enduring appeal, in the lasting power of its ancestral hauntings.

Knowing Fear, Knowing Love

In keeping with the traditional "Sleeping Beauty" tales, "The Lady of the House of Love" also ends with the heroine waking to love. For Carter's sleeping beauty, however, it is not the hero's love that awakens the Countess but rather her own; she is freed by her love for another, not by the hero's fairy-tale love for her. Although the dominant legacy of the Grimms' "Little Brier Rose" and Disney's *Sleeping Beauty* may prepare us to see the hero's innocent kiss as awakening the Countess from her somnambulist existence, it is actually the *Countess's* "improvisation" in the scripted ritual that prompts the "unexpected, mundane noise of breaking glass [that] breaks the wicked spell in the room, entirely" (Carter, 1993: 106). In the Countess's awakening to life and thus to death, in escaping the liminality of her simultaneously masochistic and sadistic being, she approaches the redemptive love that Carter describes in *The Sadeian Woman*, the love that strikes fear among libertines because of its potential to overturn the dominant order, to bring about the true "emancipation of women."

Throughout "The Lady of the House of Love" Carter is careful to emphasize the hero's inability to know fear and therefore his inability to know this love. He is a virgin, unknowing, rational.[15] He "does not yet know what there is to be afraid of . . . he cannot feel terror; so he is like the boy in the fairy tale, who does not know how to shudder, and not spooks, ghouls, beasties, the Devil himself and all his retinue could do the trick" (Carter, 1993: 104), and it is precisely "this lack of imagination [that] gives his heroism to the hero" (104).[16] Limited by both his inability to feel terror and his lack of imagination (for Carter the sure characterization of traditional fairy-tale heroes), the hero simply cannot know the terrifying but liberating love the Countess approaches; he can offer nothing but a fairy-tale love, a love that promises only another death in his desire to whisk her away to Zurich, to make her over into "the lovely girl she is" (107).

With "The Lady of the House of Love" Carter simultaneously exposes the dark allure of the "Sleeping Beauty" tales—particularly the Grimms' version with its especially passive, deathlike princess—and the cultural power of the patriarchal narrative legacy of which they are a part. Freed by her own love from the eternal imprisonment of this narrative tradition, the Countess's only option is a literal death, because for her there is simply no alternative; there is not yet an outside, not yet an escape into a true freedom, only the deadly, deadening confines of a sexist society. Through the Countess's desire for death, her desire to escape the erotic, necrophiliac impulses of the "Sleeping Beauty" tradition, Carter highlights the doubly grim attraction of the Grimms' "Little Brier Rose," the cultural desire for the literal and the metaphoric dead woman. In the end, Carter and the Countess might share fleeting moments of freedom, but the erotic fascination with the beautiful corpse endures.

At the same time, through its intertextual richness, and in particular its recuperation of Le Fanu's "Carmilla," "The Lady of the House of Love" offers a glimpse of another knowing: a queer knowing in which the vampire Countess and Sleeping Beauty might find a more productive disidentification[17] that allows them to survive the cultural confines of heteronormativity even as they literally perish within its exegetical strictures. The moment when Carter's vampire Countess awakens to death is also the moment she joins her ancestral Sleeping Beauties in narrative eternity, much as Carmilla endures in Laura's longing and imagination. This joining forever provokes the uncanny recognitions that bring the Countess and the sorority of Sleeping Beauties together to challenge the compulsive heterosexuality of the fairy tale, of their patriarchal lineages, thus enacting what Case sees as the inherently oppositional nature of queer discourse in the "trope" of the lesbian, the way "'she' is the wounding, desiring, transgressive position that weds, through sex, an unnatural being. 'She' is that bride. 'She' is the fanged lover who breaks the ontological sac" (1991: 8). Although Carter's "stories about fairy stories" are not about lesbian sexuality as defined by the hegemonic, the vampire Countess reminds us that Carter certainly revels in "queer" portrayals of gender, love, and sex, particularly portrayals whose "vampirish love-bite" pierces the fairy tale love that facilitates the patriarchal investment in a pornographic culture.

6

Erotic Infidelities

The Wolf Trilogy

The erotic always carries with it a certain discontent. Circumscribed by the hegemonic, it can only ever be a profound disappointment so long as it remains mired in heteronormative gender conventions, limited by, or to, phallocentric fantasy. Audre Lorde calls this patriarchal erotic "the confused, the trivial, the psychotic, the plasticized sensation" (1984: 53), and, even in her perhaps overly romantic redefinition in terms of women's "lifeforce," she reminds us of the social, political, and sexual confines of the dominant erotic. Such is the erotic implicit in one sense of an *erotic infidelity*, an infidelity to this (or any) singular erotic. But, I also mean to invoke a second sense of erotic infidelity, an *erotic* infidelity—that is, the way Carter's infidelity to her source tales and intertexts is animated by an erotic energy. In this second sense, then, the acts of betrayal are themselves sites for an emergent other erotic. Of course, the two are not entirely distinct but rather double up on each other, one erotic derived from a betrayal of the other.

In this context infidelity is powerful, subversive, transgressive, and, most significantly, gendered. Jane Gallop's incisive rendering of Lacan's twining of the biological (the paternal) and the linguistic (the patronym) in the authorized, the Name-of-the-Father, makes clear the feminist underpinnings of any such infidelity.

> Infidelity then is a feminist practice of undermining the Name-of-the-Father. The unfaithful reading strays from the author, the authorized, produces that which does not hold as a reproduction, as a representation. Infidelity is not outside the system of marriage, the symbolic, patriarchy, but hollows it out, ruins it, from within. (Gallop, 1982: 48)

Carter's wolf trilogy—"The Werewolf," "The Company of Wolves," and "Wolf-Alice"—performs this unfaithful reading, a ruination from within. Although the final three stories in *The Bloody Chamber* are not explicitly framed as a trilogy, I refer to them as such in order to hold them together as necessarily conjoined and intertextually inseparable, a slightly more insistent naming than what Cristina Bacchilega (1997) terms the "women-in-the-company-of-wolves stories" in her own intertextual reading of the three tales. The wolf trilogy is a set of "Little Red Riding Hood" (ATU 333) stories born of unfaithful readings, marked by multiple rewritings, and full of intricate and intimate betrayals: of Charles Perrault's patriarchal "Little Red Riding Hood," of the Grimms' subsequent literary version, of oral versions such as "The Story of Grandmother," of the feminist desire to "eroticize" the classic tales,[1] of Carter's own restagings even. Infidelities upon infidelities, a luxurious promiscuity.

Carter's betrayal begins with the *seemingly* faithful act of translation, with the infidelities that creep into the version of "Little Red Riding Hood" she translated for *The Fairy Tales of Charles Perrault* (1977). To translate Perrault's tales, Carter had to make him a familiar, had to inhabit his language, wrap herself in his elocutions, feel the very texture of his tales. Translation is the ultimate fantasy of fidelity, a fantasy that seeks to obscure the arbitrary nature of signification, an arbitrariness made explicit when the inevitable excesses and failures of language reveal the necessary slippage between two systems. Ironically, however, the act of translation—that ultimate fantasy of fidelity—may itself be the prelude to infidelity, a point that was not lost on Carter, who, tellingly, quotes from Theodor Adorno's *Minima Moralia* in one of her journals: "The fidelity exacted by society is a means to unfreedom, but only through fidelity can freedom achieve insubordination to society's command."[2] First a translation, then a reimagining. Carter's intimate knowledge of Perrault's collection and her translation of *The Fairy Tales of Charles Perrault* only accentuate the erotic infidelities of her wolf trilogy and *The Bloody Chamber* as a whole.[3]

Not only does Carter write away from Perrault—embracing Little Red Riding Hood's sexual agency in the tale's seduction, overturning the bourgeois morality of his coda in verse—but she also plays with versions from the oral tradition and writes and rewrites her own versions throughout the trilogy in an attempt to author differently. As layered and intertextual versions of "Little Red Riding Hood," the tales in Carter's wolf trilogy resist foreclosure, beckoning instead to their companion tales and, in the process, gesturing toward an important instability that works to "hollow out" (to use Gallop's phrase) Perrault's voice and the authority of the traditional tales. In part, the wolf trilogy is important as trilogy precisely because of its recursive power; rather than replace Perrault's "Little Red Riding Hood" with a "feminist" version, a different authority, Carter implies an infinite chain of infidelities, beginning with infidelities to her own tales.

Carter's desire to voice instability, to tell tales with a multivocal tongue, distinguishes the wolf trilogy, and *The Bloody Chamber* in general, from the more recent trend of women rewriting fairy tales in an explicitly "erotic" register. Carter's fairy tales, like those of Anne Sexton, Margaret Atwood, Djuna Barnes, and Olga Broumas, covet and create tensions with the hegemonic erotic; they challenge readers to find an other erotic in a dramatically different, often disturbing, sexual imagination. They are, as Bacchilega contends, "doubling and double: both affirmative and questioning, without necessarily being recuperative or politically subversive" (1997: 22), more invested in the hollowing out, the ruining from within, than in any simple reversals. Infidelity over recuperation. Women's "erotic" fairy tales, on the other hand, are generally premised on the idea of such a recuperation and seek to recast the dominant erotic in a feminine voice. I situate Carter's wolf trilogy as a counterpoint to these feminine and feminist erotic rewritings because their preponderance attests to a certain feminist desire in and for the fairy tale as a potentially transformative genre, a desire I want to ascribe to Carter but in a radically different way. I read Carter's wolf trilogy against this feminist yearning for an alternate erotics, suggesting instead that her stories undermine, complicate, and defy this feminist longing even as they approach the pleasures of an other erotic.

The sheer number of erotic fairy-tale collections written and edited by women is a statement in itself: Mitzi Szereto's *Erotic Fairytales: A Romp Through the Classics*, Alison Tyler's *Naughty Fairy Tales from A to Z*, Hillary Rollins's *The Empress's New Lingerie*, Cecilia Tan's *Of Princes and Beauties: Erotic Fairy Tales for Adults*, Isabelle Rose's *Naughty Fairy Tales* (Volume I), Nancy Madore's *Enchanted: Erotic Bedtime Stories for Women*, Joan Elizabeth Lloyd's *Naughty Bedtime Stories*, and of course, Anne Rice's erotic *Sleeping Beauty Trilogy* published under the name A. N. Roquelaure. The only erotic tale collections written or edited by and/or for men are by the same person, Michael Ford, who has two relevant collections: *Once Upon A Time: Erotic Fairy Tales for Women* and *Happily Ever After: Erotic Fairy Tales for Queer Men*. Importantly, neither of these collections is intended for heterosexual men, a point that underscores all these collections' interest in rewriting the dominant, patriarchal erotic at the heart of the traditional tales.

Along these lines women writers seem to have found in fairy tales a means of rearticulating women's sexual agency by calling attention to our positioning within a culture that fetishizes young girls as objects of sexual desire. The cultural fascination with Lolita-like girls and the related sexualization of adult women through tropes and markers of this fantasy have been well documented by psychologists (e.g., Walkerdine, 1997) and, more recently, by the American Psychological Association Task Force on the Sexualization of Girls (2007) and media scholars (e.g., Merskin, 2004 and Kilbourne, 1999a, 1999b). Heterosexual male fantasies, as expressed in pornography, strip clubs, and even mainstream media, often revolve around Lolita's appeal, whether she is in pajamas, a schoolgirl uniform, or a cheerleader's getup.[4]

Within this context women who write erotic fairy tales might be understood as shifting the terms of titillation by choosing a genre that is frequently associated with children—and, in the American context, with girls in particular. The transformation of the fairy-tale genre into erotica suggests a transgression that might at first seem to accord with the heterosexual male pedophilic fantasies about sexually precocious young girls. Titles such as *Naughty Fairy Tales*, *Naughty Bedtime Stories*, and *Enchanted: Erotic Bedtime Stories for Women* all recognize and play on such transgressions, bringing together the "naughtiness" of such a transformation with the childlike innocence of "bedtime" stories. Catherine Orenstein makes a similar point about fairy-tale pornography: "The titillation factor of these videos is in part through transgression—fairy tales are meant, we believe, for children; and meant, we believe, to express morality" (2002: 211). However, rather than further reinscribe dominant male fantasies, as fairy-tale pornography might be seen to do, women who write erotic tales call attention to the dominant cultural fetishization of young girls and the sexualization of women according to such tropes in order to rewrite desire in such a way that it prioritizes women's sexual agency as they see it. The genre itself thus becomes essential to the feminist project of dismantling patriarchal understandings of women's sexuality. Through these acts of rewriting both the tales and themselves as sexual agents, these women writers also redefine the erotic so that it appeals to their own sexual desires and fantasies, not patriarchal fantasies of women's sexual desires and fantasies.

The question, of course, is whether such erotic reimaginings of classic fairy tales exceed patriarchal definitions of the erotic or whether these women are producing a sexual agency that exists alongside and perhaps operates with and through a dominant erotic. Based on my readings of these erotic fairy tales, I would suggest that, even as these authors contest the cultural fetishization of sexually precocious young girls and their own status as adult women within such a hegemonic sexual system, they also tend to reproduce fairly traditional patriarchal definitions of the erotic as related to sexual arousal and desire. Rewriting their sexual selves through the "naughtiness" created by the cultural resonances of the genre itself might be analogous to the relatively current fashion of adult women wearing short pleated skirts with knee-high socks and Mary Jane shoes.[5] Both are ways in which women engage the set of male fantasies that converge in the figure of the nymphet. Regardless of the degree to which we might read agency and play into such acts, however, this repositioning of women's sexual agency is not in itself enough to escape the patriarchal sexual order.

Defying these ostensible subversions—as well as Perrault's authorship, Perrault's authority, the patriarchal authoring of our entextualized fairy-tale inheritance—Carter's wolf trilogy flirts with another erotic, an erotic that simultaneously acknowledges and contests the complex, ambivalent potentialities inherent in the power of the phallus.

The Phallus Reconsidered: "The Werewolf"

The opening story in Carter's wolf trilogy, "The Werewolf," is not an obvious variant of "Little Red Riding Hood." The title itself suggests another set of narrative relations, a different storytelling genealogy, and the first third of the tale elaborates on this implicit association with legend, superstition, and folk belief. For the people of this "northern country" who "have cold weather [and] . . . have cold hearts" (Carter, 1993: 108), werewolves are no more extraordinary than vampires, witches, the Devil who might be glimpsed feasting at midnight in the local graveyard, "a blue-eyed child born feet first on the night of St. John's Eve [who] will have second sight" (108). About women and witches Carter writes: "When they discover a witch—some old woman whose cheeses ripen when her neighbours' do not, another old woman whose black cat, oh, sinister! *follows her about all the time*, they strip the crone, search for her marks, for the supernumerary nipple her familiar sucks. They soon find it. Then they stone her to death" (108; emphasis in original).

With only the transition "Winter and cold weather" (Carter, 1993: 109), however, Carter transforms the tale from one of superstition and stoning witches to one that clearly recalls "Little Red Riding Hood."

> Go and visit grandmother, who has been sick. Take the oatcakes I've baked for her on the hearthstone and a little pot of butter.
> The good child does as her mother bids—five miles' trudge through the forest; do not leave the path because of the bears, the wild boar, the starving wolves. Here, take your father's hunting knife; you know how to use it. (109)

In keeping with the "Little Red Riding Hood" tradition, the "good child" does indeed encounter a wolf as she makes her way to grandmother's house. Unlike the clever, fast-talking wolves of Perrault and the Grimms, however, this wolf goes straight for her throat. She responds quickly, severing its paw with her father's hunting knife, at which point the wolf limps off. The young girl wraps the paw, puts it in her basket, and carries on to her grandmother's house. When she arrives, grandmother is feverish, sick; being the good child that she is, she removes the cloth encasing the wolf's paw, intending to make a cold compress for her sick grandmother, but when the paw falls from the cloth, it is not a paw but a hand: "It was a hand, chopped off at the wrist, a hand toughened with work and freckled with old age. There was a wedding ring on the third finger and a wart on the index finger. By the wart, she knew it for her grandmother's hand" (109). Pulling back the sheet to verify her discovery, Little Red Riding Hood awakens her grandmother—now "squawking and shrieking like a thing possessed" (109)—and is forced to restrain her with her father's hunting knife until the neighbors come rushing in, alerted by the girl's cries of horror at her grandmother's bloody stump. Grandmother is chased from her home and stoned to death, and Carter ends this first tale with a happily-ever-after of sorts: "Now the child lived in her grandmother's house; she prospered" (110).

When the girl takes over her grandmother's house, her grandmother's life, "The Werewolf" calls to mind "The Story of Grandmother," perhaps the most well-known oral variant of "Little Red Riding Hood."[6] In this variant the wolf first asks the girl which path she plans to take to her grandmother's house—the path of pins or the path of needles—and then he hurries along the other path to beat her there. When the girl arrives, the wolf-as-grandmother invites her to eat and drink the meal he has prepared, which turns out to be the grandmother's flesh and blood. He then tells her to undress and join him in bed, at which point the girl ritually removes her clothes, throwing them piece by piece onto the fire, before climbing into bed with the wolf-as-grandmother. She eventually escapes by feigning the need to relieve herself outdoors. Drawing on multiple oral versions and her ethnographic fieldwork in a village in the Chatillonais region of northern France, where the tale was commonly shared in the oral tradition, Yvonne Verdier (1997) reads "The Story of Grandmother" as a tale of female initiation in which the girl's encounter with the wolf, her eating the flesh and blood of her grandmother, her striptease, and her escape through her own guile (sometimes assisted by a group of washerwomen) all represent her socialization into womanhood, domesticity, and adult sexuality. Even though the conclusion of "The Werewolf" articulates what is only ever implicit in "The Story of Grandmother"—that is, the girl's assumption of her grandmother's life—Carter's truncated version restages the girl's initiation such that it is motivated by the grandmother-werewolf's aggression, *not* by the male stranger wolf's sexual predation.

As the first story in the wolf trilogy, "The Werewolf" structures the ways in which we read the next two stories, and Carter's positioning of the grandmother as werewolf against a vast history of predominantly male werewolves—the name itself betrays the sexing of this tradition (the Old English *wer* or *were* means "man" as biological category)—serves an important function both within the context of the story itself and within the context of the trilogy as a whole. If the "Little Red Riding Hood" tales consistently warn young girls to stay clear of predatory men, "wolves" in the long-standing vernacular tradition, what might Carter be saying in casting the grandmother in the traditional role of male sexual predator and not simply innocent postmenopausal victim? Here, the grandmother is literally wolf, not just the traditional wolf in grandmother's clothing.

Keeping in mind the primacy of "The Werewolf" in the wolf trilogy, its status as originary tale, I want to suggest that in writing the grandmother into werewolf, in transgendering both figures, Carter creates a phallic mother, herself something of a myth of origination, the supposed omnipotent master of the child's desire and the child's eventual initiation into language and the Symbolic Order. In describing Julia Kristeva's project of demythologizing the omnipotent Mother, Gallop foregrounds the importance of Kristeva's insistence on the phallic mother in denaturalizing the "ideological solidarity between phallus, father, power and man" even as she "expose[s] the phallus of the phallic mother ... theatricalize[s] her, give[s] her as spectacle, open[s] the curtain" (1982: 117–18). The existence of Carter's grandmother-as-werewolf similarly calls into question the ideological solidarity of phallus and masculine authority. But, like

Kristeva, Carter also resists substituting one (less obvious) phallic authority for another (more obvious) one. Rather, she too theatricalizes the phallic mother in the character of the grandmother and thus reveals her phallus for a sham: As wolf, she is "a huge one, with red eyes and running, grizzled chops . . . [who] let out a gulp, almost a sob, when it saw what had happened to it"; grandmother awakens and struggles, "squawking and shrieking like a thing possessed" (Carter, 1993: 109). When the neighbors arrive to help Little Red Riding Hood, "they [know] the wart on her [grandmother's] hand at once for a witch's nipple" (109–10). In her moment of exposure, granny no longer embodies the transsexuality of her werewolf persona but becomes simply witch, categorically "some old woman," like those described at the outset of the story.

If the phallic mother is "more dangerous because less obviously phallic . . . more phallic precisely by being less obvious" (Gallop, 1982: 118), it can be little surprise that Carter first conjures her to subvert the naturalization of the phallus-penis equation before killing her off, laying her bare. Granny as simultaneously werewolf, witch, and woman embodies the failures of language: She cannot be contained by the singularity of any given category. Instead, her constant slipping between werewolf, witch, woman, from male to female, offers a glimpse into the gaps that belie the myth of an omnipotent language, of total signification. In slashing the werewolf, cutting off her paw in a trauma that leads to her grandmother's eventual death, Little Red Riding Hood opens up a range of possibilities in which girls, women, might exist in the Symbolic Order, might even "prosper" there. No longer subject to the aggressions of the phallic mother—the predatory moves that a phallogocentric language in wolf's clothing make on a young girl—Little Red Riding Hood can inhabit her grandmother's house and prosper in an alternative fairy-tale ending. This heroine separates from her family only to live alone, able to protect herself, prosperous.

And yet for Carter such an act depends on Little Red Riding Hood's own phallic power, her mastery of her "father's hunting knife" (Carter, 1993: 109), the phallic object with which she both protects herself and renders her grandmother impotent. Given Little Red Riding Hood's obvious phallic power in this specific tale and the widespread understanding of the sexual innuendo implicit in the wider "Little Red Riding Hood" tradition,

"The Werewolf" might thus also be read as an Oedipal conflict. In this case granny, as both phallic mother and traditionally masculine werewolf, is simultaneously object of desire and symbolic authority. Little Red Riding Hood's encounter with her, with the wolf-witch-woman, is a complicated one, run through with the competing desires to both possess her and kill her off so as to replace her. As Carter's rendering of both granny as phallic mother and Little Red Riding Hood as phallic power suggests, the phallus occupies a certain primacy in her vision of a different relationship among power, desire, and sexuality, one that unhinges the phallus from its "ideological solidarity" with the father, with man, and considers women's independence and subjectivity as its own type of power.

Through this oedipalization of Little Red Riding Hood's drives, Carter again uses the initial place of "The Werewolf" in her wolf trilogy to establish the theoretical and thematic foundations of the three stories in their intertextual entirety. Thus, although "The Werewolf" does not foreground an explicitly alternate erotics as the next two stories in the trilogy do, it does succeed in establishing the erotic infidelities at play in Carter's intricate metamorphoses: metamorphoses of women, wolves, and witches as well as of theories, tales, and language. In this context Carter's writing both grandmother and werewolf differently, together with her killing off of that otherly inscription and all that it represents, helps her move toward the more sensual and sensory paradigms at work in the next two stories.

Pornography Reconsidered: "The Company of Wolves"

In the spirit of erotic infidelities, Carter does not just build on the implicit theoretical assumptions of "The Werewolf" as introduction to her second story, "The Company of Wolves." Rather, she returns to the thorny question of woman's signification within a phallogocentric Symbolic Order, questions she theorizes directly with respect to sexual categories in *The Sadeian Woman*, where she explores what it might mean to be a "moral pornographer."

> The moral pornographer would be an artist who uses pornographic material as part of the acceptance of the logic of a world

of absolute sexual licence for all the genders, and projects a model of the way such a world might work. A moral pornographer might use pornography as a critique of current relations between the sexes. His [sic] business would be the total demystification of the flesh and the subsequent revelation, through the infinite modulations of the sexual act, of the real relations of man and his kind. Such a pornographer would not be the enemy of women, perhaps because he might begin to penetrate to the heart of the contempt for women that distorts our culture even as he entered the realms of true obscenity as he describes it. (Carter, 2006: 19–22)

Carter's oft-quoted and frequently debated project is not so much to demarcate the moral boundaries of pornography but rather to suggest that pornography might offer a mode of interrogating any and all sexual acts in their specific historical and material contexts. In this sense Carter's "moral pornography" refers to a pornography that accounts for the power relations and material realities implicit in every sexual act, not to a pornography whose content might meet ambiguous determinations of arbitrary moral standards. Context over content: an important distinction in reading Carter's wolf trilogy as a moral pornography committed to an alternate erotics motivated by amoral sexual drives.

The Sadeian Woman also helps to contextualize Carter's move into a more visual and sensory mode of writing. Given the feminist critique of both Lacanian psychoanalytic theory and the phallogocentric Symbolic Order as overly focused on the visual—on the phallus as that which can be seen—Carter's centering of "The Company of Wolves" in a visual paradigm reproduces anew her desire to write and think between and beyond the authorities of both feminist theory and patriarchal culture. In this context I read "The Company of Wolves" as an other pornography, as Carter's moral pornography, an alternative pornography that must first engage a more traditional hegemonic gazing.

Once again, Carter opens her version of "Little Red Riding Hood" with a lengthy devotion to the lore of wolves: thick physical descriptions, tales of transformation, stories in which the wolf is always sexed male. Against this backdrop and, again, amid the "winter and cold weather,"

Carter introduces the Little Red Riding Hood of this story in the conventional pornographic tropes surrounding the sexually desirable young girl discussed earlier.

> This one, so pretty and the youngest of her family, a little latecomer, had been indulged by her mother and the grandmother who'd knitted her a red shawl that, today, has the ominous if brilliant look of blood on snow. Her breasts have just begun to swell; her hair is like lint, so fair it hardly makes a shadow on her pale forehead; her cheeks are an emblematic scarlet and white and she has just started her woman's bleeding, the clock inside her that will strike, henceforward, once a month.
>
> She stands and moves within the invisible pentacle of her own virginity. She is an unbroken egg; she is a sealed vessel; she has inside her a magic space the entrance to which is shut tight with a plug of membrane; she is a closed system; she does not know how to shiver. (Carter, 1993: 113–14)

Carter's description plays up Little Red Riding Hood's childlike desirability—"her breasts have just begun to swell," "her cheeks are an emblematic scarlet and white"—and her virginity is fundamental to that desirability.

As Little Red Riding Hood makes her way through the forest, she meets up with a handsome stranger, shortly after hearing the "freezing howl of a distant wolf" (Carter, 1993: 114). They have a flirtatious exchange in which he, characteristically, encourages her to leave the path and follow him through the woods on a shortcut to her grandmother's house. She is demure, hesitant; instead, they wager on who will get there first. Again, Carter casts Little Red Riding Hood in the role of sexual nymphet, typical object of male fantasy, in their flirtatious exchange.

> Is it a bet? he asked her. Shall we make a game of it? What will you give me if I get to your grandmother's house before you?
> What would you like? she asked disingenuously.
> A kiss.

> Commonplaces of a rustic seduction; she lowered her eyes and blushed. (115)

She is, of course, both innocent and knowing, and that is exactly what makes her so highly desirable in the typical male fantasy.

But Carter is just toying with that fantasy, writing her own moral pornography as a way to further dismantle a world of sexual absolutes. As Carter writes her, Little Red Riding Hood is ultimately a sexual agent more akin to Tex Avery's stripteasing Red than to Perrault's innocent. Early on, Carter hints at her emergent phallic power: "Her father might forbid her, if he were home, but he is away in the forest, gathering wood, and her mother cannot deny her" (Carter, 1993: 114). Despite (or perhaps because of?) her enticing innocence, Little Red Riding Hood shares her father's power, participates in his authority over her mother. Having insisted on traveling alone to her grandmother's house, she dawdles along the way to ensure that the handsome stranger will win the wager. Meanwhile, the stranger, a ravenous young man with beastly eyes, arrives at grandmother's house. He begins to remove his disguise, and it is at this moment that Carter fully shifts her moral pornographer's gaze. He—ambiguously described as wolf, as man—is now the object of the gaze.

> He strips off his shirt. His skin is the colour and texture of vellum. A crisp stripe of hair runs down his belly, his nipples are ripe and dark as poison fruit but he's so thin you could count the ribs under his skin if only he gave you the time. He strips off his trousers and she can see how hairy his legs are. His genitals, huge. Ah! huge. (116)

Upon devouring granny, he is barely disguised, somewhere between wolf and man, awaiting Little Red Riding Hood's arrival. She arrives and realizes the wolf has eaten her grandmother, temporarily the scared child once again. Realizing, however, that fear will do her no good, she ceases to be afraid, returns to her knowing. And, then, piece by piece, she begins to strip, coyly asking the stranger-wolf for direction.

> What shall I do with my shawl?

> Throw it on the fire, dear one. You won't need it again.
>
> She bundled up her shawl and threw it on the blaze, which instantly consumed it. Then she drew her blouse over her head; her small breasts gleamed as if the snow had invaded the room.
>
> What shall I do with my blouse?
>
> Into the fire with it, too, my pet.
>
> The thin muslin went flaring up the chimney like a magic bird and now off came her skirt, her woolen stockings, her shoes, and on to the fire they went, too, and were gone for good. The firelight shone through the edges of her skin; now she was clothed only in her untouched integument of flesh. This dazzling, naked she combed out her hair with her fingers; her hair looked white as the snow outside. (117–18)

It is as though Carter is describing Little Red Riding Hood for the script of a traditional pornographic film, the desirable young nymphet caught in the male gaze. Yet even as she zooms in on Little Red Riding Hood, she continues to grant her sexual agency, an agency that resonates with the "Little Red Riding Hood" tales that exist around the edges of Perrault's essentially authoritative version.[7] Wendy Swyt likewise points out that "when she disrobes and throws her clothes into the fire she transcends the symbols that would contain her in the story and embraces the becoming-woman" (1996: 322), thus challenging what Carter's critics have read as the tale's hegemonic masculine desire and voyeurism.[8]

Bacchilega locates Little Red Riding Hood's act of stripping and burning her clothes, piece by piece, in a European variant from the oral tradition of the Middle Ages (1997: 54), wherein the heroine escapes just as often as she is eaten by the wolf. Carter's own journal notes for her wolf stories specifically highlight the girl's slow stripping in the oral versions collected by Paul Delarue. By the time Perrault writes her story, however, Little Red Riding Hood's stripping becomes a much more banal act: "Little Red Riding Hood took off her clothes and went to lie down in the bed" (Perrault, 1977b: 26). As Carter stages it, Little Red Riding Hood's striptease is much more playful, a slow and sweet seduction, as thrilling in its act as in its defiance of both Perrault's moralizing tale and the cautionary old wives' tales.

"Clothed only in her untouched integument of flesh," Little Red Riding Hood begins to undress the wolf; she gives him the kiss she owes him as "every wolf in the world now howl[s] a prothalamion outside the window" (Carter, 1993: 118). Despite the consummation implicit in the wolves' prothalamion, Little Red Riding Hood and the stranger-wolf go through some of the tale's ritual exchange—my what big arms you have, my what big teeth you have. But, when the stranger-wolf replies "All the better to eat you with," "the girl burst out laughing; she knew she was nobody's meat" (118). This assertion is critical for Carter. In reading Sade's exploration of the limits of sexual behavior (and perhaps adding her own commentary on marriage), she makes an important distinction between flesh and meat: "Flesh has specific orifices to contain the prick that penetrates it but meat's relation to the knife is more random and a thrust anywhere will do" (2006: 162). Unlike the meatiness of Sade's characters—"He writes about sexual relations in terms of butchery and meat" (163)—Carter's Little Red Riding Hood laughs in the face of anyone misinterpreting her thus. The fact that Little Red Riding Hood is "nobody's meat" removes her from the realm of patriarchal pornography—the dominant tropes with which Carter first describes her—and resituates her in what Carter calls "the world of absolute sexual licence for all the genders" (22).

After proclaiming herself nobody's meat, Little Red Riding Hood continues to undress the stranger-wolf, throwing *his* clothes into the fire in a move that ensures he will remain forever wolf: "If you burn his human clothing you condemn him to wolfishness for the rest of his life" (Carter, 1993: 113). And then she seduces him; outside the blizzard rages and calms as nature mimes their sexual appetites, their long-awaited consummation. For Carter it is another happily-ever-after, or at least the lingering afterglow of a blissful intimacy: "See! sweet and sound she sleeps in granny's bed, between the paws of the tender wolf" (118). In choosing to burn the stranger-wolf's human clothing, Little Red Riding Hood opts for the bestial, and Carter seems to suggest that such a choice also reveals Little Red Riding Hood's own animal drives. Bacchilega similarly reads this scene as a testament to Little Red Riding Hood's desires: "By acting out her desires—sexual, not just for life—the girl offers herself as flesh, not meat.... Both carnivores incarnate, these two young heterosexual beings satiate their hunger not for dead meat, but flesh, while at the same time embodying it" (1997: 64).

For Carter, the virginal, sexually precocious nymphet is not so much desired object of patriarchal projection but rather desiring subject, as bestial as the stranger-wolf: "She will lay his fearful head on her lap and she will pick out the lice from his pelt and perhaps she will put the lice into her mouth and eat them, as he will bid her, as she would do in a savage marriage ceremony" (Carter, 1993: 118). While Little Red Riding Hood's initial seductions of the stranger-wolf—her "freely" given kiss, her stripping him—might still be perceived according to the logic of a pedophilic fantasy (the nymphet as seemingly innocent in her knowing seductions), her picking and eating the lice of his pelt cannot be so understood. Through this other erotic, this animal intimacy, Carter unveils the hegemonic order of heterosexual relations. In its stead she offers "the infinite modulations of the sexual act, the real relations of man and his kind," a sexual moment no longer chained to a dominant erotic that limits the sexual possibilities of men and women but one that emerges from our deepest drives.

Language Reconsidered: "Wolf-Alice"

If Little Red Riding Hood acts on her animal desires in "The Company of Wolves," she is all animal desire in "Wolf-Alice." Feral child, raised in the company of wolves until found in a den beside "the bullet-riddled corpse of her foster mother" (Carter, 1993: 119–20), Wolf-Alice is not quite child, not quite wolf: "Nothing about her is human except that she is *not* a wolf; it is as if the fur she thought she wore had melted into her skin and become part of it, although it does not exist" (119; emphasis in original). Like "The Werewolf," "Wolf-Alice" gestures toward other narrative traditions: to legends of feral children, to myths of famous children raised by wolves, Romulus and Remus for instance, to Lewis Carroll's *Alice in Wonderland* and *Through the Looking Glass* even (see, e.g., Schanoes 2012). Bacchilega helps to place "Wolf-Alice" in the "Little Red Riding Hood" tradition, citing the medieval poem "De puella a lupellis seruata" ("About a Girl Saved from

Wolf Cubs") in which the heroine "tames the wolves thanks to her red tunic" (1997: 65), a version that Jan M. Ziolkowski argues "should be registered somewhere on the ['Little Red Riding Hood'] family tree" (quoted in Bacchilega, 1997: 65). Carter further inscribes Wolf-Alice in this tradition, drawing parallels between her own earlier images of Little Red Riding Hood and Wolf-Alice: "Her panting tongue hangs out; her red lips are thick and fresh. Her legs are long, lean and muscular" (Carter, 1993: 119). Once again, Carter plays with the pornographic, with the male fantasy of the nymphet, and reminds us that Little Red Riding Hood's animal desires link her directly to Wolf-Alice.

But Wolf-Alice is of a necessarily different order from the Little Red Riding Hoods of "The Company of Wolves" and "The Werewolf." Carter uses this third story to draw together the considerations of phallogocentric language, dominant erotics, and the visual that center the first two stories in her wolf trilogy. With "Wolf-Alice" Carter more explicitly engages and critiques psychoanalytic theories of language, the senses, and desire in a complex and final erotic infidelity. Unlike the first two Little Red Riding Hoods, Wolf-Alice does not speak, a point Carter makes in the story's opening sentence: "Could this ragged girl with brindled lugs have spoken like we do she would have called herself a wolf, but she cannot speak" (Carter, 1993: 119). Even more significant, neither does she "look."

> Two-legs looks, four-legs sniffs. Her long nose is always a-quiver, sifting every scent it meets. With this useful tool, she lengthily investigates everything she glimpses. She can net so much more of the world than we can through the fine, hairy, sensitive filters of her nostrils that her poor eyesight does not trouble her. (119)

Outside the dominant paradigms of speech and sight, Wolf-Alice smells her way through the world, thus recalling the Freudian association between feminine sexuality and the olfactory, an association whose logic Gallop makes clear: "The penis may be more visible, but female genitalia have a stronger smell" (1982: 27).[9] Deeply connected to women, to women's smells, to the smell of menstruation, the olfactory is marginalized by the privileging of the visual, is made "odious, nauseous, because it threatens to undo the achievements of repression and sublimation, threatens to return the subject to the powerlessness, intensity and anxiety of an immediate connection with the body of the mother" (27). Carter writes against the dominant discourses in which the smell of women, women's smelling, threatens the stability of the Symbolic Order, positing instead an entirely different world for Wolf-Alice to inhabit, a world of sensual embodied pleasure.

Removed from the den where she is found beside the corpse of her wolf-mother, Wolf-Alice is taken to a convent where she is "taught a few, simple tricks" (Carter, 1993: 120); however, when the Mother Superior tries to teach her "to give thanks for her recovery from the wolves"—that is, tries to push her into language, make her a speaking subject—"she arched her back, pawed the floor, retreated to a far corner of the chapel, crouched, trembled, urinated, defecated—reverted entirely, it would seem, to her natural state" (120). This resistance to language is her bridge to the Duke, a night-prowling, corpse-eating zombie-werewolf who has "ceased to cast an image in the mirror" (120). Pawned off on the equally incomprehensible Duke, living in his castle, Wolf-Alice and the zombie-werewolf Duke lead entirely separate lives, and Carter alternates their stories as though to underscore the parallel but largely untouching nature of their coexistence. In her part of the tale, Wolf-Alice is safely ensconced in the extralinguistic world of her imaginary.

> In the lapse of time, the trance of being of that exiled place, this girl grew amongst things she could neither name nor perceive. How did she think, how did she feel, this perennial stranger with her furred thoughts and her primal sentience that existed in a flux of shifting impressions; there are no words to describe the way she negotiated the abyss between her dreams, those wakings strange as her sleepings. (122)

It is only Wolf-Alice's coming-of-age, her first menses, that shifts her world, that brings her in contact with a mirror, though, importantly, not one that heralds an identity in the Symbolic Order. In her search for "rags to sop the blood up" (122), Wolf-Alice discovers linens and old ball gowns in the closets of the Duke's castle as well as the burial clothes of his recently disentombed victims scattered about his "bloody chamber"; in the process, she also "bump[s] against that mirror over whose surface the Duke passed like wind on ice" (123). Here, in the mirror whose reflection she cannot fathom, the mirror that cannot perceive him, the narrative paths of the two characters cross for the first time; but Wolf-Alice finds a different companion in the mirror.

> First, she tried to nuzzle her reflection; then, nosing it industriously, she soon realized it gave out no smell. She bruised her muzzle on the cold glass and broke her claws trying to tussle with this stranger. She saw, with irritation, then amusement, how it mimicked every gesture of hers. . . . She rubbed her head against her reflected face, to show that she felt friendly towards it. (123)

Over time, marked by her budding sexuality, the adolescent development of her body—"She examined her new breasts with curiosity. . . . She found a little diadem of fresh hairs tufting between her thighs" (124)—she comes to recognize her reflection in the mirror for what it is, an intimate disappointment.

> This habitual, at last boring, fidelity to her every movement finally woke her up to the regretful possibility that her companion was, in fact, no more than a particularly ingenious variety of the shadow she cast on sunlit grass. . . . A little moisture leaked from the corners of her eyes, yet her relation with the mirror was now far more intimate since she knew she saw herself within it. (124)

Wolf-Alice recognizes herself in the mirror not as the ideal-I, the coherent self of Lacan's mirror stage (for Lacan, a misrecognition) but rather as shadow, as reflection, and it is this different recognition that keeps her from entering into the Symbolic Order, keeps her outside of language. Yet narratively it is also this moment of recognition—her abandonment of an Other, a playmate, the one who "gave out no smell"—that sends her out into the world beyond the Duke's castle, out into the world where olfaction structures meaning for her and ultimately reveals the danger that the local villagers pose to the Duke. With both Wolf-Alice and the Duke in the graveyard, Carter contrasts their sensory awarenesses in an explicitly gendered way so as to overturn the hierarchy that insists on the ocular over the olfactory; Wolf-Alice's orientation to the world through smell clues her into the villagers' proximity, the danger they bring, whereas the zombie-werewolf Duke remains oblivious until hit by a bullet that "drags off half his fictive pelt" (125).

Back at the castle, Wolf-Alice's response to the injured Duke—"locked half and half between such strange states, an aborted transformation, an incomplete mystery, now he lies writhing on his black bed" (Carter, 1993: 126)—is both tender and erotic. She circles his bed, sniffs at his wound, then "she leapt upon his bed to lick, without hesitation, without disgust, with a quick, tender gravity, the blood and dirt from his cheeks and forehead" (126). Wolf-Alice's erotic care brings to mind Little Red Riding Hood's earlier picking and eating of the lice from the stranger-wolf's pelt: feminine desires exercised on the bodies of wolf-men. But Wolf-Alice's licking has yet another effect.

> As she continued her ministrations, this glass, with infinite slowness, yielded to the reflexive strength of its own material construction. Little by little, there appeared within it, like the image on photographic paper that emerges, first, a formless web of tracery, the prey caught in its own fishing net, then in firmer yet still shadowed outline until at last as vivid as real life itself, as if brought into being by her soft, moist, gentle tongue, finally, the face of the Duke. (126)

Here, Carter's final description of Wolf-Alice's licking is slow and sensual, an erotically charged literary tumescence, building, ultimately, to the Duke's presence in the mirror. Wolf-Alice has ushered him into existence, escorted him into the Symbolic Order, but it is her symbolic, a world outside of language though still shaped by the tongue.[10] As in "The Tiger's Bride," the alternative, erotic use of the tongue creates a momentary enchantment in which two beings, two subjects, might discover an intimate recognition and a mutual pleasure beyond the scripted limits of heterosexual love and desire.

Nestled in the heart of the "Little Red Riding Hood" tradition is a mutual desire almost completely overshadowed by the wolf's interpellation as sexual predator, the cultural presumption of his dangerous and antisocial desires. At the same time, the patriarchal imaginary that explicitly structures the literary tradition and implicitly frames the oral tradition denies girls and young women their own active desires. But beyond the wolf's naturalized *maleness* and his voracious appetites, beyond the assumption of the girl as innocent victim or as seductive nymphet who gets what she deserves, are hints of another desire, an agential longing between the girl and the wolf that goes almost entirely unrecognized in the tales and the critical literature.

Jack Zipes locates one example of this mutual attraction in Gustave Doré's set of canonical illustrations for an 1862 edition of Perrault's tales, wherein Little Red Riding Hood's "longing if not seductive look" (Zipes, 1983a: 91) and the "proximity of wolf and girl who appear to be touching and to be totally absorbed in an intimate *tête-à-tête*" (92) suggest "the desire of the girl and wolf for one another" (92). Although Zipes goes on to argue that, in capturing the girl's full face and seductive look, "Doré also suggests that it is primarily she who is asking for it" (92), he nonetheless points to the possibility of their mutual desire, a mutual desire that Doré not only recognized in the tale but also animated through the intimacy of his portrayal.[11]

The underlying mutual desire between the girl and the wolf—the recognition of the girl's desire for the wolf alongside his assumed desire for her—also surfaces in Verdier's (1997) interpretation of the path of pins and needles in the oral versions of the tale. Drawing on her ethnographic research, Verdier accounts for this seemingly odd choice of paths through the symbolic meaning of pins and needles that emerges out of the local customs and practices associated with feminine sexual maturity: girls apprenticing as seamstresses, courting customs involving the exchange of pins, and the folk speech that articulates these apprenticeships with preparation for courtship, marriage, and adult sexuality. Against this cultural backdrop, the language of pins and needles for the choice of paths reframes the meeting of girl and wolf as a flirtatious and dangerously thrilling encounter, one that hints at their mutual desire even if such longing is foreclosed at the end of the tale.

Whereas Zipes argues that Perrault and the Grimms "transformed an oral folk tale about the social initiation of a young woman into a narrative about rape in which the heroine is obliged to bear the responsibility for sexual violation" (1983a: 78), Carter rejects such a progressive genealogy and instead incorporates elements from the oral and the literary traditions in ways that underscore the fact that both traditions ultimately suppress the possibility of a reciprocal desire. Carter's wolf trilogy releases the intense mutual attraction denied by both the oral and the literary tales, providing the girl and the wolf with opportunities to act on their desires, opportunities to explore an alternate erotic, even as it seeks to account for the power relations of every sexual coupling. The detailed bodily encounters that animate these stories—a girl who severs a charging wolf's paw, a grandmother's stoning, a long absent husband who returns and transforms himself into a wolf to punish his "whorish" wife, the exhumation and devouring of a bride-corpse—reiterate the material and corporeal nature of power and the ways it moves through and across the shifting relationships and moments of contact between women, wolves, and strange others. It is precisely through such an attention to the dangers of power and its differentials that Carter grounds her alternate erotics in the material reality of gender relations.

At the same time, Carter's women and wolves slip between categories—male, female, human, child, animal, witch—in a way that confuses the sexed ideologies of the phallic and the Oedipal, that confuses the sexed conventions of power, authority, and symbolic representation. Such a confusion—the infinite metamorphoses of Little Red Riding Hood, her grandmother, the men they encounter, and their lupine counterparts—(re)imagines animal drives, sexual drives, free from systems of sex and gender. In so doing, Carter begins to dismantle the phallocentric underpinnings of both sex and language. In creating a series of constantly shifting women, constantly shifting wolves, Carter fantasizes an alternative to the dominant myth of singularity. Her endless transformations—from sex to sex, state to state, story to story—indulge a certain arbitrariness in denial of a hierarchical ordering, in defiance of any linear progression. As such, her infinite becomings uphold her erotic infidelities, ensure that her infidelities remain infidelities, never to become the fidelities of another set of definitive interpretations.

If Carter's women and wolves prove slippery, so too do their tongues. Good for "squawking and shrieking," flirting with the bestial, howling a collective prothalamion, howling a wolf-girl's loneliness, good for licking with "a quick, tender gravity," the tongues of Carter's women and wolves move them away from language, speech, articulation, and into a more sensory realm, inspiring us to consider the affective and corporeal possibilities of an expanded sensorium. Carter's feminine tongues, her wolfish tongues, bring into being an other erotic, much as Wolf-Alice's tongue brings the zombie-werewolf Duke into another symbolic, an erotic outside language as we know it, language as it knows us. Through these tongues, Carter writes erotic possibility, not simply a prescription for a new erotic, a new definition, but rather a space where both women and men can express their animal drives, can enact their desires beyond their cultural inscriptions, can embrace their erotic selves in a "world of absolute sexual license for all the genders" (Carter, 2006: 22).

Epilogue
Enchanting Possibilities

Wolf-Alice's wonderfully transformative tongue is just one of the many enchantments Carter imagines in *The Bloody Chamber*.

> Maternal telepathy.
> The stain on a bloody key transferred to the heroine's forehead.
> The Beast's licking away a girl's skin to reveal her underlying pelt.
> A self-playing fiddle that discloses a mother-daughter-lover's murderous intentions.
> A girl born of a Count's desire.
> A somnambulist beauty awakened to death by a young man's kiss.
> The intimate afterglow of a seductive girl and a werewolf-turned-wolf.

Carter's delightfully twisted enchantments refashion tradition to imagine love and erotic possibility outside of banal convention, to disrupt the legacy and shift the burden of the fairy tale as enduring narrative.

The Gender of Enchantment

Enchantment is deeply gendered in Western fairy tales. A survey of the Grimms' *Kinder- und Hausmärchen*, for instance, suggests that the logic of enchantment parallels the gendered logic of speech and silence that Ruth Bottigheimer articulates in her article "Silenced Women in the Grimms' Tales" (1986). That is, boys and young men tend to remain active even when enchanted, whereas girls and young women are generally rendered passive, if not catatonic. Thus, for instance, in "The Seven Ravens" (KHM 25), when the seven brothers are transformed into ravens, they are able to make a life for themselves as the "lord ravens," who inhabit a glass mountain where they are served by a dwarf. Similarly, in "The Six Swans" (KHM 49), when the king's six sons are transformed into swans by their evil stepmother, they take up residence in a cottage in the forest and are able to shed their swan skins for fifteen minutes each day. As ravens and swans, the enchanted boys of both tales spend their days away from home, presumably in some activity of their choosing, and their avian forms seem to interfere little in the quality of their lives. In contrast, the heroines of "Little Brier Rose" (KHM 50) and "Snow White" (KHM 53), two of the Grimms' most well-known tales, must suffer a deathlike passivity. Even more, when girls and young women are not themselves the victims of wicked enchantments, they must nonetheless endure similarly extreme passivity, particularly in the form of multiyear injunctions against speaking or laughing, as one of the primary conditions for disenchanting their brothers or the prince.[1]

    This gendered logic of enchantment not only pertains to the structure of the Western fairy tale but also underlies many of the popular interpretations that contribute to its broader cultural understanding, such as Bruno Bettelheim's *Uses of Enchantment* (1976), Robert Bly's *Iron John* (1990), and Colette Dowling's *Cinderella Complex* (1982). Bettelheim's interpretation of "Sleeping Beauty," for instance, is itself structured by precisely this gendered logic, despite the fact that he makes a point of denying "sexual stereotyping" in fairy tales (1989: 226). In his psychoanalytic reading of the tale, male and female protagonists represent the two challenges that every adolescent must negotiate in order to develop selfhood, specifically the "inner world" represented by Sleeping Beauty's lengthy slumber and the "outer world" represented by the hero's "aggressive" interactions with the world. The fact that Bettelheim fails to recognize the ways that these different paths to selfhood are gendered does not mean that they do not reproduce the sex-based stereotypes at their core *even if* individuals, regardless of gender, must ultimately work to overcome both internal and external trials.

Beyond this particular blind spot, Bettelheim's rather essentializing interpretation of "Sleeping Beauty" further extends and naturalizes the gendered logic of fairy-tale enchantment. The tale's message, he claims, is much like the message of "Snow White": "What may seem like a period of deathlike passivity at the end of childhood is nothing but a time of quiet growth and preparation, from which the person will awaken mature, ready for sexual union. It must be stressed that in fairy tales, this union is as much one of the minds and souls of two partners as it is one of sexual fulfillment" (1989: 232). Setting aside Bettelheim's unquestioningly romanticized understanding of the fairy-tale union as a joining of the minds, souls, and bodies of the two partners (one of his claims with which Carter certainly "quarrels"), his equating the "period of deathlike passivity" with "a time of quiet growth and preparation" assumes that girls—the only ones whose enchantments entail deathlike passivity—are preparing only for sexual and romantic partnering. Their job is to be passive, to await the prince whose active battle with the external world will eventually prompt Sleeping Beauty and Snow White from what he characterizes as their narcissistic internal focus, represented by their enchanted passivity.

Bettelheim himself makes these gendered assumptions explicit as he continues with his analysis: "Only relating positively to the other 'awakens' us from the danger of sleeping away our life. The kiss of the prince breaks the spell of narcissism and awakens a womanhood, which up to then has remained undeveloped. Only if the maiden grows into woman can life go on" (1989: 234). Although Bettelheim begins his interpretation with an attempt at gender neutrality—we must *all* awaken from the danger of sleeping our life away—he quickly slips into the sexist narrative that ensues from a gendered logic of enchantment. The *prince* must break the spell of narcissism in order to awaken the proper *womanhood*. I offer this brief critique of Bettelheim—one could write an entire book challenging his interpretations, and indeed, Carter has done just that with *The Bloody Chamber*—not only to contest the particularities of his argument about "Sleeping Beauty" but also to show the cultural reach of the gendered logic of fairy-tale enchantment, the way that enchantment's taken-for-grantedness within and around fairy tales obscures its ideological workings.

Feminist Disenchantments

Outside of fairy-tale studies and popular interpretations of fairy tales, the question of enchantment has been taken up by feminist and critical cultural theorists. Provoked by Max Weber's famous 1918 claim that "the fate of our age is characterized by rationalization and intellectualization and, above all, by the disenchantment of the world" (quoted in Lassman, 2000: 97), these theorists turn to enchantment in order to contemplate ways of generating meaning—and meaningful subjectivities—in a secular, rational, commodified world. In their introduction to the special issue of *Women's Studies Quarterly* devoted to interdisciplinary perspectives on enchantment, Ann Burlein and Jackie Orr capture well the ethic driving the feminist interest in enchantment as praxis: "How to imagine a world in which one could flourish? What might be the serious and playful role of enchantments in materializing that world? We experiment with enchantment as both a content of thought and as a way of thinking because the present so desperately requires the fabrication of escape routes that are not escapist" (2012: 13). The special issue of *Women's Studies Quarterly* and the questions that Burlein and Orr invoke to frame it are inspired in large part by the tenth anniversary of political theorist Jane Bennett's *The Enchantment of Modern Life* (2001).

In *The Enchantment of Modern Life* Bennett seeks to identify everyday enchantments within the contemporary social and material world—moments of intermingling pleasure, surprise, awe, and the uncanny—that exist amid the disenchanted world that Weber describes, a world she recognizes as run through with "inequity, racism, pollution, poverty, violence of all kinds" (2001: 8). Explicitly resisting an understanding of her theory as one of *re*-enchantment, Bennett is more interested in "calling attention to magical sites already here" (8), to enchantment as "an affective force" (3). For her, enchantment includes a "condition of exhilaration or acute sensory activity"; it is to be in "a state of wonder . . . to be transfixed, spellbound" (5).

Bennett is motivated by more than simply identifying fleeting moments of enchantment in the modern world, however; rather, she locates in enchantment an ethical significance, the possibility that its affective force might "aid in the project of cultivating a stance of presumptive generosity (i.e., of rendering oneself more open to the surprise of other selves and bodies and more willing and able to enter into productive assemblages with them)" (2001: 131). In her compelling discussion of the intersection of enchantment and ethics, Bennett offers a number of brief case studies involving interspecies and intraspecies crossings: Andoar, the goat-kite in Michel Tournier's novel *Friday*; Rotpeter, the ape-man in Franz Kafka's short story "A Report to an Academy"; Alex, a parrot capable of abstract thinking; and Deleuze and Guattari's body-without-organs. Through careful readings, Bennett draws out the ways in which becoming-otherwise and mobile subjectivities resist "purist identities of ethnicity, race, gender, or nation" (29), offering instead "a more radical permeability" that "extends to nonhuman animals, the wind, rocks, trees, plants, tools, machines" (29). How, Bennett wonders, might self-morphing affect the politics of identity, not just for marginalized groups but also for more privileged hegemonic groups? For her, "metamorphing creatures enact the very possibility of change; their presence carries with it the trace of dangerous but also exciting and exhilarating migrations" (17), and this, she argues, might "render one more open to novelty, less defensive in the face of challenges to norms that one already embodies, and thus more responsive to the injustices that haunt both cross-culture and cross-species relations" (29).

It might seem easy to dismiss Bennett's theory of enchantment as overly naïve or romantic, but she anticipates and responds to these potential criticisms by insisting that her theory of enchantment is grounded in a "stance that consists, above all, in the acknowledgement of human finitude" (2001: 76). Drawing on Simon Critchley's work on death in philosophy and literature, Bennett argues that an acknowledgment of human finitude depends on accepting the fact that one's death is meaningless, that it happens for no reason; in so doing, we accede to what we cannot understand, which in turn contributes to what Critchley refers to as the "unworking of human arrogance." For both Critchley and Bennett this arrogance is epitomized by the assumption that we might know the Other when, in reality, any such knowledge simply reduces the alterity of the Other to the self. Bennett summarizes Critchley's argument beautifully when she writes, "Owning up to death, then, raises the chances that the radical alterity of the Other will make a 'claim on me' and change and challenge 'my self-conception'" (76).

The subjects of Carter's animal-human transformations, couplings, and mutual becomings animate the promise of enchantment as Bennett theorizes it. When the heroine of "The Tiger's Bride" overcomes her "most archaic of fears, fear of devourment" (Carter, 1993: 67) and when Little Red Riding Hood burns the werewolf's human clothes to keep him in wolf form so she might sleep, "sweet and sound . . . between the paws of the tender wolf" (118), Carter imagines love as the meeting of two beings beyond the confines of "human arrogance," two beings whose fundamental otherness insists on a mutual recognition that calls hegemonic ideologies of self and subjectivity into question. Suspended in a productive ontological liminality, Carter's characters perform the "exciting and exhilarating migrations" that Bennett finds so critical to enchantment's political and ethical power. The heroine of "The Tiger's Bride," like the werewolf-turned-wolf, like Wolf-Alice, like the zombie-werewolf Duke, relishes her interspecies crossing just as the heroine of "The Erl-King" embraces her own intraspecies crossing from daughter to mother. In truly challenging the traditional paradigms of love and desire, Carter's stories of enchantment depend on the radical alterity of the Other to push enchantment into a new, ethical space of potential freedom and equality.

Implicit in *The Bloody Chamber* is a critique of the gendered logic of fairy-tale enchantment, and Carter's alternative enchantments obviously move in different directions to recuperate enchantment's capacity to inspire wonder and to render our familiar world "utterly strange."[2] Whereas traditional fairy-tale disenchantments awaken young women to adult heteronormative femininity or transform them from animals into ready bride-prizes, Carter's peculiar enchantments release them from the strictures of hegemonic femininity, transforming them instead into animals, animal hybrids, and the eager sexual partners of animals. With such fantastic metamorphoses and unexpected couplings, Carter suggests that the traditional enchantments reserved for women and girls in fairy tales run in parallel with the limiting norms that dictate gendered performance in everyday life. Moreover, as she demonstrates so forcefully throughout *The Bloody Chamber*, it is in our everyday lives as adult women that we are destined to live these fairy-tale enchantments unless we disenchant ourselves by inviting interactions with radical forms of alterity. Only by taking seriously the power of enchantment as both theory and praxis—a particularly Carteresque enchantment—might we resist the pull that fairy tales and other enduring narratives continue to exert over us, thus allowing for the pursuit of freedom, desire, and an alternate erotics.

Notes

Chapter 1

1. See, for instance, Dimovitz (2010), Engle (1999), Fabian (2011), Geoffroy-Menoux (1996), Kaiser (1994), Losada Pérez (n.d.), McLaughlin (1995), Pyrhönen (2007), and Sheets (1991).
2. Notepad, MS 88899/1/101 [1972], Angela Carter Papers, British Library.
3. Referring to the *Bloody Chamber* stories in an interview with John Haffenden, Carter claims that she wanted to "extract the latent content from the traditional stories and to use it as the beginning of new stories" (1985: 84); her definition of psychoanalysis as "looking at this world, seeing it as utterly strange" strikes me as operating in similar fashion.
4. See, for instance, Armitt (1997), Gamble (1997), Kaiser (1994), and Makinen (1992).
5. Kathryn Bond Stockton, personal communication, 2005.
6. Journal, MS 88899/1/94 (1972), Angela Carter Papers, British Library.
7. Journal, MS 88899/1/87 (1961–1962), Angela Carter Papers, British Library.
8. Journal, MS 88899/1/93 (1969–1970), Angela Carter Papers, British Library.
9. See Gamble (2006) for an extended analysis of the mutual influences of Carter's fiction and autobiographical writings. Reading the two together, Gamble insightfully argues that neither is a reflection of Carter's life; rather, both reflect her self-consciously constructed "endlessly shifting identity" (9), "just another story" (197). Although Gamble does not draw from Carter's unpublished journals and thus refers only to her published autobiographical writing, I want to follow Gamble's warning against simply reading Carter's fiction as a reflection of her life or vice versa. That said, Gamble claims that "in much of what she wrote from the seventies onwards, Carter is mimicking in fiction what she was also doing with her own life story" (197), and Carter's journals bear this out as well; phrases, images, and characterizations from the *Bloody Chamber* stories often appear first in poems and entries dedicated to or describing her lovers.

Chapter 2

1. In Perrault's "Bluebeard," Bluebeard is an extremely wealthy man with a frightful blue beard. At the start of the story he is looking to marry one of his widowed

neighbor's two daughters, but neither will have him on account of his beard; in addition, the girls are suspicious because he had previously been married but nobody seems to know what became of his former wives. To befriend and impress the young women, Bluebeard throws a lavish week-long party at one of his country estates, after which the younger daughter finds him to be a fine gentleman and his beard to be much less blue. As soon as they return to town, the two are married. Shortly after the marriage, Bluebeard is called away on business, but before he leaves, he entrusts his key ring to his wife. He describes the treasures protected by each key and encourages her to explore the mansion freely, save for a single room, which he expressly forbids her to enter despite providing her with the key and its explicit location. With Bluebeard away on business, his young wife begins to explore the mansion and its riches but is quickly bored by what she finds; her curiosity is, of course, piqued by the forbidden room. Unable to resist any longer, she enters the room and finds a bloody chamber in which Bluebeard has stored the bodies of his murdered wives. In shock and horror, the newest bride drops the key on the bloody floor, the blood leaving a telltale sign of her transgression on the key. Bluebeard returns unexpectedly the next day and, upon seeing the bloody key, condemns his wife to join the others she has discovered. She asks him for some time to pray and prepare for death, and when alone, she calls to her sister, Anne, to see whether anyone is coming who might save her. Just as Bluebeard has raised his cutlass to decapitate his wife, her brothers rush in and kill him. His wife, now rich, marries her sister off, commissions her two brothers, and finally settles with a true gentleman. Perrault completes the tale with two morals. The first chastises women for their curiosity, suggesting that it mainly leads to regret; the second emphasizes the fact that the tale is old and that no modern husband would be so terrible as to "demand of his wife such an impossible thing as to stifle her curiosity" because "it's easy to see which of the two is the master" (Perrault, 1977b: 41). Whereas most critics have understood Perrault's "Bluebeard" as Carter's primary fairy-tale intertext, Barzilai (2009) argues that Carter is most clearly engaging and elaborating on Anne Thackery Ritchie's *Bluebeard's Keys*.

2. Carter also saw Bluebeard in Sade. For instance, in her notes for *The Sadeian Woman*, she conflates Sade and Bluebeard in her description of Sade's chateau: "If you go to the Vaucluse, in the South of France, you can see the ominous ruins of Sade's chateau from a great distance away. It broods upon a hilltop among beautiful fields of lavender, the chateau of la Cost—Bluebeard's Castle, where the Marquis, his wife, five young maidservants, a secretary, a dancer named Du Plan, engaged as a housekeeper, two kitchenmaids and a cook, spent the winter of 1775 with the drawbridge down only for a few hours in the middle of the day" ("The Sadeian Woman" 3, MS 88899/1/71 [n.d.], Angela Carter Papers, British Library).

3. The reference to the scimitar in this pornographic illustration and to another image that the heroine finds in the Marquis's library, *The Adventures of Eulalie at the Harem of the Grand Turk* (Carter, 1993: 17), attest to the eighteenth-century

orientalizing of "Bluebeard." See Hermansson (2009) for a discussion of the tale's orientalization. For a more specific reading of the tale's orientalizing in "The Bloody Chamber," see Sheets (1991), Bacchilega (1995), and Roemer (2001). Sheets reads this scene as Carter's calling attention to the tale's history of orientalizing. Bacchilega looks to Carter's nonfiction writing about her time in Japan—itself orientalist (Bacchilega leaves open whether this is intentional or not)—to explore the ways that those experiences influence descriptions of sadomasochism in "The Bloody Chamber." Roemer draws parallels between "The Bloody Chamber" and Christopher Marlowe's *Tamburlaine, the Great*.

4. For more on the association between Gilles de Rais and Bluebeard, see Hyatte (1984) and Hermansson (2001).

5. For readings of "The Bloody Chamber" as a "Beauty and the Beast" tale (in addition to a "Bluebeard" story) and the collection as a whole as a series of retellings of that particular tale, see Bacchilega (1997: 141), Brooke (2004: 68–69), and Cavallaro (2011: 124). Margaret Atwood also connects "The Bloody Chamber" with the two "Beauty and the Beast" stories, although she holds them together under the heading of meat-eating felines (2007: 138).

6. For a discussion of how Carter carries this theme throughout *The Bloody Chamber*, see Bacchilega (1997: 141).

7. See, among the many examples, Buchel (2003: 38), Gamble (2008: 31), and Manley (2001: 85).

8. Elaine Jordan (2007) recounts a letter in which Carter describes exactly this desire to draw the reader into the discomforting world where women might be seduced by wealth and transgression: "Replying to a letter of mine about attacks on her work by some feminists, Angela Carter wrote that the title story in *The Bloody Chamber* is 'a deliberate *homage* to Colette': 'I wanted a lush fin-de-siècle décor for the story, and a style that . . . utilizes the heightened diction of the novelette, to half-seduce the reader into this wicked, glamorous, fatal world'" (208–209).

9. See, for example, Bacchilega (1997), Day (1998), Gamble (2008), Jordan (1998), Makinen (1992), and Sheets (1991).

10. Although most feminist critics read Perrault's morals as sexist, Martine Hennard Dutheil de la Rochère and Ute Heidmann (2009) draw out some of the intertextual play that might add nuance to the morals; in addition, they intervene in the "critical consensus" that understands Carter as subverting Perrault. Rather, they argue, Carter's translations of Perrault's *contes* and her own rewritings, particularly in *The Bloody Chamber*, provide "a means to pursue and develop a complex and productive dialogue with Perrault" (41). That said, Carter herself finds Perrault's "Bluebeard" to be "overdetermined, the latent content put too squarely at the service of rational socialization" (Notepad, MS 88899/1/105 [n.d.], Angela Carter Papers, British Library), and in her essay "The Better to Eat You With" she elaborates on this point: "The ghastliness of the rest of the Bluebeard story is clearly almost too much for Perrault: the dismembered wives lying in their own blood in the secret chamber, the

bloodstained key that won't wash clean. . . . It's easy to see all this took place long ago, consoles Perrault in his moral tag at the end of the story. Modern husbands wouldn't dare to be so terrible. He blithely dismisses all the Freudian elements in the tale that galvanise the twentieth century. The troubling and intransigent images are incorporated into a well-mannered scheme of good sense" (1998b: 453). For an excellent analysis of the misogyny underlying Perrault's *contes* and other writings, despite feminist attempts to read him as sympathetic to women, see Duggan (1996).
11. For feminist discussions of this affiliation, see, for example, Jacobson (1993), Renfroe (2001), Tatar (1987), and Warner (1994).
12. Many critics have noted Carter's engagement with Lacan's theories of subjectivity, particularly through her use of mirrors, in her short stories and novels. For discussions that address *The Bloody Chamber* in particular, see, for example, Cavallaro (2011), Day (1998), Dimovitz (2010), McLaughlin (1995), Pyrhönen (2007), and Schanoes (2009, 2012).
13. See Losada Pérez (n.d.) and McLaughlin (1995) for a discussion of the Marquis as Žižek's anal father; for additional readings of the Marquis in relation to God and/or the heroine's father, see Bacchilega (1997: 124), Hennard Dutheil de la Rochère and Heidmann (2009: 53), and Renfroe (2001: 101).
14. See also Bacchilega (1997) and Sheets (1991) for similar readings.
15. See Henke (2013) for an extended discussion of shame—and its recuperation—in *The Bloody Chamber* as a whole.
16. I would argue that the caustic responses to *The Sadeian Woman* by Anglo-American antipornography feminists are, at least in part, based on misreadings of Carter. Although Carter finds in Sade's work the *potential* for a moral pornography and an important "refusal to see female sexuality in relation to its reproductive function" (2006: 1), she ultimately reads him as too cowardly to grant the mother's full sexual pleasure and too cowardly to face the possibility of the "holy terror of love" (176). Many antipornography feminists see Carter as only upholding Sade's ideas. See Sheets (1991) for a detailed discussion of the Anglo-American antipornography feminist response to *The Sadeian Woman*.

Chapter 3

1. By "beastly subjects" I mean both characters and topics.
2. Beaumont's "Beauty and the Beast" involves a recently impoverished merchant and his three daughters, the youngest of which is of incomparable beauty and kindness. Upon learning that one of his ships may have returned safely to port, the merchant sets off with the hopes of recovering his wealth and reinstating his daughters to the luxuries of bourgeois life. Before leaving, he asks each daughter what gift she would like should his wealth be restored; the older two ask for expensive clothing and jewels, but Beauty requests only a rose. After learning that his ship has not returned and that he is indeed ruined,

the merchant sets off on his return journey only to get lost in a storm; seeking shelter, he finds his way to a magical palace where he is fed and pampered by invisible forces. As he departs for home, he plucks a rose from the garden, which inspires the wrath of the Beast, who tells him that he must return or send one of his daughters in his place. Beauty, who is both devoted to her father and self-sacrificing, convinces him to send her in his place. At the castle she is treated royally and eventually comes to love the Beast, although she misses her family. The Beast allows her to visit her family and to care for her ailing father, and Beauty promises to return. Once home, however, her sisters prevent her from returning until it is nearly too late; when she finally returns, she finds the Beast on his deathbed and suffering from grief over her absence. Declaring her love, she simultaneously saves and disenchants the Beast, who becomes a prince and marries Beauty.

3. For a detailed discussion and breakdown of the "Beauty and the Beast" tale type, see Uther (2004: tale type 425C). Uther's classification system is based on the system developed by Antti Aarne and Stith Thompson.

4. Fairy tales and their themes are often characterized as "timeless" (see, e.g., Bettelheim, 1989: 97; Griswold, 2004: 17; Rowe, 1979: 251; and Russell, 2002: 114), but this sense of timelessness was specifically invoked to frame this tale in Disney's animated version, *Beauty and the Beast*, whose theme song is titled "Beauty and the Beast (Tale as Old as Time)." In addition, Disney later issued a book titled *Tale as Old as Time: The Art and Making of* Beauty and the Beast (Solomon, 2010).

5. "The Sadeian Woman" 4, MS 88899/1/72 (n.d.), Angela Carter Papers, British Library.

6. "The Sadeian Woman" 4, MS 88899/1/72 (n.d.), Angela Carter Papers, British Library.

7. The work on gender and the male gaze, voyeurism, and scopophilia is extensive. I have found the following works to be especially useful in providing an overview: Freud (1962), Gallop (1982), Heru (2003), Irigaray (1985), Metzl (2004), and Mulvey (1975).

8. Sylvia Bryant (1989) points out that to break the curse, the Beast need only marry *a* beautiful girl; thus it makes sense that he loves beauty, in general, over Beauty, the individual.

9. These lines have been much discussed in Shakespeare criticism because of the controversy about whether the intended word is *Indian* or *Iudean* (Judean); in this case, Carter's use of *Indian* and the specific context seem to point to the common interpretation in which the "savage" Indian does not recognize the value of gems and thus casts them away. That said, Carter may very well have been familiar with the scholarly debates around the word and the interpretation of the lines, and she may be playing with this ambiguity and likening the father's loss of his daughter in a game of cards to Judas's betrayal of Jesus. For more on the debate over *Indian* and *Iudean*, see Levin (1982) and Seaman (1968).

10. Here, Carter may be citing Cocteau's film wherein Beauty's tears turn to diamonds. However, in casting The Beast as the one to produce the diamond tears, Carter invokes them to signal a space outside the dominant scopophilic economy. In Carter's story The Beast's two diamond tears (from his requests to see the heroine naked) are made into earrings that she refuses to wear until they have entered into a reciprocal relationship as subjects outside the Symbolic Order.
11. Carter makes explicit the relationship between psychoanalysis and Western culture exemplified in male erotic violence and the myth of the female wound in *The Sadeian Woman*: "The whippings, the beatings, the gougings, the stabbings of erotic violence reawaken the memory of the social fiction of the female wound, the bleeding scar left by her castration, which is a psychic fiction as deeply at the heart of Western culture as the myth of Oedipus, to which it is related in the complex dialectic of imagination and reality that produces culture" (2006: 26).
12. Here Carter offers yet another inversion of "The Courtship of Mr. Lyon." In that story the father's promise of furs distracts Beauty from returning to the beastly Mr. Lyon, from the "possibility of some change," whereas in "The Tiger's Bride," the heroine's furs are disenchanted—the social sign of elite culture is shown to be nothing more than a pack of rats—when she opts to go to The Beast instead of returning to her father. Of course, Carter further reproduces this inversion at the story's end when the tiger licks away the heroine's "skins of a life in the world" to reveal her own fur.
13. See, for instance, Bacchilega (1997: 99), Buchel (2003: 66), Day (1998: 146), and Gamble (2008: 42).
14. Although the term *animal* in relation to *human* obscures the continuity between them, including, obviously, humans' animal status, I use the term *animal* to refer to nonhuman animals for its terminological efficiency and ease.
15. Although some feminists may interpret Carter's associating women and animals as reproducing long-standing patriarchal stereotypes, her awareness of such hegemonic articulations—as indicated by this passage, for instance—allowed her to play with them in order to try to get at women's animal drives as a component of sex and sexual relations outside their dominant tropes and conventions. In her journals Carter draws on such associations in her own self-descriptions: She refers to her overwhelming sexual desire as being "on [in] heat" (Journal, MS 88899/1/95 [1973], Angela Carter Papers, British Library), attributes the failure of one romantic relationship to the fact that "Bill doesn't smell right" (Journal, MS 88899/1/94 [1972], Angela Carter Papers, British Library; emphasis in original), and even characterizes a moment when her despair led her to unexpected animal behavior: "Soon, to my great surprise, I crouched on all fours, yelped continuously & began to scrabble at the tatami with my fingernails" (Journal, MS 88899/1/93 [1969–1970], Angela Carter Papers, British Library).

16. Although it is possible to read the werewolf-grandmother and the feral wolf-girl in "Wolf-Alice" as examples of Carter's fairy-tale animals, both wolf-women and Wolf-Alice's zombie-werewolf companion inhabit a much more liminal space that does not address the desiring relationship between humans and animals in quite the same way I am discussing here.
17. In another scene of writing that takes place after their first sexual liaison, Master still struggles with language: "He sits, for a while, and scribbles; rips the page in four, hurls it aside" (Carter, 1993: 79).
18. Carter's moral, while keeping with the structure of Perrault's "Puss-in-Boots" (which contains two morals), departs dramatically from the ideological points of Perrault's "Moral" and "Another Moral." The "Moral" reads, "A great inheritance may be a fine thing; but hard work and ingenuity will take a young man further than his father's money." "Another Moral" states, "If a miller's son can so quickly win the heart of a princess, that is because clothes, bearing and youth speedily inspire affection; and the means to achieve them are not always entirely commendable" (Perrault, 1977b: 53).

Chapter 4

1. See Engle (1999) for an extended and insightful reading of the metaphor of the labyrinthine woods as Carter's commitment to "effect[ing] a radical reformulation of the very notion of intelligibility by presenting a model for reading and identity formation which insists upon the reader's acknowledgment of being always already located inside a labyrinthine social structure" (19). This reading accords, to some degree, with my reading of "The Bloody Chamber" and also points to Carter's ongoing play with Lacanian theories of language, although Engle is not as concerned with the role of desire.
2. In Goethe's "Erlkönig," a father and his young son are riding home on horseback during the night. The son is anxious and seems to hear and see things that his father attributes to the mundane world around them. For instance, when the father asks the boy why he hides his face in fear, the son replies by asking whether the father does not see the Erlkönig; the father then dismisses what he takes to be the boy's imaginative fears, saying that it's just a wisp of fog. The poem continues through a series of the son's fears as the Erlkönig pursues him, but the father repeatedly attributes these "sightings" to natural phenomena. At the end of the poem, after the son has cried out that the Erlkönig has him in his grip, the father arrives home only to find that his son is dead in his arms.
3. "The Bloody Chamber and Other Short Stories" 2, MS 88899/1/34 (1975–1979), Angela Carter Papers, British Library.
4. In the unattributed translation of Goethe's "Erlkönig" transcribed in Carter's journal, the child cries, "Erl-King has done me grievous harm!" (Journal, MS 88899/1/95 [1973], Angela Carter Papers, British Library).
5. Lacan contends that the phallus is a signifier (i.e., a position in language) and thus is decoupled from biology, but in practice he theorizes about men and

women in ways that seem to ignore their own status as signifiers. Homans characterizes this sleight of hand as a confusion of "trope and material condition": "That Lacan's narrative originates in male experience shouldn't necessarily invalidate it as a description of a daughter's relation to sexuality and language. But his narrative depends upon a disingenuous confusion of trope and material condition. On the one hand, 'phallus,' 'masculine,' and 'feminine' are all argued to be tropes or positions in language, which anyone, male or female, can occupy. On the other hand, he himself applies what he has said about the trope 'woman' to actual women, in a remark in which gender has obviously become a material condition: 'There is no woman who is not excluded by the nature of things, which is the nature of words, and it must be said that, if there is something they complain a lot about at the moment, that is what it is—except that they don't know what they are saying, that's the whole difference between them and me.' While Lacanian language assumes the lack of the phallus, it is only those who can lack it—those who might once have had it, as sons believe their fathers have—who are privileged to substitute for it symbolic language; daughters lack this lack" (Homans, 1986: 9).

6. Ana María Losada Pérez (n.d.) casts the Erl-King and the Marquis in "The Bloody Chamber" as Slavoj Žižek's "anal father," the simultaneously seductive and horrific monstrous father figure who challenges the Law of the Father by virtue of his excessive and sadistic pleasure. Although some of the details of Losada Pérez's reading are quite compelling, including the way in which the anal father represents "what is 'in me more than myself'" (Žižek, 1992, quoted in Losada Pérez, n.d.) and consequently physically marks the women after he has been killed off (the stain on the heroine's forehead in "The Bloody Chamber," the "crimson imprint of his love-bite" on the freed bird-girls in "The Erl-King"), her overall analysis fails to account for the intertextual specificity of each of the stories and for Carter's ongoing interrogation of the importance Lacan grants the Law of the Father.

7. See Linkin (1994) for an alternative interpretation of the extended scene ("The wind stirs the dark wood. . . . Yet when he shakes out those two clear notes from his bird call, I come, like any other trusting thing," Carter, 1993: 87–88), which she reads as the heroine's fear of dependence as opposed to a fear of her desire and what that desire represents. For Linkin the "romantic subjugation of the female to the male" implicit in this scene derives from the Erl-King's resonances with the "Shelleyan persona" of his "Ode to the West Wind" and suggests that, although the heroine recognizes her complicity in the Erl-King's seductive call, she does not know how to resist it (Linkin, 1994: 316).

8. Lorna Sage describes Ophelia as "one of the images that haunts [Carter's] fiction, one of her most poignant and persistent borrowings . . . the image of crazy, dying Ophelia, as described by Gertrude in Shakespeare's *Hamlet*, and (possibly even more) as painted by Millais: waterlogged, draped in flowers, drifting downstream to her virgin death" (1994: 33). Christina Britzolakis

also highlights Carter's frequent invocation of Ophelia, particularly in her early fiction: "The text [*Love*] is preoccupied with representations, fantasies and icons of female madness, a point underscored when Lee buys Annabel a print of Millais's 'Ophelia.' . . . Carter's later novels leave behind the Ophelia plot (though it is worth noticing that *Wise Children* resurrects it in the figure of Tiffany)" (1997: 48). And, in an early version of "The Tiger's Bride" titled "La Bestia," Carter describes the heroine's mirror image through the trope of Ophelia: "She swam on the transparent depths of the glass; she swam, upheld by the white lace, like drowning Ophelia" ("The Bloody Chamber and Other Stories" 2, MS 88899/1/34 [1975–1979], Angela Carter Papers, British Library).

9. Ophelia's own descent into madness, when read in conjunction with her father's and brother's efforts to ensure her proper feminine behavior, encapsulates the doubling dramatized by nineteenth-century women writers and challenges the patriarchal definition of women's madness. Indeed, in her madness Ophelia undoes the patriarchal constraints represented by the lessons in gendered propriety that Polonius and Laertes force on her. These lessons, traditionally collected in *anthologies* (from the Greek for "bouquet") of proverbial wisdom, are metaphorically destroyed when Ophelia, at the height of her madness, tears apart her bouquet to distribute the individual flowers. I am grateful to Sean Keilen for providing this insight.

10. For alternative readings of this shift in tense, see Engle (1999), Fludernik (1998), and Linkin (1994). Linkin and Fludernik both interpret it in relation to the heroine's authorial voice, whereas Engle reads the "unintelligibility" of the final sentence, together with this shift in tense and voice, as fostering a productive "sense of incompleteness and possibility" (42–43).

11. Gerardo Rodríguez Salas (2010) also reads in "The Erl-King" an intentional ambiguity; however, he argues that Carter's intentional ambiguity permeates the story and creates an alternative feminism capable of mediating the conflicting critical positions on Carter's feminist politics.

12. Cristina Bacchilega insightfully reads this scene as a "highly concentrated and parodic version of the traditional fairy-tale heroine's initiation" (1997: 37). She argues that the Snow Child's death and rape, the impossibility of her rebirth into adult sexuality, underscore her status as nothing more than "passive object of the Count's desire" (38).

13. Bacchilega (1997) notes that the summary of this version of "Snow White" uses the German term *mädchen*, meaning both "maiden" or "girl," as Bettelheim translates it, and "child," to refer to the articulation and eventual materialization of the Count's desire.

14. By emphasizing the Countess's exteriority and thus implying such a possibility, Carter once again advances a mother-daughter relationship outside the hegemony of female rivalry, as she does in "The Bloody Chamber." Carter's discussion in *The Sadeian Woman* of the ways that Western European culture and psychoanalytic theory foster competition and rivalry between women is relevant to both examples. See Chapter 1 for a more detailed discussion.

15. The Sleeping Beauty, as trope and as allusion, appears in a number of Carter's novels and short stories, including *The Infernal Desire Machines of Doctor Hoffman* (1972), *Nights at the Circus* (1984), "The Fall River Axe Murders" (1985), "The Loves of Lady Purple" (1974), and of course, "The Lady of the House of Love," discussed in Chapter 5. For an extended reading of the "Sleeping Beauty" motif in *The Infernal Desire Machines of Doctor Hoffman*, see Mikkonen (2001).
16. Journal, MS 88899/1/95 (1973), Angela Carter Papers, British Library.
17. Barchilon also suggests that the Count's rape of the Snow Child is his attempt to revive her: "What can the father do? In Angela Carter's surreal world of sortilege, mouth to mouth resuscitation will not do. A stronger medicine is administered by the desperate and grieving father" (1988: 221). However, in an early draft of the story, Carter makes clear that the Count's rape is not an attempt to resuscitate the Snow Child as a material girl but rather "to keep his desire alive as long as he could" (Journal, MS 88899/1/96 [1977], Angela Carter Papers, British Library).

Chapter 5

1. Perrault's version continues through a series of trials prompted by the prince's ogre-mother's attempts to eat Sleeping Beauty and their children.
2. Although the Grimms' *Kinder- und Hausmärchen* was first published in 1812 and 1815, Jack Zipes's 1987 translation, *The Complete Fairy Tales of the Brothers Grimm*, is based on their final 1857 version.
3. In Basile's version, Talia eventually wakes when one of the twins unintentionally removes the splinter from her finger while seeking to suckle and finding her finger instead of her breast. The tale continues much as Perrault's version after Talia's awakening, although the antagonist is the King's wife, not his ogre-mother.
4. See, for instance, Mikkonen (2001), Peng (2004), Sage (2001: 72, 76), Sceats (2001), and Wisker (1997). Mikkonen traces the intertextual references to "Sleeping Beauty" and to the tales of E. T. A. Hoffmann in Carter's novel *The Infernal Desire Machines of Doctor Hoffman*, underscoring the necrophiliac impulses that structure the plot and drive both of the main characters: Desiderio "makes love to this 'beautiful somnambulist' when she is sleeping, then goes to see pictures of sleeping beauties in peep show machines the following morning, and is finally charged with the murder of this fairy tale–like woman," whereas Doctor Hoffmann embalms his dead wife and keeps her in his castle, his "love for a corpse . . . another instance of necrophilia" (2001: 176).
5. Even though Carter sees in Sade a potential for moral pornography, Sade ultimately fails to deliver on that full potential because he never breaks free of patriarchal society. For Carter this is particularly evident in Sade's limited view of the mother in *Philosophy in the Boudoir* and his ultimate fear of the redemptive power of love. See Carter (2006: 135–59 and 176).

6. See Hennard Dutheil de la Rochère (2011) for a countervailing reading of the story with Perrault's version as the primary fairy-tale intertext.
7. In *The Sadeian Woman* Carter distinguishes between meat and flesh by emphasizing their differences in relation to sensuality (2006: 161–63). In this case Carter inverts the more common cultural practice of rendering women's flesh as meat in a move consistent with her characterization of the hero in terms more traditionally reserved for fairy-tale princesses (e.g., "He has the special quality of virginity, most and least ambiguous of states: ignorance, yet at the same time, power in potentia," Carter, 1993: 97). In general, Carter's characterization of the hero as naïve and virginal serves to highlight the predatory qualities of the Countess.
8. See, for instance, Jordan (1998), Makinen (1992), Peng (2004), Sage (2001), and Tucker (1998) for discussions of the mixed responses to Carter's stories.
9. In her radio play *Vampirella*, a precursor to "The Lady of the House of Love" (Crofts, 2003: 27–28), Carter makes explicit the sexual *and* marital desire for a corpse. The character Henri Blot explains to a judge his reason for taking corpses from the cemetery for his personal pleasures: "Corpses don't nag and never want new dresses. They never waste all day at the hairdressers, nor talk for hours to their girl-friends on the telephone. They never complain if you stay out at your club; the dinner won't get cold if it's never been put in the oven. Chaste, thrifty—why, they never spend a penny on themselves! and endlessly accommodating. They never want to come themselves, nor demand of a man any of those beastly sophistications—blowing in the ears, nibbling at the nipples, tickling of the clit—that are so onerous to a man of passion. Doesn't it make your mouth water? Husbands, let me recommend the last word in conjugal bliss—a corpse" (Carter, 1976). Carter takes her necrophiliac brothel scene from Léo Taxil's 1890 *La corruption fin-de-siècle* (1973).
10. Hagopian (2007) reads the "House of Love" in this manner and then interprets it in relation to the story of Eros and Psyche in Apuleius's tale.
11. See, for example, Belford (1996: 9), Demetrakopoulos (1977: 105), Miller (2006), Pikula (2012: 283, 299), and Signorotti (1996: 623).
12. Signorotti (1996) details the many ways that Stoker diminishes women's agency in marriage by situating them in male systems of power. One especially notable example is when Lucy's mother, the widow Mrs. Westenra, transfers her estate (and Lucy's inheritance) to Lucy's fiancé, Arthur Holmwood, even before their wedding, thus "[ensuring] Lucy's total dependence on her future husband" (623).
13. Although Carmilla is killed by a group of men who represent a range of patriarchal institutions—Laura's father, General Spielsdorf, a baron familiar with Carmilla's history, a priest, and representatives of the legal Inquisition—Laura is not present for the staking and beheading, thus allowing Carmilla to live in her imagination. As she writes at the conclusion of her narrative account, "To this hour the image of Carmilla returns to memory with ambiguous alternations—sometimes the playful, languid,

beautiful girl; sometimes the writhing fiend I saw in the ruined church; and often from a reverie I have started, fancying I heard the light step of Carmilla at the dressing-room door" (Le Fanu, 2003: 148). Thus, despite consigning Carmilla to literal death, Le Fanu allows Carmilla, and Laura, to escape complete patriarchal control.

14. For Carter the killing off of women's sexual desire and agency is especially clear as women become mothers; in *The Sadeian Woman* Carter argues that it is in Sade's refusal to grant Eugenie's mother any pleasure that his conservatism and limitations as a possible moral pornographer are most evident. Thus for Carter fairy-tale love and marriage are especially deadly in a sexist society because they imply motherhood and the death of sexual desire and pleasure.

15. Carter's description of the hero's rationality calls to mind the hyperrationality of Stoker's Crew of Light and Dr. John Seward in particular: "A fundamental disbelief in what he sees before him sustains him, even in the boudoir of Countess Nosferatu herself; he would have said, perhaps, that there are some things which, even if they *are* true, we should not believe possible. He might have said: it is folly to believe one's eyes" (Carter, 1993: 103–104; emphasis in original). This passage echoes Van Helsing's words to Seward as he tries to convince him of Lucy's vampirism: "You are a clever man, friend John; you reason well, and your wit is bold; but you are too prejudiced. You do not let your eyes see nor your ears hear, and that which is outside your daily life is not of account to you. Do you not think there are things which you cannot understand, and yet which are; that some people see that that others cannot?" (Stoker, 2011: 178). Although Van Helsing is forced to challenge Seward in order to convince him of Lucy's vampirism, once convinced he and the Crew of Light continue to rely on technology, scientific observation, and reason in order to conquer Dracula. Thus throughout *Dracula* Stoker furthers the cultural myth of the rational male and the emotional/embodied female, a myth that Carter questions and dismisses with her similarly rational but ultimately ineffective hero.

16. In the Grimms' fairy tale "The Story of a Boy Who Went Forth to Learn Fear" (ATU 326), the boy learns to shudder only in marriage, when his wife, the princess awarded to him for redeeming the haunted castle, tires of his talking about his inability to shudder and throws a bucket of cold water full of minnows on him while he sleeps. In noting that her hero "will learn to shudder in the trenches" and in drawing attention to this fairy tale, Carter seems to imply a certain equation between marriage and war, another critique of fairy-tale romance and the cultural myth of marriage as a relationship of love (as opposed to one of power and labor, as she contends in *The Sadeian Woman*, 2006: 7–15).

17. "Disidentification" is José Muñoz's term for the "survival strategies" (1999: 4) that allow for a complex (re)engagement with dominant interpellations.

Chapter 6

1. Wendy Swyt reads "The Company of Wolves" in similar fashion. Arguing against Robert Clark's patriarchal reading "in which the wolf is 'essentially coercing her' to perform a 'strip tease' for him which she agrees to with '*surprising* readiness'" (1996: 322; emphasis in original), Swyt suggests that "the girl's alliance with the wolf attests to more than just a rewritten feminist ending" (315).
2. Journal, MS 88899/1/95 (1973), Angela Carter Papers, British Library.
3. See Hennard Dutheil de la Rochère (2013) for an excellent and detailed analysis of how Carter's research for and translation of *The Fairy Tales of Charles Perrault* influenced *The Bloody Chamber* and her other fairy tales.
4. Carter describes the appeal of the "Good Bad Girl," epitomized by Marilyn Monroe, in a section titled "The Blonde as Clown" in *The Sadeian Woman* (2006: 65–81). In a particularly relevant passage, she writes: "The Good Bad Girl is celebrated for her allure but this allure is never allowed to overwhelm the spectator. Besides, she has not got enough self-confidence to overwhelm men. She has to rely on a childlike charm, she has more in common with Mary Pickford than with Mae West; she must make up to the paedophile in men, in order to reassure both men and herself that her own sexuality will not reveal to them their own inadequacy" (76–77).
5. Micah Perks offers an insightful political reading of this trend in relation to the post-9/11 emergence of a regressive femininity in her essay "All Tied Up: *Homeland* and the Female Fabulists" (2013). She argues, along with Susan Faludi, that 9/11 and the ensuing war on terror inspired women to perform the role of "vulnerable maidens" (Faludi, quoted in Perks, 2013) to support the cultural fantasy of heroic hypermasculinity. As Perks makes clear, this renewed cultural desire for the childlike woman is one in which women are, at least, as complicit as men: "A few years after 9/11, I began noticing that many of my undergrads had started referring to themselves as 'girls' instead of 'women'; some began to dress like little girls as well, in knee-high socks and short skirts. Indeed, according to the website 'History of Fashion,' in the years after 9/11 women's clothes became more 'feminine, excessive and "anti-modern."' My female students often wore heavy eye make-up that made them look like 'vulnerable maidens,' too, like little match girls begging to be let in from the cold."
6. In the journal notes for her "Red Riding Hood" and werewolf stories, Carter summarizes key scenes from Delarue's "Story of Grandmother": "She undresses in front of the wolf-grandmother; after she removes each garment, she asks wolf-grandmother what she must do with it. 'Jette-le au feu, mon enfant, tu n'en as plus besoin.' The wolf asks the child: 'Quel chemin prends-tu? Celui des Épingle ou celui des Aigulles?'" (Journal, MS 88899/1/95 [1973], Angela Carter Papers, British Library). She also notes the cannibalistic aspect of the story from Lang: "In the popular version, in Brittany & the Nièv, the wolf puts the grandmother in the pot & her blood in bottles, & makes the unconscious child eat & drink her ancestors! The cock or the robin

redbreast warns her in vain, & she is swallowed" (Journal, MS 88899/1/95 [1973], Angela Carter Papers, British Library).
7. I am grateful to JoAnn Conrad for continually pushing against a progressive history of the fairy tale as moving from oral (and, implicitly, more feminist) to written (and, implicitly, more patriarchal) and for pointing out moments when I inadvertently invoke such a narrative in the previously published version of this chapter (Lau, 2008).
8. See, in particular, Clark (1987). Swyt (1996) offers a thorough and convincing rejoinder to Clark.
9. Carter was herself familiar with Freud's work on smell and civilization, particularly in the context of menstruation, and she quotes from *The Wise Wound: Menstruation and Everywoman*, by Penelope Shuttle and Peter Redgrave, on the topic in one of her journals: "Perfumes bring scenes back; it is for this reason that Freud argues that with our two-legged posture we have surmounted a primitive stage of evolution, carrying our noses proudly in the air. Therefore this archaic sense of smell will carry all the primitive dangers & energies with it" (Journal, MS 88899/1/96 [1977], Angela Carter Papers, British Library).
10. For alternative readings of this scene, see Dimovitz (2010) and Schanoes (2012). Dimovitz argues that the scene represents Wolf-Alice's entry into the Symbolic Order and thus her acquiescence to patriarchy: "With this highly syncopated syntax, a rarity for Carter, 'Wolf-Alice' ends with the image of the newly-subjected girl, who had rejected the superior mother, passed through the mirror stage and taken on the symbols of patriarchy (licking the filth from the Duke, so that *his* mirror image appeared 'as if brought into being,)" (2010: 14; emphasis in original). Schanoes, on the other hand, interprets Wolf-Alice's licking as the maternal, mature care that establishes the Duke's—and her own—humanity, a humanity dependent on the possibility of multiple subject positions within the mirror: "It is no accident that their rapprochement comes when they are both able to occupy a multiplicity of roles and subject positions, including the subjectivity of the mother" (2012: 35). Although both Dimovitz and Schanoes draw on the significance of the mirror in psychoanalytic theory to ground their interpretations of this scene, their readings differ based on their particular perspectives within psychoanalytic theory; where Dimovitz follows Lacan's theory of the mirror stage, Schanoes invokes Irigaray's theory of the mirror and maternal subjectivity. For a discussion of the mirror in relation to the fantasy genre more generally, including Carter's *Bloody Chamber*, see Schanoes (2009).
11. Zipes's identification of the mutual desire between the girl and the wolf is a minor part of his overarching argument that the literary versions of "Little Red Riding Hood" reflect Perrault's and the Grimms' patriarchal appropriation of the more feminist oral tradition; as such, he contends that they transform the story of a young woman's social initiation into a rape narrative in which the

girl is made to take the blame for her victimization. Within this context the girl's desire for the wolf can only ever be transgressive and inappropriate. See Zipes (1983b) for his extended discussion and historical analysis and Zipes (1983a) for an analysis of the illustrated history of the tale as reinforcing and perpetuating this patriarchal appropriation.

Epilogue

1. A notable exception is "The Frog Prince" (KHM 1), in which the princess's throwing the frog against the wall disenchants the prince.
2. Notepad, MS 88899/1/101 (1972), Angela Carter Papers, British Library.

Bibliography

American Psychological Association, Task Force on the Sexualization of Girls. 2007. *Report of the APA Task Force on the Sexualization of Girls*. Washington, DC: American Psychological Association.

Andermahr, Sonya, and Lawrence Phillips, eds. 2012. *Angela Carter: New Critical Readings*. London: Continuum.

Armitt, Lucie. 1997. "The Fragile Frames of *The Bloody Chamber*." In *The Infernal Desires of Angela Carter: Fiction, Femininity, Feminism*, ed. Joseph Bristow and Trev Lynn Broughton. London: Longman, 88–99.

Atwood, Margaret. 2007 [1994]. "Running with the Tigers." In *Essays on the Art of Angela Carter: Flesh and the Mirror*, ed. Lorna Sage. London: Virago, 133–50.

Bacchilega, Cristina. 1995. "Sex Slaves and Saints? Resisting Masochism in Angela Carter's 'The Bloody Chamber.'" In *Across the Oceans: Studies from East to West in Honor of Richard K. Seymour*, ed. Irmengard Rauch and Cornelia Moore. Honolulu: University of Hawaii Press, 77–86.

———. 1997. *Postmodern Fairy Tales: Gender and Narrative Strategies*. Philadelphia: University of Pennsylvania Press.

Barchilon, Jacques. 1988. "Confessions of a Fairy-Tale Lover." *The Lion and the Unicorn* 12(2): 208–23.

———. 1993. "Personal Reflections on the Scholarly Reception of Grimms' Tales in France." In *The Reception of Grimms' Fairy Tales: Responses, Reactions, Revisions*, ed. Donald Haase. Detroit: Wayne State University Press, 269–82.

Barthes, Roland. 2001 [1977]. *A Lover's Discourse: Fragments*, trans. Richard Howard. New York: Farrar, Straus & Giroux.

Barzilai, Shuli. 2009. *Tales of Bluebeard and His Wives from Late Antiquity to Postmodern Times*. New York: Routledge.

Beaumont, Marie Leprince de. 1783 [1756]. *The Young Misses Magazine, Containing Dialogues Between a Governess and Several Young Ladies of Quality Her Scholars*, 4th ed. London: C. Nourse.

Belford, Barbara. 1996. *Bram Stoker: A Biography of the Author of "Dracula."* London: Weidenfeld & Nicolson.

Bennett, Jane. 2001. *The Enchantment of Modern Life: Attachments, Crossings, and Ethics*. Princeton, NJ: Princeton University Press.

Bettelheim, Bruno. 1989 [1976]. *The Uses of Enchantment: The Meaning and Importance of Fairy Tales*. New York: Vintage Books.
Bly, Robert. 1990. *Iron John: A Book About Men*. New York: Addison-Wesley.
Bottigheimer, Ruth B. 1986. "Silenced Women in the Grimms' Tales: The 'Fit' Between Fairy Tales and Society in Their Historical Context." In *Fairy Tales and Society: Illusion, Allusion, and Paradigm*, ed. Ruth B. Bottigheimer. Philadelphia: University of Pennsylvania Press, 53–74.
Britzolakis, Christina. 1997. "Angela Carter's Fetishism." In *The Infernal Desires of Angela Carter: Fiction, Femininity, Feminism*, ed. Joseph Bristow and Trev Lynn Broughton. London: Longman, 43–58.
Brooke, Patricia. 2004. "Lyons and Tigers and Wolves—Oh My! Revisionary Fairy Tales in the Work of Angela Carter." *Critical Survey* 16(1): 67–88.
Bryant, Sylvia. 1989. "Re-Constructing Oedipus Through 'Beauty and the Beast.'" *Criticism* 31(4): 439–53.
Buchel, Michelle Nelmarie. 2003. "'Bankrupt Enchantments' and 'Fraudulent Magic': Demythologising in Angela Carter's *The Bloody Chamber* and *Nights at the Circus*." PhD diss., University of Pretoria.
Burlein, Ann, and Jackie Orr. 2012. "The Practice of Enchantment: Strange Allures." *Women's Studies Quarterly* 40(3–4): 13–23.
Burnett, Frances Hodgson. 2010 [1911]. *The Secret Garden*. London: Harper Collins.
Canepa, Nancy L., trans. 2007. *Giambattista Basile's "The Tale of Tales, or Entertainment for Little Ones."* Detroit: Wayne State University Press.
Carter, Angela. 1976. *Vampirella*. Radio 4 Original Broadcast, July 20.
———. 1985. *Come Unto These Yellow Sands*. Newcastle: Bloodaxe.
———. 1991. Review of *Beauty and the Beast: Visions and Revisions of an Old Tale*, by Betsy Hearne. *Folklore* 102(1): 123–24.
———. 1993 [1979]. *The Bloody Chamber and Other Stories*. New York: Penguin.
———. 1998a [1978]. "The Alchemy of the Word." Reprinted in her *Shaking a Leg: Collected Writings*. New York: Penguin, 507–12.
———. 1998b [1976]. "The Better to Eat You With." Reprinted in her *Shaking a Leg: Collected Writings*. New York: Penguin, 451–55.
———. 1998c [1983]. "Notes from the Front Line." Reprinted in her *Shaking a Leg: Collected Writings*. New York: Penguin, 38–43.
———. 2006 [1979]. *The Sadeian Woman: An Exercise in Cultural History*. London: Virago.
Case, Sue-Ellen. 1991. "Tracking the Vampire." *Differences* 3(2): 1–20.
Cavallaro, Dani. 2011. *The World of Angela Carter: A Critical Investigation*. London: McFarland.
Chainani, Soman. 2003. "Sadeian Tragedy: The Politics of Content Revision in Angela Carter's 'Snow Child.'" *Marvels & Tales* 17(2): 212–35.
Clark, Robert. 1987. "Angela Carter's Desire Machine." *Women's Studies* 14: 147–61.
Crofts, Charlotte. 2003. *"Anagrams of Desire": Angela Carter's Writing for Radio, Film, and Television*. Manchester, UK: Manchester University Press.
Crunelle-Vanrigh, Anny. 2001. "The Logic of the Same and *Différance*: 'The Courtship of Mr. Lyon.'" In *Angela Carter and the Fairy Tale*, ed. Danielle M.

Roemer and Cristina Bacchilega. Detroit: Wayne State University Press, 128–44.
Day, Aidan. 1998. *Angela Carter: The Rational Glass*. Manchester, UK: Manchester University Press.
Demetrakopoulos, Stephanie. 1977. "Feminism, Sex Role Exchanges, and Other Subliminal Fantasies in Bram Stoker's *Dracula*." *Frontiers: A Journal of Women Studies* 2(3): 104–33.
Derrida, Jacques. 2009. *The Beast and the Sovereign*, v. 1, trans. Geoffrey Bennington. Chicago: University of Chicago Press.
Dimovitz, Scott. 2010. "'I Was the Subject of the Sentence Written on the Mirror': Angela Carter's Short Fiction and the Unwriting of the Psychoanalytic Subject." *LIT: Literature Interpretation Theory* 21(1): 1–19.
Dowling, Colette. 1982. *The Cinderella Complex: Women's Hidden Fear of Independence*. New York: Simon & Schuster.
Duggan, Anne. 1996. "Women Subdued: The Abjectification and Purification of Female Characters in Perrault's Tales." *Romantic Review* 99(3–4): 211–26.
Duncker, Patricia. 1984. "Re-Imagining the Fairy Tales: Angela Carter's Bloody Chambers." *Literature and History* 10(1): 3–14.
Dye, Ellis. 2004. *Love and Death in Goethe: "One and Double."* Rochester, UK: Camden House.
Engle, Karen Jane. 1999. "Through a Glass Darkly, or, Intertextual Travel and Angela Carter's De/Constructions of Identity." Master's thesis, University of Alberta.
Fabian, Jenny. 2011. "Love, Terror, and Emancipation: Angela Carter's Interrogation of Authority in *The Bloody Chamber*." *London Grip*, online ed., May 6. http://londongrip.co.uk/wp-content/uploads/2011/06/Literature_Angela_Carter_Jenny_Fabian.pdf (accessed July 3, 2013).
Faulk, Malcolm. 1973. "'Frigidity': A Critical Review." *Archives of Sexual Behavior* 2(3): 257–66.
Feuerlicht, Ignace. 1959. "'Erlkönig' and 'Turn of the Screw.'" *Journal of English and Germanic Philology* 58(1): 68–74.
Fludernik, Monika. 1998. "Angela Carter's Pronomial Acrobatics: Language in 'The Erl-King' and 'The Company of Wolves.'" *European Journal of English Studies* 2(2): 215–37.
Ford, Michael. 1996a. *Happily Ever After: Erotic Fairy Tales for Queer Men*. New York: Masquerade.
———. 1996b. *Once Upon A Time: Erotic Fairy Tales for Women*. New York: Masquerade.
Freud, Sigmund. 1962 [1905]. *Three Essays on the Theory of Sexuality*, trans. and ed. James Strachey. New York: Basic.
Gallop, Jane. 1982. *The Daughter's Seduction: Feminism and Psychoanalysis*. Ithaca, NY: Cornell University Press.
Gamble, Sarah. 1997. *Angela Carter: Writing from the Front Line*. Edinburgh: Edinburgh University Press.
———. 2006. *Angela Carter: A Literary Life*. New York: Palgrave Macmillan.

———. 2008. "Penetrating to the Heart of the Bloody Chamber: Angela Carter and the Fairy Tale." In *Contemporary Fiction and the Fairy Tale*, ed. Stephen Benson. Detroit: Wayne State University Press, 20–46.

Geoffroy-Menoux, Sophie. 1996. "Angela Carter's *The Bloody Chamber*: Twice Harnessed Folk-Tales." *Para-doxa* 2(2): 249–62.

Gilbert, Sandra, and Susan Gubar. 1979. *The Madwoman in the Attic: The Woman Writer and the Nineteenth-Century Literary Imagination*. New Haven, CT: Yale University Press.

Grimm, Jacob, and Wilhelm Grimm. 1987 [1857]. "Brier Rose." In *The Complete Fairy Tales of the Brothers Grimm*, trans. Jack Zipes. New York: Bantam, 186–89.

Griswold, Jerry. 2004. *The Meanings of "Beauty and the Beast": A Handbook*. Ontario: Broadview Press.

Gubar, Susan. 1979. "Mother, Maiden and the Marriage of Death: Women Writers and an Ancient Myth." *Women's Studies* 6(3): 301–15.

Haase, Donald. 2011. "Kiss and Tell: Orality, Narrative, and the Power of Words in 'Sleeping Beauty.'" *Etudes du Lettres* 3–4: 279–98.

Haffenden, John. 1985. "Angela Carter." In his *Novelists in Interview*. London: Methuen, 76–96.

Hagopian, Katherine A. 2007. "Apuleius and Gothic Narrative in Carter's 'The Lady of the House of Love.'" *Explicator* 66(1): 52–55.

Hearne, Betsy. 1989. *Beauty and the Beast: Visions and Revisions of an Old Tale*. Chicago: University of Chicago Press.

Henke, Suzette A. 2013. "A Bloody Shame: Angela Carter's Shameless Postmodern Fairy Tales." In *The Female Face of Shame*, ed. Erica L. Johnson and Patricia Moran. Bloomington: Indiana University Press, 48–60.

Hennard Dutheil [de la Rochère], Martine. 2006. "Modelling for Bluebeard: Visual and Narrative Art in Angela Carter's 'The Bloody Chamber.'" In *The Seeming and the Seen: Essays in Modern Visual and Literary Culture*, ed. Beverly Maeder, Jürg Schwyter, Ilona Sigrist, and Boris Vejdovsky. Bern: Peter Lang, 183–208.

Hennard Dutheil de la Rochère, Martine. 2011. "Conjuring the Curse of Repetition or 'Sleeping Beauty' Revamped: Angela Carter's *Vampirella* and *The Lady of the House of Love*." *Études de Lettres* 3–4: 337–58.

———. 2013. *Reading, Translating, Rewriting: Angela Carter's Translational Poetics*. Detroit: Wayne State University Press.

Hennard Dutheil de la Rochère, Martine, and Ute Heidmann. 2009. "'New Wine in Old Bottles': Angela Carter's Translation of Charles Perrault's 'La Barbe bleu.'" *Marvels & Tales* 23(1): 40–58.

Hermansson, Casie. 2001. *Reading Feminist Intertextuality Through Bluebeard Stories*. Lewiston, NY: Edwin Mellen.

———. 2009. *Bluebeard: A Reader's Guide to the English Translation*. Jackson: University of Mississippi Press.

Heru, Alison M. 2003. "Gender and the Gaze: A Cultural and Psychological Review." *International Journal of Psychotherapy* 8(2): 109–16.

Homans, Margaret. 1986. *Bearing the Word: Language and Female Experience in Nineteenth-Century Women's Writing*. Chicago: University of Chicago Press.

Hyatte, Reginald, trans. 1984. *Laughter for the Devil: The Trials of Gilles de Rais, Companion-in-Arms to Joan of Arc*. Rutherford, NJ: Fairleigh Dickinson University Press.

Irigaray, Luce. 1985 [1977]. *This Sex Which Is Not One*, trans. Catherine Porter. Ithaca, NY: Cornell University Press.

Jacobson, Lisa. 1993. "Tales of Violence and Desire: Angela Carter's 'The Bloody Chamber.'" *Antithesis* 6(2): 81–90.

Jordan, Elaine. 1998 [1992]. "The Dangers of Angela Carter." Reprinted in *Critical Essays on Angela Carter*, ed. Lindsey Tucker. New York: G. K. Hall, 33–45.

———. 2007 [1994]. "The Dangerous Edge." In *Essays on the Art of Angela Carter: Flesh and the Mirror*, ed. Lorna Sage. London: Virago, 201–26.

Kaiser, Mary. 1994. "Fairy Tale as Sexual Allegory: Intertextuality in Angela Carter's *The Bloody Chamber*." *Review of Contemporary Fiction* 14(3): 30–36.

Kilbourne, Jean. 1999a. *Deadly Persuasion: Why Women and Girls Must Fight the Addictive Power of Advertising*. New York: Free Press.

———. 1999b. *Killing Us Softly 3: Advertising's Image of Women*. Video. Northampton, MA: Media Education Foundation.

Lang, Andrew. c. 1889. *The Blue Fairy Book*. London: Longmans, Green, 290–95. www.pitt.edu/~dash/perrault03.html (accessed July 9, 2012).

Lassman, Peter. 2000. "The Rule of Man over Man: Politics, Power, and Legitimation." In *The Cambridge Companion to Weber*, ed. Stephen P. Turner. Cambridge, UK: Cambridge University Press, 83–98.

Lau, Kimberly J. 2008. "Erotic Infidelities: Angela Carter's Wolf Trilogy." *Marvels & Tales* 22(1): 77–94.

Law, Holly. n.d. "Folklore of the Erlkonig." https://sites.google.com/site/folkloreoftheerlkonig/home/history-of-the-erlkonig-poem (accessed July 3, 2013).

Lawley, Paul. 2001. "'The Grim Journey': Beckett Listens to Schubert." *Samuel Beckett Today* 11: 255–66.

Le Fanu, Sheridan. 2003 [1872]. "Carmilla." In *Three Vampire Tales*, ed. Anne Williams. Boston: Houghton Mifflin, 86–148.

Levin, Richard. 1982. "The Indian/Iudean Crux in Othello." *Shakespeare Quarterly* 33(91): 60–67.

Lewallen, Avis. 1988. "Wayward Girls but Wicked Women? Female Sexuality in Angela Carter's *The Bloody Chamber*." In *Perspectives on Pornography: Sexuality in Film and Literature*, ed. Gary Day and Clive Bloom. New York: St. Martin's, 144–58.

Linkin, Harriet Kramer. 1994. "Isn't It Romantic: Angela Carter's Bloody Revision of the Romantic Aesthetic in 'The Erl-King.'" *Contemporary Literature* 35(2): 305–23.

Lloyd, Joan Elizabeth. 2005. *Naughty Bedtime Stories*, Harmondsworth, UK: Penguin.

Lorde, Audre. 1984 [1978]. "Uses of the Erotic: The Erotic as Power." In her *Sister Outsider: Essays and Speeches*. Trumansburg, NY: Crossing Press, 53–59.

Losada Pérez, Ana Maria. n.d. "'In Me More than Myself': The Monstrous as a Site of Fear and Desire in Angela Carter's 'The Bloody Chamber' and 'The Erl-King.'"

www.inter-disciplinary.net/wp-content/uploads/2009/08/draft_m7_analosada1.pdf (accessed August 3, 2012).

Madore, Nancy. 2006. *Enchanted: Erotic Bedtime Stories for Women*. Buffalo, NY: Spice.

Makinen, Merja. 1992. "Angela Carter's *The Bloody Chamber* and the Decolonization of Feminine Sexuality." *Feminist Review* 42(autumn): 2–15.

Manley, Kathleen E. B. 2001 [1998]. "The Woman in Process in Angela Carter's 'The Bloody Chamber.'" In *Angela Carter and the Fairy Tale*, ed. Danielle M. Roemer and Cristina Bacchilega. Detroit: Wayne State University Press, 83–93.

McCallum, E. L. 1995. "How to Do Things with Fetishism." *Differences* 7(3): 24–49.

McLaughlin, Becky. 1995. "Perverse Pleasure and Fetishized Text: The Deathly Erotics of Carter's 'The Bloody Chamber.'" *Style* 29(3): 404–58.

Merskin, Debra. 2004. "Reviving Lolita? A Media Literacy Examination of Sexual Portrayals of Girls in Fashion Advertising." *American Behavioral Scientist* 48: 119–29.

Metzl, Jonathan. 2004. "From Scopophilia to Survivor: A Brief History of Voyeurism." *Textual Practice* 18(3): 415–34.

Mikkonen, Kai. 2001 [1998]. "The Hoffman(n) Effect and the Sleeping Prince: Fairy Tales in Angela Carter's *The Infernal Desire Machines of Doctor Hoffman*." In *Angela Carter and the Fairy Tale*, ed. Danielle M. Roemer and Cristina Bacchilega. Detroit: Wayne State University Press, 167–86.

Miller, Elizabeth. 2006. "Coitus Interruptus: Sex, Bram Stoker, and *Dracula*." *Romanticism on the Net* 44(November). www.erudit.org/revue/ron/2006/v/n44/014002ar.html?action=envoyer (accessed May 11, 2012).

Moglen, Helene. 1976. *Charlotte Brontë: The Self Conceived*. New York: Norton.

Mulvey, Laura. 1975. "Visual Pleasure and Narrative Cinema." *Screen* 16(3): 6–18.

Muñoz, José Esteban. 1999. *Disidentifications: Queers of Color and the Performance of Politics*. Minneapolis: University of Minnesota Press.

Orenstein, Catherine. 2002. *Little Red Riding Hood Uncloaked: Sex, Morality, and the Evolution of a Fairy Tale*. New York: Basic Books.

Peng, Emma Pi-tai. 2004. "Angela Carter's Postmodern Feminism and the Gothic Uncanny." *NTU Studies in Language and Literature* 13: 99–134.

Perks, Micah. 2013. "All Tied Up: *Homeland* and the Female Fabulists." *The Rumpus*, online ed., April 13. http://therumpus.net/2013/04/saturday-rumpus-essay-all-tied-up-homeland-and-the-female-fabulists/ (accessed August 26, 2013).

Perrault, Charles. 1977a. [1697]. "La Belle au Bois Dormant." In *The Fairy Tales of Charles Perrault*, trans. Angela Carter. New York: Avon, 57–71.

———. 1977b [1697]. *The Fairy Tales of Charles Perrault*, trans. Angela Carter. New York: Avon.

Pichois, Claude. 1989. *Baudelaire*, trans. Graham Robb. London: Hamish Hamilton.

Pikula, Tanya. 2012. "Bram Stoker's *Dracula* and Late-Victorian Advertising Tactics: Earnest Men, Virtuous Ladies, and Porn." *English Literature in Translation* 55(3): 283–302.

Pollock, Mary S. 2000. "Angela Carter's Animal Tales: Constructing the Non-Human." *LIT: Literature Interpretation Theory* 11(1): 35–57.

Pyrhönen, Heta. 2007. "Imagining the Impossible: The Erotic Poetics of Angela Carter's 'Bluebeard' Stories." *Textual Practice* 21(1): 93–111.

Renfroe, Cheryl. 2001 [1998]. "Initiation and Disobedience: Liminal Experience in Angela Carter's 'The Bloody Chamber.'" Reprinted in *Angela Carter and the Fairy Tale*, ed. Danielle M. Roemer and Cristina Bacchilega. Detroit: Wayne State University Press, 94–106.

Roemer, Danielle M. 2001 [1998]. "The Contextualization of the Marquis in Angela Carter's 'The Bloody Chamber.'" Reprinted in *Angela Carter and the Fairy Tale*, ed. Danielle M. Roemer and Cristina Bacchilega. Detroit: Wayne State University Press, 107–27.

Rollins, Hillary. 2001. *The Empress's New Lingerie and Other Erotic Fairy Tales*. New York: Harmony.

Roquelaure, A. N. [Anne Rice]. 1999. *Sleeping Beauty Trilogy*. New York: Plume.

Rose, Isabelle. 2010. *Naughty Fairy Tales*, v. 1. Self-published.

Rossetti, Christina. 1970 [1863]. *Selected Poems of Christina Rossetti*, ed. Marya Zatursenka. New York: Macmillan.

Rowe, Karen E. 1979. "Feminism and Fairy Tales." *Women's Studies* 6: 237–57.

Russell, David L. 2002. "Young Adult Fairy Tales for the New Age: Francesca Lia Block's *The Rose and the Beast*." *Children's Literature in Education* 33(2): 107–15.

Sage, Lorna. 1994. *Angela Carter*. Plymouth, UK: Northcote House.

———. 2001 [1998]. "Angela Carter: The Fairy Tale." In *Angela Carter and the Fairy Tale*, ed. Danielle M. Roemer and Cristina Bacchilega. Detroit: Wayne State University Press, 65–82.

———. 2007 [1994]. "Introduction." In *Essays on the Art of Angela Carter: Flesh and the Mirror*, ed. Lorna Sage. London: Virago, 20–41.

Salas, Gerardo Rodríguez. 2010. "No More Lullabies for Foolish Virgins: Angela Carter and 'The Erl-King.'" *English Studies: Revista de Filología Inglesa* 31: 223–31.

Sceats, Sarah. 2001. "Oral Sex: Vampiric Transgression and the Writing of Angela Carter." *Tulsa Studies in Women's Literature* 20(1): 107–21.

Schanoes, Veronica. 2009. "Book as Mirror, Mirror as Book: The Significance of the Looking-Glass in Contemporary Revisions of Fairy Tales." *Journal of the Fantastic in the Arts* 20(1): 5–23.

———. 2012. "Fearless Children and Fabulous Monsters: Angela Carter, Lewis Carroll, and Beastly Girls." *Marvels & Tales* 26(1): 30–44.

Seaman, John E. 1968. "Othello's Pearl." *Shakespeare Quarterly* 19(1): 81–85.

Sheets, Robin Ann. 1991. "Pornography, Fairy Tales, and Feminism: Angela Carter's 'The Bloody Chamber.'" *Journal of the History of Sexuality* 1(4): 633–57.

Signorotti, Elizabeth. 1996. "Repossessing the Body: Transgressive Desire in 'Carmilla' and *Dracula*." *Criticism* 38(4): 607–32.

Simpson, Helen. 2006. "Femme Fatale." *The Guardian* (June 23). www.guardian.co.uk/books/2006/jun/24/classics.angelacarter (accessed August 14, 2012).

Solomon, Charles. 2010. *Tale as Old as Time: The Art and Making of* Beauty and the Beast. White Plains, NY: Disney Editions.

Stoker, Bram. 2011 [1897]. *Dracula*, ed. Roger Luckhurst. Oxford: Oxford University Press.

Swyt, Wendy. 1996. "'Wolfings': Angela Carter's Becoming-Narrative." *Studies in Short Fiction* 33: 315–23.

Szereto, Mitzi. 2001. *Erotic Fairy Tales: A Romp Through the Classics*. Berkeley, CA: Cleis Press.

Tan, Cecilia, ed. 1995. *Of Princes and Beauties: Erotic Fairy Tales for Adults*. Cambridge, MA: Circlet Press.

Tatar, Maria. 1987. *The Hard Facts of the Grimms' Fairy Tales*. Princeton, NJ: Princeton University Press.

———. 2004. *Secrets Beyond the Door: The Story of Bluebeard and His Wives*. Princeton, NJ: Princeton University Press.

Teverson, Andrew. 1999. "'Mr. Fox' and 'The White Cat': The Forgotten Voices in Angela Carter's Fiction." *Hungarian Journal of English and American Studies* 5(2): 209–22.

Tiffin, Jessica. 2009. *Marvelous Geometry: Narrative and Metafiction in Modern Fairy Tale*. Detroit: Wayne State University Press.

Tracy, Robert. 1966. "The Owl and the Baker's Daughter: A Note on Hamlet IV.v.42–43." *Shakespeare Quarterly* 17(1): 83–86.

Tucker, Lindsey. 1998. "Introduction." In *Critical Essays on Angela Carter*, ed. Lindsey Tucker. New York: G. K. Hall, 1–23.

Turner, Kay, and Pauline Greenhill, eds. 2012. *Transgressive Tales: Queering the Grimms*. Detroit: Wayne State University Press.

Tyler, Alison, ed. 2004. *Naughty Fairy Tales from A to Z*. Harmondsworth, UK: Penguin.

Uther, Hans-Jörg. 2004. *The Types of International Folktales: A Classification and Bibliography Based on the System of Antti Aarne and Stith Thompson*, v. 1. Folklore Fellows Communications 285. Helsinki: Suomalainen Tiedeakatemia Academia Scientiarum Fennica.

Verdier, Yvonne. 1997 [1980]. "Little Red Riding Hood in Oral Tradition," trans. Joseph Gaughan. *Marvels & Tales* 11(1–2): 101–23.

Walkerdine, Valerie. 1997. *Daddy's Girl: Young Girls and Popular Culture*. Cambridge, MA: Harvard University Press.

Warner, Marina. 1994. *From the Beast to the Blonde: On Fairy Tales and Their Tellers*. London: Chatto & Windus.

Waugh, Patricia. 1995. *Harvest of the Sixties: English Literature and Its Background, 1960 to 1990*. Oxford: Oxford University Press.

Wisker, Gina. 1997. "Revenge of the Living Doll: Angela Carter's Horror Writing." In *The Infernal Desires of Angela Carter: Fiction, Femininity, Feminism*, ed. Joseph Bristow and Trev Lynn Broughton. London: Longman, 116–31.

Zipes, Jack. 1983a. "A Second Gaze at Little Red Riding Hood's Trials and Tribulations." *The Lion and the Unicorn* 7–8: 78–109.

———. 1983b. *The Trials and Tribulations of Little Red Riding Hood*. London: Heinemann.

Index

anal father, 160n6
Andermahr, Sonya, 6–7
animal: charmers, 76; desires, 13, 42; and female drives, 107–8, 114, 119, 136, 138; and human intimacy, 137; and human relations, 64, 66; and women, 61–62, 158n15
Armitt, Lucie, 5, 15–16

Bacchilega, Cristina: on "Bluebeard," 23, 30; on Carter's time in Japan, 155n3; on Carter's wolf tales, 123–24, 135–38; on masochism, 27–28, 30; on "Snow Child," 99, 161n12; on "Snow White," 161n13; on victimhood, 26, 29
Basile, Giambattista, 103–4, 108, 162n3
Baudelaire, Charles, 19–23, 26
beast: Beast, the ("Courtship of Mr. Lyon"), 5, 44, 46–50, 52, 53; Beast, The ("Tiger's Bride"), 54–60, 63-64; and libertinism, 21–22; and sovereign, 61–63
Beaumarchais, Pierre, 65–66, 69
Beaumont, Marie Le Prince de, 42–53, 55–56, 156n2
Belle et la Bête, La (Cocteau), 47
Bennett, Jane, 11, 148–50
Bettelheim, Bruno, 94, 95–96, 146–47
"Bloody Chamber," 12, 17–41, 63, 108, 112
Bloody Chamber and Other Stories, 2–11, 15–16, 95, 145, 150–51

Bond Stockton, Kathryn, 8
Britzolakis, Christina, 2–3, 160–61n8

"Carmilla" (le Fanu), 111–13, 120–21, 163–64n13
Carter, Angela, Oedipal complex in, 29, 32; pornography in, 37–38, 131–32, 156n16; sword as phallus in, 34
Carter, Angela, works of:
—"Bloody Chamber," 12, 17–41, 63, 108, 112
—*Bloody Chamber and Other Stories*, 2–11, 15–16, 95, 145, 150–51
—*Come Unto These Yellow Sands*, 2
—"Company of Wolves," 15, 123, 131–37
—"Courtship of Mr. Lyon," 12–13, 42–54, 58, 72, 158n12
—"Erl-king," 13–14, 73–94, 150, 160nn6–7, 161n11
—*Fairy Tales of Charles Perrault*, 4, 123–24
—"Lady of the House of Love," 14, 100–101, 103–21, 163n9
—"Puss-in-Boots," 12–13, 42, 64–72, 159n18
—*Sadeian Woman*: constrained desire in, 28; flesh and meat in, 51; love in, 2, 40, 65, 114
—"Snow Child," 13–14, 73–74, 94–99, 161n12, 162n17
—"Tiger's Bride," 12–13, 54–64, 87, 150, 158n12, 161n8
—"Werewolf," 15, 123, 127–31

177

178   INDEX

—"Wolf-Alice," 15, 123, 137–44, 166n10
Case, Sue-Ellen, 104, 116–17, 121
Cecilia, Saint, 25, 29
Clark, Robert, 26–27, 165n1
Come Unto These Yellow Sands, 2
"Company of Wolves," 15, 123, 131–37
"Courtship of Mr. Lyon," 12–13, 42–54, 58, 72, 158n12
Crunelle-Vanrigh, Anny, 44

Day, Aidan, 25, 37, 46
Derrida, Jacques, 61–63, 65
Dimovitz, Scott, 3, 166n10
Dracula (Stoker), 110–13, 163n12, 164n15
Duncker, Patricia, 26–27, 37

enchantment, 11, 88, 145–51
"Erl-king," 13–14, 73–94, 150, 160nn6-7, 161n11
"Erlkönig" (Goethe), 76–77, 159n2
Eve, 17, 29–32

Fairy Tales: "Beauty and the Beast," 42–49, 51–53, 59, 156n2; "Bluebeard," 12, 17–18, 23–24, 29–31, 36, 153–55nn1-3, 155n10; "Jack and the Beanstalk," 108; *Kinder- und Hausmärchen*, 94, 102, 145, 162n2; "Little Brier Rose," 102–8, 120, 146; "Little Red Riding Hood," 15, 123–24, 127–30, 135, 137–38, 142, 166n11; "Puss-in-Boots," 159n18; "Sleeping Beauty," 99–104, 115–17, 119–20, 146–47; "Story of the Boy Who Went Forth to Learn Fear," 164n16; "Story of Grandmother," 123, 128–29, 165n6
Feuerlicht, Ignace, 77
Freud, Sigmund: and fetish, 38; and *fort/da* game, 33–34; and Oedipal complex, 3, 35, 92–93, 98–99; and Oedipal phase, 29, 32–33; on the olfactory, 138; on women's frigidity, 95

Gallop, Jane, 92, 98, 122–23, 129, 130, 138
Gilbert, Sandra, 82–83
"Goblin Market" (Rossetti), 89–90
Grimm, Jacob and Wilhelm, works of: *Kinder- und Hausmärchen*, 94, 102, 145, 162n2; "Little Brier Rose," 102–8, 120, 146; "Story of the Boy Who Went Forth to Learn Fear," 164n16
Gubar, Susan, 82–83, 85

Hamlet (Shakespeare), 81, 89–90, 160n8
Henke, Suzette, 37
Hennard Dutheil [de la Rochère], Martine, 4, 22, 155n10
Hermansson, Casie, 23
Homans, Margaret, 13, 78–79, 87, 159n5
Huysmans, J. K., 20–21

identificatory metamorphosis, 4, 62, 72
Irigaray, Luce, 58, 166n10

jouissance, 10, 60, 64

Kristeva, Julia, 129–30

labyrinth: language as, 11–12, 17–18; gender as, 29, 40
Lacan, Jacques: and desire, 71, 78, 80, 96; and ideal-I, 48, 58, 140; and the Law of the Father, 13, 34, 79; and the male gaze, 34; and the mirror stage, 58, 140, 166n10; and the phallus, 3, 13, 33, 38, 78, 132, 159–60n5; and the Symbolic Order, 10, 66, 93, 132
"Lady of the House of Love," 14, 100–101, 103–21, 163n9
le Fanu, Sheridan, 111–13, 163–64n13
Lewallen, Avis, 26–27, 37
libertine, 17–18, 21–22, 38–40, 118–19
Linkin, Harriet, 74–76, 78, 80–81, 85, 91, 160n7, 161n10

love: as cliché, 1–11; as emancipation, 40, 114, 118; and flesh, 92–93; fruits of, 103; heterosexual, 8–10, 68, 141; and orgasm, 40; romantic, 44–45, 54, 68, 84, 115; and Romanticism, 75, 88–90; and sex, 65, 71; and torture, 23, 26; waking to, 119

madness, 81–82, 89–91, 160–61nn8–9
Makinen, Merja, 27
male gaze, 34–36, 46–50, 50–60, 67, 137
male violence, 29–30
Marquis, the ("Bloody Chamber"): as anal father, 160n6; castle of, 5, 63–64; former wives of, 108, 112; and the male gaze, 34–36; and orgasm, 39–40; and sadism, 18–26; and trauma, 38
marriage: arranged, 44; as exchange, 44, 54–56; as myth, 45, 164n16; and patriarchy, 36, 53; and women's agency, 163n12, 164n14
Marriage of Figaro (Beaumarchais), 65–67, 69
maternal telepathy, 12, 35
meat, 51, 107, 115, 136–37, 163n7
menstruation, 138, 166nn9–10
mirrors, 10, 25, 48–49, 139–41
mirror stage. *See under* Lacan, Jacques
Mitchell, Juliet, 79
Moglen, Helene, 79, 84

necrophilia, 14, 99, 103–4, 109, 162n4
nymphet, 126, 133, 135, 137–38, 142

Oedipal complex: Carter's critique of, 92–93, 96; and incest, 98; and Lacan, 78; as phase, 32–33; and pedophilia and necrophilia, 99; and phallic mother, 35, 131; and story of Eve, 29
Oedipus, myth of, 158n11
Ophelia, 81–82, 89–90, 160–61nn8–9
Orenstein, Catherine, 126
orgasm, 39–40, 64, 70, 71

Othello (Shakespeare), 55-56

passivity, 10, 103–4, 115, 146–47
pedophilia, 99, 109, 126
Perrault, Charles, Carter's translation of, 4, 123–24
Perrault, Charles, works of: "Bluebeard," 17–18, 153–54n1, 155–56n10; "Little Red Riding Hood," 135–36, 142–43; "Morals," 30, 159n18; "Puss-in-Boots," 71, 159n18; "Sleeping Beauty in the Wood," 102–3, 108
Persephone, myth of, 84–85
phallic mother, 12, 35, 129–31
phallus: in "Bloody Chamber," 32, 34, 38; in "Company of Wolves," 132; and language, 78; as signifier, 13, 159–60n5; in "Tiger's Bride," 56, 58, 62; in "Werewolf," 129–31
Phillips, Lawrence, 6–7
Pollock, Mary, 62
pornography: in "Bloody Chamber," 18–24 passim, 26–29, 37–41; in "Company of Wolves," 131–38; and the fairy tale, 126; in "Lady of the House of Love," 104, 114; moral, 131–32, 156n16; in "Puss-in-Boots," 69–70
psychoanalysis, 2–3, 158n11. *See also* Freud, Sigmund; Irigaray, Luce; Lacan, Jacques
"Puss-in-Boots" (Carter), 12–13, 42, 64–72, 159n18

Rais, Gilles de, 21
Romantic poetry, 13–14, 74–75, 78–94, 95–96, 98
Rossetti, Christina, 89–90

Sade, Marquis de: in "Bloody Chamber," 18, 21, 26, 33, 38, 40, 154n2; in "Company of Wolves," 136; in "Courtship of Mr. Lyon," 51; and Juliette, 104, 107, 110; and Justine, 18, 28, 50–51, 104; in "Lady of the House of Love," 104, 107, 110; and masochism, 24, 26, 104; and pornography, 70, 71, 104, 156n16, 162n5, 164n14; in "Puss-in-Boots," 70; and sadism, 20, 23, 24, 26, 38, 104

Sadeian Woman: constrained desire in, 28; flesh and meat in, 51; love in, 2, 40, 65, 114; Oedipal complex in, 29, 32; pornography in, 37–38, 131–32, 156n16; sword as phallus in, 34

Sage, Lorna, 5, 15, 80, 160n8

Schanoes, Veronica, 166n10

scopophilia. *See* male gaze

Secret Garden, The (Burnett), 76

Shakespeare, William: *Hamlet*, 81, 89–90, 160n8; *Othello*, 55–56

Sheets, Robin Ann, 18, 21, 28, 31, 34, 37, 41

smell, 138–40, 166n9

"Snow Child," 13–14, 73–74, 94–99, 161n12, 162n17

somnambulist, 104–5, 110, 119

Stoker, Bram, 110–13, 163n12, 164n15

Swyt, Wendy, 135, 165n1

Teverson, Andrew, 53

"Tiger's Bride," 12–13, 54–64, 87, 150, 158n12, 161n8

tongues, 60–61, 63, 141, 144

torture. *See* sadism

vagina dentata, 98, 106

vampires, 100–121 passim

virtue, 28, 51-52

Waugh, Patricia, 3

"Werewolf," 15, 123, 127–31

"White Cat" (d'Aulnoy), 52–53

"Wolf-Alice," 15, 123, 137–44, 166n10

Zipes, Jack, 142–43